The Piñata-Maker's Daughter

Book One of the Marisol Trilogy

For my mother and my father,
who taught me that there is nothing in life
too hard to try.

The Piñata-Maker's Daughter

by

Eileen Clemens Granfors

The Piñata-Maker's Daughter

Copyright © 2013 by Eileen Clemens Granfors

Cover art copyright: Donna Dickson

All rights reserved. No part of this book may be reproduced or transmitted in any form or by any means without written permission of the author. This is a work of fiction. No person, place, or event is based on historical fact, including Western Pacific Concordia University and the sorority, Tri Chi. All are a product of the writer's imagination.

ISBN-13: 978-1456341213

ISBN-10: 1456341219

Key words: college life—fiction; Hispanic women—fiction; Hispanic Americans—fiction; Southern California—fiction; title, fiction

Other works by Eileen Granfors

Breathe In, 2013
Sydney's Story, 2012
Burst, 2012
Stairs of Sand, 2011
Flash Warden and Other Stories, 2011
Some Rivers End on the Day of the Dead, 2010
And More White Sheets, 2010

Prologue

Mama and I sat for hours on a burping bus full of chickens in cages, round-eyed babies on round mothers' laps. Young boys played cards or dice with slouching teenagers, hooting at one another with their jibes. I drowsed and dreamed, memories of my birth city, of walking with Mama to the market on the way to school in the morning, of lingering over the limes and oranges, of her gentle scoldings that I would be late to school. The clarity of the air, the colors that washed the buildings, Mama's hand in mine, even today, this is what I remember of San Miguel de Allende. We left in 1976 when I was ten.

In Mexico City, I felt like a sparrow among flocks of parakeets, the colorful clothes and the chatter of thousands of people. Mama spread her striped *serape* to draw me close and keep me safe. I trembled against her like a shy toddler.

A taxi driver, a fat, old man with stinky breath and angry eyes, took us from the bus station to the airport. Mama argued with him about the taxi cost even though Mama was not the arguing kind of person when I was little. The taxi man shook his fist, yelling loud, until a policeman came to help us. Inside the airport, we found a ticket seller where Mama counted out the money she had saved and saved for so long.

The airplane took us to San Diego in the United States. Aunt Ines waved at us in the lobby, her baby Salvador in her arms. She drove us to San Ysidro, a place where she said no one would notice two more Mexicans. I found out in American school that my classmates would be mostly other Mexicans if we stayed in San Ysidro. Some had been born U.S. like Salvador; others arrived, like me, in Mexico one moment, in the U.S. the next.

In the new neighborhood, the children spoke a mixture of English and Spanish. I helped Mama with the piñatas. The first year, I stole candy for my pockets so that I would have friends. When Gayla moved in across the street, she became a true friend, someone who didn't care about candy. She cared more about me and boys and her favorite books by Sydney Sheldon and Jacqueline Susann. She said the books taught her about life, meaning love and romance, money and drugs and sex.

Mama's business grew and so did I. In junior high and high school, she needed me more and more, but the more she needed me, the more I longed to find another life, a life not sticky with paste, my hands not blistered from cutting paper, Mama not driving a broken down Chevy truck that backfired so that children made fart noises when she drove by. I knew I could become more than the Piñata-Maker's daughter.

If my father had stayed with my mother, they would have handled the business together like a normal couple, and Mama wouldn't have relied on me so much. I never knew my father. Mama didn't talk of him except to say he left San Miguel to go to Colorado. I thought Colorado was part of Mexico, another state like Sonora or Durango. In American school I learned the American states. I learned that Colorado is not so far from California, but I didn't choose to find my father. He left us. He left Mama with a baby to raise, a baby who would have a paper father, a name on a birth certificate. Why would I chase him? Mama said only that I must use his name for all my school forms, so that I am Principia, not Gracia, so that I had an easier road to citizenship.

My Mexican-American friends called the white children here the White Bread. American children's lives were limited by white: white walls, white cars, white flowers, white blouses for girls and white shirts for boys. Their houses were surrounded by white picket fences behind white mesh gates that locked against the world. Mexico is hot pink, purple, fuschia. It is red and gold bougainvillea climbing stuccoed walls painted blue.

Someday, who knows when, I will breathe again the pure mountain air of my birthplace and reach out for the bright stars that hang so close to San Miguel.

I rock in our creaky swing on the front porch, facing Gayla's house, humming a lullabye from long ago:

Duérmete mi niño
Duérmete mi amor.

The baby in my arms stops fussing to listen, coo, and gurgle.

Chapter One

September, 1984

Our dented red Chevy truck labors up the hill near San Clemente. If it overheats, the engine won't be the only thing that needs to cool off. I had begged Mama, couldn't I please take our sedan? It's not as old and bashed up. I need a car. But she said no, if we're driving through LA, she might as well make a business trip of it. She likes the bargains downtown and the shops in East LA.

She's spending the night with Uncle Luis and Aunt Rosa. I have their phone number in my wallet in case I get homesick. Mama forgets that their boot shop is listed in the Yellow Pages. She wants me to tell everyone about their boots. She doesn't get it that there are people in the world who see Mexican boots and their heads spin tales of *banditos*. Plus, you'd think I was asking her to drive me and my friends to a boy band, she's so grumpy about the whole thing.

It's only college. It's only the beginning of my real life. I wish I had gone through sorority rush a week ago to gauge how people would treat me. I sent the forms in, but then I chickened out. What if no one asked me back after the first day? What if they said from the start I would never belong with them? Rejection would have sent me crying home to Mama.

I roll down the window and lean my head out. The wind is hot. I worry more about the truck. It backfires every thirty seconds.

"Carmenita, close the window. You're making a mess of your new hair cut. Look how the wind is blowing all those bags you had to bring."

The bed of the truck is strewn with my possessions. Everything I might need at college, my stuffed animals, my new bedspread and pillows, my typewriter, my clothes packed in bags, all have tipped over under a flapping tarp.

"I needed a trunk to pack things in, Mama."

"Yes, you told me. And did you look at my check book? Did you see extra money for fancy luggage?"

"Why don't you make people pay you on time so we'll have enough money?"

"Because that's not what a piñata is about, *mi hija.* Piñatas are our culture. God gave me the gift to make the best piñatas. How can I brush off God's plan for me? Everyone pays me eventually, you know that."

I frown at her and think. Yeah, I know that. I know our neighbors will bring over extra tamales, people from across town will pay up by Christmas. Money in, money out. Real piñatas take more time and more money to create than those cheap things people buy in Tijuana. San Ysidro isn't exactly a tourist destination. People come through running from the law or playing tourist without going into Mexico or to buy Mexican insurance for their car before crossing the border. At least these visitors pay cash for Mama's piñatas.

We chug down the long hill into San Clemente. Then the freeway turns away from the sea. It's hotter. I'm angrier. I want to be excited. I want to feel grown up and free, not like a new kid at school with the rich clique laughing behind their hands about my boots. The traffic slows to a stop near El Toro. The engine gauge climbs. Just when I'm sure an explosion is near, Mama swings to the right, ignoring the outraged horns honking and squealing tires as others stop. She pulls the truck onto the shoulder of the road.

"Mama, why didn't you take the off-ramp? You passed the gas station sign back there." She frustrates me with these sudden decisions, not even asking what I think we should do.

"I have water. I know this truck like *masa* for tamales." She checks the rearview mirror and hops down. I roll my head against the seat, check my watch, bite my cheek, say a prayer. "Please, God, help me get to my university."

Mama opens the hood. She climbs in the back, tossing things around until she finds the water jug. When she opens the radiator, I hear a hissing and a yell. Something smells acrid. I rush out.

The engine's steam spews into the smoggy air. Mama is cradling her arm, her lips pinched with pain. "Ay yi yi, Carmen. I thought it would be okay. Look at this."

She holds her arm up. The skin is red and blistered. I don't know what to do.

"Get the first aid kit from the glove box," she says, mouth tight with pain. "See if we have some gauze."

I throw myself back into the cab and open the glove box. It's empty. I yell back to her, "It's not here."

She heaves herself up from the pavement, still cradling her arm. She comes to look at the empty glove box with me. "I think I loaned the kit to Magdelena when she took her June vacation."

"See how you are about people and borrowing things and paying for things? Now we should find a drugstore. There's a call box up there. I'll go."

I run away from the truck, the traffic slowing to looky-loo at our problem. At the call box, I pick up the phone. The line is dead. The Golden State is once again behind in road repairs. I walk back with the sun broiling my face and shoulders. If I ever arrive at the U, I'm going to be a big mess, just great for first impressions.

Mama has sat back down on the side of the road in a clump of pickle weed. The scent of the pickle weed, smelling of summers past, brings tears to my eyes. Maybe Mama is right that I am reaching too far, too high, too soon. She told me again and again how long she saved to bring us to San Ysidro. I'm not that patient. I'm not waiting ten years to get on with life after high school. Mama didn't agree without a fight.

The sun crawls higher. Traffic is loud. We wait and sweat and hope. No one stops to help us.

"Should I wave a red towel? Maybe the Highway Patrol will come?" It does no good to nag at Mama. She will make a plan sooner or later.

But now that we've set out, the troubles of this trip remind me of the fights Mama and I had all spring long, once the fat WPC envelope came.

We were working on a piñata for my cousin Miguel, an eagle for his rank in Boy Scouts. She glanced at the envelope and told me to put it away, not be in such a rush.

"I will be in a rush. I will go to a big name college. You never encourage me." I opened the letter and read the admissions news with a blue and white peechee folder that said *WPC* in a script font with the silver stamp of the Western Pacific Concordia University Crusaders.

"*Mi hija*, put all your important papers on your desk. Help me finish this piñata. After we deliver it, we can discuss your plans again. But don't expect a miracle."

"It's already a miracle, Mama. I've been accepted." I wanted to call my high school counselor, who suggested I should apply for Concordia, but I came back and sat cross-legged on the floor.

"Which part should I work on?" I asked.

"You do the eagle's bill and his wings. You are so artistic, Carmen. I have big dreams for your designs."

"I have big dreams too, not about paste and piñatas, about a college degree and a big career. I will be someone important."

"I told you, talk later."

We worked together to give the eagle his wings. The piñata got wings. From Mama, I got *de nada.* Tears filled my eyes, and I blinked them away. Mama doesn't mind if I cry, but I knew it would give her another reason to keep her little girl home.

She had the main pottery bowls ready, one smaller for the head and one larger for the body. The legs and feet dangled from the bottom of the main bowl. We worked for an hour to align the wings. The eagle's wings spread out, as if in flight. That's what I wanted--to be in flight.

"Which candy would the boys like best?" asked Mama. "Bubble gum or chocolate?"

"Either one. They're boys. They won't care.

"More profit if we use bubble gum," she said, dumping three sacks of Double Bubble into the main pot. We attached twine around the neck of the smaller pot with a long length left free. "Oh, my back aches," Mama said as she stood to hang the finished eagle to dry.

"Mine too," I agreed. "If I go to college," I started, but Mama held up her hand.

"Enough. Later. I told you twice."`

My face burned with anger. "What time is Miguel's eagle landing?" My tone of voice wasn't very polite.

"Keep your temper."

"Sorry." I sighed. "What time do you need me?"

"I need you all day because there's also the flowered piñata for Easter. But okay, you go. Come back with a better attitude."

"Where are the keys?" I asked, fingers crossed.

"Why drive?"

"To Ashley's."

"The rich friend?"

"Please, Mama."

"No, when you go there, you're late coming home. We can't be late for Miguel's delivery. Walk over to Gayla's. She's a nice girl."

I shared the news with Gayla. She was happy for me and sad for herself. I became more obstinate about making this dream come true. Mama chattered on the phone about her selfish, mule-headed daughter, who thought she was already smarter than her mother, who thought she had to be the fancy college girl.

We fought all spring until the financial aid package arrived. All my fees, paid. Dorm, paid. I would have an on-campus job.

Mama could find no more excuses. I would fly off to college even if my flight depended on a miracle for our broken-down Chevy truck.

We have been sitting here, frying in the sun and the pickle weed for an hour. Mama puts her finger to her lips every time I try to make a suggestion. I'm ready to concede this one when a miracle occurs. A shiny blue Mazda Miata pulls off the freeway. "See," says Mama. "Never lose faith."

My heart bangs in my chest. What if he's some weirdo? "No matter what he says, Mama, we're not getting into that car, do you understand me?" She nods, holding her arm like a broken wing.

"Hey, what's the trouble?" the guy says when he is close enough to hear. He is not very tall, maybe five-eight. He has a buzz cut, which is hilariously old-fashioned. His brawny, tanned shoulders show through his muscle tank tee shirt. He has on surfer shorts and sandals. His smile is pretty dreamy.

"Engine overheated. My mom got burned," I say, pushing my short hair behind my ears. Is he the kind of guy who will notice dangly gold earrings?

"Let me take a look," he says, and instead of going to the truck like I expect, he sits down by Mama. He breaks off some pickle weed and squeezes the juice on her arm. "Aloe," he says.

"That feels good." Mama tears out more pickle weed.

"Wait." He retrieves a shirt from his car, tears it into strips. "To wrap with the aloe until you get something better."

"Thank you. My daughter doesn't like my wasting so much time on this journey."

"Glad to help. I'm Joe by the way."

"I am Lucia. My daughter is Carmen. She is supposed to move into her dorm today."

"Cal State Dominguez Hills or Long Beach?"

"WPC," I say. "No Cal States for me. How much farther anyway?"

"Me too! Where you from?"

"Chula Vista," I say without hesitation just as Mama says, "San Ysidro."

He looks confused. "I'm local, Laguna Beach."

He rubs his hands across his buzz cut. "So back to your question. In miles, probably another 160 miles. But the traffic is slow, not just because of your truck here. So, I don't know, at least two hours, maybe three?"

"Maybe you could take Carmen?" my mother asks, and I shake my head no, no, no. Doesn't she remember I said we're not getting in the car with him? Besides, my stuff won't fit, and I definitely do not want to call attention to my lack of luggage.

"Don't worry about it, Joe. I may be late, but as soon as the truck starts, I'll drive, and Mama can rest her arm." I give her the look that means *leave it to me.*

"You sure?" Joe peers into the engine. "I think I can fix this. I'll take out the thermostat so it shouldn't overheat again this trip." He goes back to his car, grabs a tool box, and starts his little project.

"Look, my arm's not so red now," says Mama. She's right. It does look better. "We can get you to school if only the truck starts and stays cool."

Joe turns around, smiles, and says, "Start her up." I turn the ignition. The truck belches some black smoke, but it does start.

"Thank you, Joe," I say. "See you around campus."

"Maybe. Twelve thousand people, sometimes it's hard to find who you're looking for. What dorm are you in?"

"Ortega."

"Good one, closer to campus."

"Yeah, that's what I thought. Are you in the dorms?"

"Not this year, I pledged Kappa. The house is right across the street. Come on over and ask for me when you get settled. I'll buy you a sundae at Al's."

"Al's?" It sounds like a dive bar.

"Al's Place at the student union. Everybody hangs there. Gotta go if you ladies are okay. We have some frat business this afternoon." As he leaves, he sees the bumper sticker. "Hey, the *La Raza* people hang out on Crusader Commons. *Viva La Raza*?" he says as if it's a question, pronouncing *Raza* with a long *A*. He waves, guns the Miata, and disappears into traffic.

I look at Mama, Mama looks at me, we both shrug, and then we laugh. We wrap her arm in strips of tee-shirt. I hug Mama. I'm so relieved it's going to be okay. Twelve thousand students at WPC, and now I know one.

"Don't be ashamed of your hometown, Carmenita," says Mama.

"Why would you say that?" I ask, full of false innocence. "Wow, Laguna Beach, this Joe guy must be rich."

"You're going to meet a lot of rich people in college. Rich doesn't make them better."

"Sure." I can picture the looks of people the first time I answer, "So what does your mom do?" and I tell them, "Oh, she makes piñatas." As if piñata-making is perfectly normal in their world. I remind myself to say she's an artisan. Yeah, artisan sounds totally righteous.

Chapter 2

Sweat slides between my shoulder blades. Mama gave me a hug, dropped me and my possessions in front of the dorm, tooted the horn, and drove away. She didn't cry like some of the moms I see standing by mounds of luggage and trunks or unloading their Mercedes Benzes. Mama didn't even care if she saw my room. Coming here was my idea, and now I have to succeed. She did check twice that I have Uncle Luis and Aunt Rosa's phone number.

The doors to the dorm are propped open to receive the freshmen for UR-U orientation. I see mothers carrying pink-tasseled throw pillows and dads carrying television sets. I stand at the curb a moment, watching Mama trying to merge into the circling traffic. She has already turned up the radio, mariachi music blaring out. Thank God no one here can connect me to her.

"Hey, need a hand?" A tall blond girl with a springy pony tail arrives by my side. "I'm Teri, one of the UR-U counselors. You ready for the big adventure? What's your name? What floor are you on? What's your major? Where are you from?"

She talks so fast, I just shake my head. "I'm Carmen. I don't know what I'm supposed to do first."

Mama has come around the circle one more time. She stops, and the truck rattles as the engine goes off. She jumps out in her frumpy, flowered dress. "Carmen? You have the phone number?"

I am so embarrassed. "Yes, Mama. You can go now. See, Teri is here to help me." Mama throws her waist-length braid behind her, waves at Teri, and decides a wave is not enough. She reaches out to give Teri a hug, which I know smells of chiles and B.O. Mama doesn't believe in chemicals on her body. She hugs me too. "Bye, Mama. Drive safely," I tell her, trying not to sound impatient. She grinds the ignition a couple of times before the engine turns over, and she swings back into traffic. Teri grabs my hand.

"C'mon. First you go to that table and get your keys for your room. Put your driver's license into your pocket because you're going to need it for everything today. They'll tell you your roommate's name. Then, we cart your stuff upstairs."

I sign in with the room key person, another blond who looks like Teri except her bangs are about a mile long and fluffed back in feathery perfection from her face. I'll be on the fifth floor. My roommate's name is Shirley Wooster. That's just terrific. At least my name isn't Laverne or Tootsie. I can hear the cat calls for a Tootsie and Wootsie show.

Teri and I grab as many paper sacks as we can carry. We go to the elevator line and watch the lights blinking from the seventh floor back to G for ground. A wave of people floods out, everybody talking at once.

We shoulder our way in, not able to see over the top of the bags we're carrying.

"Somebody push five for us, please," yells Teri.

The elevator stops at the second floor. People boo. "You can walk up one flight of stairs. This elevator won't ever be stopping at two again after move-in day, so live it up," Teri tells the offender. I'm embarrassed for her. How are we supposed to know that? It wasn't in any brochure they sent. I know because I read each one 100 times. Then I look at the top of the floor tracker. "This elevator does not stop at 2" is clearly marked in big felt pen letters.

We get to five. There's more room now as people step off. All of a sudden, I'm kind of sick to my stomach. What if my roommate is a rich snob? What if she hates me because I'm Mexican? Teri pushes me in the back to get moving.

"Down this hall," she points to a long, long hallway measured off in doors along the outside and bathroom doors on the interior wall. Here we go.We find my room and unlock the door. Nobody is in there.

"Cool. You get first dibs on the beds. What do you choose?"

"Right side," I say for no reason. What difference would it make? "Where's the bed?"

Teri pulls the beds out from their spaces under the book shelves. Once they're out, there's not much room in the room. "Hope your roommate doesn't snore like mine did. When both beds are out, there's about twelve inches between them."

We throw the bags on the beds. I'm about to go to the elevator when Teri yanks my tee-shirt. "Stairs down—way faster."

We jog down the stairs with a dozen other pairs of new girls, parents, and helpers. At the parking circle, my junk is still lined up in its pathetic grocery store brown bags. This is going to take forever.

"Hey, Teri," yells a guy. "I knew I could count on you to be helping. Here, let me lend a hand and then we can boogie."

"Cool, Lance," she says. "Room 507."

He's really big like a football player. He can carry six of my bags. Teri and I stand by the elevator, but he takes the stairs. Before we get on, he's already back and has picked up another six bags. "I think I've got the last of it," he says as he runs by.

The elevator finally arrives and deposits us. My roommate still isn't here. The room seems really full. Teri says there's nothing required today except putting our rooms in order, so she takes off for lunch. I am alone. I look out the window and see tennis courts. I open the window to catch the breeze. "Here I am," I say to the palm trees. "I can do this. Watch me."

I start unpacking my junk, books, clothes, purse, wallet, records, record player. I try to keep mostly to my side of the room. I put a few pictures on the bulletin board to prove I have friends somewhere. I wonder if I should leave my door closed or prop it open. I peek out into the hallway. It's still busy with arriving people. At the far end of the hall there's someone behind a stack of hat boxes. Hat boxes? What? I pop back into the room, closing the door.

Someone's fumbling at the lock. This is it. I'm about to meet my roommate. I start arranging my books and records and hold my breath.

A gray-haired man enters. He is string-bean skinny and would be tall except his back is noticeably hunched. He has a huge duffel bag slung over his shoulder. Behind him, the hatboxes come forward. A tiny gray-haired lady is carrying them. I wait. No one says anything, so I say, "Hello. Are you Shirley's parents?"

They laugh. "Shirley's grandparents. She's coming. Are you Carmen? Nice to meet you. We are Rolf and Brenda Wooster. Um, not to be rude, but could you move some of these bags out of the way? Shirley brought so much." The grandmother drops the hat boxes. "Where is that girl?" She peeks down the hall. Rolf props the door open by sliding the bracket on the door's hinge. Brenda sits down on the left side of the room at the desk, rummages through a box, finds pictures and thumbtacks and starts decorating the bulletin board. Now, me, that would fully piss me off. My mom keeps her hands off my stuff.

The grandfather begins emptying the duffel bag. The first thing he pulls out is an oversized stuffed horse wearing Mickey Mouse ears, which he puts on the desk. He digs around some more. "Brenda, what about this?" He's holding up a prosthetic leg made of pink plastic. It goes from the knee to the foot,

The person who must be Shirley arrives at the door on crutches. She sees the leg and yells, "Grandpa, I'm enough of a freak without you waving my leg around." She puts out her hand to me, "I'm Shirley, your roommate. I had cancer. Now I don't. The hat boxes have wigs 'cause my hair is growing back all weird. Cancer cost me a leg and normal hair, not an arm and a leg. I hope it doesn't gross you out."

I blink about twenty times and try to hold my voice steady. I really don't want to shake her hand, but there's no way out of that so I give her a three-fingered shake. "No, of course it doesn't gross me out," I lie. "I'm Carmen Principia, your roommate. Looks like we have a big year ahead."

"You have no idea," Shirley says with a wink. She leans on her crutch and shoves a hand into her jeans pocket. She flashes me a palmed reefer. "It helps with pain. It's good you like having the windows open."

Chapter 3

The room is too crowded with the Wooster family squeezed in there with me. I tell them I am going to scope out the hall a bit. My stomach growls. I know there is no way for me to look more like a loser than showing up at the dining hall alone on this first day. Way, way too scary for me.

The bathroom is a few steps away. I lock myself into one of the toilets and just sit there with my feet up. What I expected at the U was a whole lot different than what I've been living the past two hours. Who needs a roommate with one leg? Maybe it's fair though because I seem to have half a brain.

Girls' voices echo off the tiled floor and ceiling. Now I'm really stuck unless I'm just going to give it the old college try and say hi. That's when I hear the showers running. I slip away. I tell myself to walk all the way around the floor one time to see who is here.

I go towards the far window that overlooks the new track stadium. There's a door there. I open it and find myself on an outdoor landing. I love it! I breathe in deeply and open the doorway to the opposite hall. Unlike my hallway, this one is silent as Mrs. Myerson's classroom during a test. Not one door is open. Walking past each one, I tilt my head to listen. No people. This must be the non-freshman side of our floor. So I complete my lap of the halls and head back to our room.

"Hey, girl!"

I turn and look into the room three doors from ours.

"Hey," I say. I try to smile, but my mouth is dry.

"Do you have your roommate yet?"

I nod. "Yeah, her name is Shirley."

"Is yours Laverne?"

"Good one. Never thought of that. No, I'm Carmen."

"My roommate's not here yet. It's creepy alone."

"Creepy?"

"Like I'm an outcast." She pouts her plump lips, lips shining with a hot pink lip stick. Her blonde hair is sprayed into a big hair hairdo. She's skinny. She's wearing a really mini-mini-skirt and a low-cut halter top. I doubt she's ever been an outcast. She reminds me of some movie star.

"How about going for lunch?" I offer. "I'm Carmen, by the way. From down south."

"Really? Why didn't you go to UCSD? That's where the hot surfer guys are."

"I wanted out of San Diego. Surfing's not my thing." I don't tell her that Mexicans and the beach are a sure fight if the surfers are around protecting their territory.

"Got it. Yeah, let's go for lunch. It's probably time to start our freshman fifteen."

This remark doesn't register with me at all. "Is it an eating club? I didn't like that about Stanford."

"Stanford? What are you a brainiac? The fifteen is the pounds you'll gain on the crappy dorm food this first semester."

"No way."

"Yes, totally."

"I still want lunch." I'm glad she told me about gaining weight because all I have to do is look at chocolate or ice cream and I gain a size. I look at her again. Except for the double D boobs, she's probably a size four. "C'mon, let's check it out. What's your name?"

"Norina. My parents liked that song "Corina, Corina." She rolls her eyes. "I go by Norine. My parents are so weird."

"Whose aren't? I think I was named for Carmen Miranda, that lady who dances in those huge, ugly headdresses? Nothing like being named for some grapes and a banana."

Norine starts laughing, and I do too. Now I remember. She looks like Sally Field in the *Gidget* movies Aunt Ines watched with me. Norine, like Sally Field, is so petite and cute. I feel like a Neanderthal next to her.

We take the stairs down because the elevators are still full of arriving people. Across the lobby, there's a line, which is bound to be the food line.

"Do you have your meal card?"

"What's that?"

"Carmen, I'm not sure this is the right school for you if you don't know what a meal card is. We'll get it after lunch. Show them your room key. They'll let you do that once."

"How do you know all this stuff? We haven't had even one UR-U meeting."

"My sister was in this dorm last year. Now she has an apartment. I used to stay with her on weekends for fun, you know, meet guys, go to football, get drunk. Marnie would get her roommate's meal card for me for the weekend."

I have so much to learn. It's a good thing we have three days of UR-U before classes start and I have to start stuffing my head with facts. I don't know what to say about her casual references to boys and getting drunk. That's not how Mama brought me up. "Norine, you're scaring me."

"Relax. You're cute. I love your hair. The guys will too. When we get through the food line, follow me. We have a chance to check out the freshmen boys. The older guys tend to look at us like we're lunch, if you know what I mean. Fresh, sweet young num nums waiting to be devoured or deflowered, take your pick."

My face turns red. Sometimes I talked about sex with Gayla at home, usually reading some hot part of a book out loud, but I've never talked like that with a person I met ten minutes ago. Norine has picked up a tray and starts choosing things from under the glass shelves. She passes the desserts, takes a salad, and goes right past the spaghetti and meatballs.

Spaghetti and chocolate cake! I haven't eaten since a quick breakfast at five this morning. I'll go light at supper.

Norine disappears into the noisy dining room. She stops for a minute to look back for me, eyes my tray and shakes her head. "Over there," she says, and moves forward to put her tray down next to three really cute, preppy boys. She immediately asks them questions about where they're from, what their majors are, and their SAT scores. I sit mutely, trying to figure out how to get spaghetti into my mouth without dripping sauce all over my tee-shirt. The guys have their eyes on Norine's boobs, and I basically disappear.

"Wait," Norine says. "Got milk?"

The guys crack up and point to a big stainless steel dispenser. Glasses sit by its side. "You want white milk or the chocolate? You won't believe how cold they serve the milk here.

"Big whoop," says Norine. "Half a glass of regular. Carmen?"

"You know that brown girl wants some brown milk," says the tallest guy. He winks at me like it's a big joke. I try to smile. Racial jokes are part of college. I read that somewhere. I look around. I don't see any black kids. I don't see any other Mexicans either. They're probably all at UCSD or San Diego State. That's what Mama told me, like she was an expert on college. I'm going to find some *amigos* if it's the last thing I do on this campus. Joe said the Commons and *La Raza*. I make a mental note to go that way to class.

I pick up my tray, wave goodbye, and go to the food tray dump off. I wrap my cake in a napkin. Chocolate makes up for almost anything when I feel bad. But maybe Shirley's grandparents will be gone, and Shirley and I can sit around getting to know each other. I have my record player and some albums. Music always works. I'll find friends, besides Norine, who's too pushy with guys.

When I get back to our room, the door is locked. Every door has a chalk/cork board. Shirley divided ours into two with red tape. She left a note on her side saying, "Went to Al's with a friend."

Whatever. I open the door and flop on my bed. Shirley left her leg behind leaning against her desk chair, so it must be a pretty good friend.

Hey, God, I know I've shown the world some bad manners lately and I haven't been humble or obedient, but if You hear me, I could use one girlfriend. Until He answers, there's chocolate cake, and I don't have to split it with Shirley.

Chapter 4

A runner flies down the hallway, yelling into each room, "Get together at 5 p.m. with the guys from seventh floor. Food and volleyball."

"Food and volleyball" echoes.

Crap! like I want to jump around and get sweatier. Up the hall and down, the echoing squeals of girls sound like the screams of peacocks at the San Diego Zoo. There are only four shower stalls per bathroom so it's better to shower now. I grab my stuff, glad that I listened to my Tia Ines, who bought me a plastic carry box for all my bath junk. The clock says 3:30. I have enough time to wash and dry my hair. The cold water practically sizzles off my hot skin, and even though I have reached this big dream of mine, I start crying. Crying in the shower is good, too much other noise for anybody to notice, easy to dry off the tears.

My hair wrapped in a towel, I slip on my bathrobe. The hall is clear, and the noise has died down. I flip flop my way back to my room that isn't my room, it's our room. Shirley is still gone. I find an outfit I like, running shorts and a cut-off sweatshirt, lay it out on my bed. I start blow drying my hair and singing "Hotel California." I'm about to slip my robe off, but I keep looking at Shirley's prosthetic leg. It's right there. I pick it up. It's not too heavy. When I sniff it, it smells funky, like sweat and oil.

The door opens. Shirley crutches in with her friend, a boy. I drop the leg like it's red hot. There's nothing that says college freak like getting caught with your nose in an artificial limb that doesn't belong to you.

"It doesn't bite, at least not that way," says Shirley. "I'd let you try it on, but you have to bend your leg into a grotesque position to get it to fit." She starts giggling. "I know this guy from high school. Hairy head here is Morton. Everybody calls him Salt."

He laughs with her. Their eyes are red. Their clothes reek of pot. "Dude, are you Shirley's roommate? Are you

Laverne?" asks Salt. They laugh like it's the most hilarious joke ever.

I pull my robe around me more tightly. "Uh, yeah, hi. Shirley, there's this dorm floor exchange party at five with volleyball first."

She leans against Salt and takes a swing at an imaginary ball with her crutch. "No volleyball for me. Softball's cool. Or that Mexican game where you break this thing and candy falls out." She giggles again.

"Piñata. I don't think we'll be singing the piñata song anytime soon here. I really need to get dressed."

"Don't mind us," Salt says. He has a moon face and bright blue eyes with red streaks. He reminds me of my Eagle Scout cousin, skinny, dweeby Miguel.

"Sorry. I do mind." They don't react, so I grab my clothes to get dressed in the bathroom. A loud laugh follows me out the door. When I'm dressed, I leave my robe on a hook in a shower and take the elevator downstairs. I couldn't wait for Shirley to get back and now I can't wait for her and her buddy to leave and crap, I walked out without my wallet so unless I go back upstairs, I can't even go buy notebooks for fall quarter. I make myself small on a couch in one of the lounges. Luckily, somebody left a schedule of classes.

Flipping through the pages gives me a headache. All the buildings have abbreviations that mean nothing to me. The times and days I can deal with if I make a chart. Down on my hands and knees, I'm stretching to reach a pencil under the coffee table, when somebody snaps the elastic of my shorts, which are low enough to flaunt an embarrassing amount of butt crack.

When I sit up, I thunk my head against the table. Joe is leaning over the couch, balanced on the back of it. He rolls forward, laughing.

"Hey," he says, and the skin around his eyes crinkles.

He's really tan.

"Aren't you in a frat?"

"Yeah, service project to get over here and help people move in. Managed to miss most of the rush."

"Slacker."

"I beg your pardon? My reputation as a Kappa is at stake here. I can't help it if all these freshmen girls are early birds. Anyway, oh, skeptical one, may I assist you in any way? If not, I'll be moving along."

I want to ask him to explain the catalog or take me on a campus tour. But that might appear pushy. "I was working on my schedule," I say, hinting he could help.

"First, don't get your hopes up for any nice mid-morning classes because as a freshman, you won't get them. And don't set your heart on any classes that you need for your major. Those fill up first thing. Find the weirdest stuff, like the music and dance of Bali, and fit your schedule around things like that.

"What a waste of a quarter's credits. I need to graduate on time."

"Ha! Once you've been here long enough, you'll be stretching out your college career over seven years like everybody else."

"I will not."

"Trust me. Just set up a schedule. Your advisor has to sign off on it anyway." Joe grabs the booklet out of my hands. "Why don't you take ice skating? I took it last spring. It's at night and pretty fun."

"Let me see. That's funny that it's taught by Professor Rink."

"Dork. The venue is listed, not the prof. It's a grad student in PE teaching it. In fact, I know him. He still lives at Kappa house."

"You led me into that one. Thanks a bunch, Joe."

"At your service, my Chicano friend."

"Chicana."

"Say again?"

"Spanish, female nouns end in *A*. Like Santa Monica. But San Diego."

"No wonder I'm taking Japanese."

"Really?"

"Why not? The next twenty years are forecast to be all about Asia. Are you going to freeload your way through Spanish?"

"It's not freeloading because my Spanish stinks. It's street Spanglish, not Castilian. How should I know what I'll be taking anyway?"

Joe rolls the schedule up and bops me on the head. "Gotta jet. Take a look at the multicultural classes. They're so easy it's disgusting and that will give you one class you won't have to study for. Don't forget to put ice skating in your schedule. See you, ah, what's your name again? Margarita? Principalitas?"

"Carmen Principia."

"I think I'll call you Caramel."

"Big joke. Can you see me laughing?"

"Hang loose, baby! Bye, Caramel. See you at Professor Rink's." He splits a gut and lopes over to the guys' elevator, which sweeps him upward. The light doesn't stop once until he gets to the top, level seven. I wonder who he knows up there and if he's coming to the volleyball game/barbeque. If he spreads that Caramel nickname, maybe the other guys will think it's cute.

Chapter 5

Guides are leading a tours around the dorm, so I fall into a pack. The leader treks us around, showing off the dorm library, the dorm computer for occupational surveys, and the offices of the Residence Advisors. She says how nice they are and not to tick them off by breaking rules.

We turn a corner, completing the loop of the dorm, and she says to give our mailboxes a try. They have built in locks, set with our room number, ready to accept new codes. I won't be getting any mail, but I go ahead and program the box with my high school locker combo. The group disperses to the dining room. The campus bells toll the half hour. Thirty minutes until my floor's party-game-barbeque.

On impulse, I go back and knock on the opened door of the Residence Advisor. She looks up over her glasses. "Need some help? Come in."

"Yeah, sort of. Um, I was wondering if I could change roommates?"

She takes her glasses off. "Why would you do that on the first day?"

"I was hoping for a Hispanic roommate, somebody I'd have a lot in common with."

"You don't like your assigned roommate?"

"She's okay."

"Then why hurt her feelings?"

"I don't think she'd care."

"Who is she?"

"Shirley Wooster, the girl who had cancer."

"I know Shirley. She's been through a lot."

"Yeah, of course. I was just wondering."

"You try this arrangement for five weeks. Come to see me if you're still not okay with your roommate in five weeks."

"That's like forever."

"Sometimes it is, sometimes it isn't." She flips through note cards on her desk. "And Carmen, one thing about WPC is that we try to get you to walk in the other person's shoes for a bit."

"That goes both ways, right?"

"It does."

"I don't think Shirley knows much about being Hispanic."

"Beautiful. You can teach her. She probably has a few things on her mind. It's not easy being her, you know. Think about that."

"Right. Sure. Sorry. I'll definitely try to walk in her shoe," I say as I exit. I picture trying to put her prosthetic leg on. Now the RA is going to think I'm a brat and a whiner. Norine and Salt wave me over. They break away from their tour to tell me Norine's roommate arrived, that she's a fox with a boyfriend who has an apartment, and we'll probably never see her again. Her name is Jennifer something. I rush outside.

It's cooler now. The freshly cut lawn smells sweet with clover and alyssum. There's something else in the air too, coconut oil? On the deck, girls in bikinis are catching some last rays on their beautifully tanned, skinny bodies. They work on getting to the color I have been since birth. Weird how that works.

Three guys open the equipment shed. They pull out a volleyball net and argue about which way to place it, north to south or east to west. I listen because frankly I don't know which direction is which. They decide on north to south to avoid the glare of the setting sun. Before they get the whole thing on its stanchions, the tallest guy is testing the middle, trying to see if he can block if he jumps high. He's in the middle of his zillionth show-off move when his friends pull the posts out and ambush him. He's rolled into the net like a tuna on Miguel's boat They are busy prodding their catch with their sneakers, not hard enough to hurt, just joking around.

"Call the border patrol, and report Franco here," the first guy says. He's got on a baseball cap, shades, and no shirt. I admire his massive muscles and a hairy chest.

"I surrender," says the tuna. He is a Mexican, long dark black hair pulled into a pony tail, worn-out jeans, and a school tee-shirt. "Let me out. No *La Migra*." He plays right along with them.

They unroll the nets and set them up again, leave for more stuff from the dorm. I wander over and pick up a volleyball, bumping it to myself. When I miss, the ball rolls down a hill. By the time I'm back, so are the guys, returning with a silver ice chest. They walk in a chain with each of the bulky guys carrying one handle and the tall Mexican guy in the middle carrying on each side. Every now and again, both sides veer out, pulling the Mexican in both directions at once. My mom and aunts used to do that with me when I was little.

Setting the ice chest next to the barbeque, they look around. "Where's the party? Where are the girls? You promised us girls, Franco."

Franco points at me. "One! Hey, girl? Where are your floor mates?"

I walk over. "They're coming. It's not five yet."

"Yeah, dickheads. It's not five yet."

"Besides," I say, "I thought you *A-Team* guys in the rooms with a view would have more than three superstars at their own party. So what's in the cooler?"

Franco opens it and hands me a Coke. An elevator must have landed on the ground floor because we're suddenly surrounded by girls. They grab diet Cokes. Someone lights the grill, and our floor leader gets us playing volleyball. The game heats up when Franco spikes one off my head. I shake off the worried looks and rotate around to serve. First serve, net. Nerd girl strikes again.

We play, the guys win, and they tell us that means we have to coordinate next month's floor exchange.

"Exchange?" Norine sidles up to the muscled guy. "What are we exchanging? Like, I don't know, fluids?"

I blush.

The boys find the remark hilarious, and suddenly they all surround her like she's Marlene the Lumberjack in *Sixteen Candles*. I sit on the grass with my plate, two hot dogs and chips and another Coke. I lean against the brick wall. The bricks are warm through my tee-shirt even with a cool breeze picking up. Franco breaks off from the man-pack to sit by me.

"Sorry I slammed your head on that block."

"Were you aiming for me?"

"No way. I jump and hit. Look out below!"

He smiles with big white teeth. His brown eyes are like mine, a little more almond shaped. He pulls his hair out of the leather tie, runs a comb through it, and puts it back up.

"I used to have hair like yours," I say.

"I bet it was cute."

"Got sick of it. The whole Latina sterotype. New do, new me."

"Really? You better join *La Raza*. We'll help you be yourself here. Those white breads aren't going to respect you more for trying to mayo out your heritage."

"That's a thought. I heard you making fun of yourself, that talk about *La Migra*."

"I'm not advocating a Mexicans-only existence. I'm just sayin', don't sweat being who you are."

"Yeah, cool. So who's your roommate?"

"The jock."

"Is that okay?"

"Why not?"

"He seems like such a show off."

"Only in front of the ladies. Is that foxy girl your roommate?"

"Norine? I met her down the hall. She's very, um, she's very friendly and outgoing."

"Probably a man-eater."

"Totally At least that's what she wants people to think."

"So where's your roommate?"

I scan the mob of students. Shirley sits at a table with Salt. She has on long jeans and didn't bring her crutches. I point. "Over there with a friend from home."

"You like her okay?"

"So far, yeah, fine," I lie. I don't want to bring up the subject of her leg. That would be disloyal and rude. I can't mention the pot either because you never know who's a narc. "Want to meet her?"

"Later. I have to get going, need trash bags for the clean-up crew. What's your name anyway?"

"Carmen."

"Really? Joe was talking about some girl named Caramel. I'm Franco."

"So I heard when you were squirming around in the net. Now you let them use you like a bus boy? I don't think that's a good precedent."

"What did you score on your SAT? Precedent? God, show off."

"1250. And my math score was pathetic. I'm majoring in Art or English Lit."

"Why not Spanish Lit? Or Hispanic Studies?"

"I like to go against stereotype."

"Me too. I'm a chem major, pre-med with a philosophy minor. So if you get in some logic or math class and need help, I'm your man."

"Thanks, I'll need it. I want to prove Latinas aren't baby factories with no brains."

"That's the spirit! With the short hair and all *Viva La Raza*!" He gets up, brushes the grass of his butt.

"Hey, Franco?"

"Yeah," he says walking backwards.

"Could you help me with my schedule? I have to meet my advisor tomorrow."

"Breakfast at seven? That gives us a couple hours. The profs never show up until nine."

"Seven? Who in college gets up at seven?"

"Me. So if you want some help, be there. If you're okay, if you find someone else, no sweat. I like breakfast. I'd rather eat hot food than Frosted Flakes."

"I doubt the dorm serves *huevos rancheros* like *abuelita* used to make."

"I bring my own hot sauce." He's shouting now because he's pretty far away, still walking backwards.

Norine yells, "Hey, honey! I like it with hot sauce!" She licks her lips.

Franco gives her that beautiful smile. As he turns, he crashes into another guy. Joe, Joe Sneed.

Chapter 6

Joe blocks my view. I lean left to finish watching Franco walk away. Franco has the cutest butt. His glossy pony tail shines like spangled satin. Whew, gorgeous man.

"Hey, Caramel. What's so interesting over there?"

"Nothing. You're cutting off my rays, Schmo!"

"What?"

"You call me Caramel. I'm calling you Joe Schmo. Schmo for short."

"Not nice. WPC will be all over you."

"I doubt it."

"Okay, true, Carmen. So the *seniorita* gets a chili pepper up her ass when she doesn't get her way."

"Thank you, Mr. Sneed. By the way, in my culture, we don't go around talking about female body parts to women. Is that a cultural cue I should learn from you? Or perhaps you could learn it from me?"

"Christ, Carmen. Who poured the hot sauce on your tongue tonight?"

"The whole story or the shortened version?"

"Let's walk to campus. I'll buy you that ice cream at Al's. Tell me what's up."

The sun is lower, and it's like San Ysidro here, the fog has come rolling in. I shiver.

"Let me get a sweatshirt. I'll be right back." I bound up the stairs, open our room, and grab my WPC sweatshirt that Tia Ines bought me back when Mama was still pushing junior college.

The drawer to my desk is open, which is weird. Looking in, I have to slap myself. My wallet is gone. All the money I saved to spend this week before financial aid comes, it's all gone. Shit, shit, shit, shit, shit. Maybe I put it somewhere else? I know that's just bull. Somebody, probably somebody named Shirley or her creepy friend, Salt, has my wallet. I'm in college and now I'm playing Charlie's Angel? Nothing like having a one-legged thief for a roommate.

The elevator drops me off in the lobby. Joe is right there, straight ahead of me when the door opens.

"What would you have done if some other girl had come out?"

"Said hi."

"You're so weird."

"You're so uptight. Relax, it's only college. It's only the rest of your life. This is the fun part. When classes start, then you can get uptight."

"Yeah, I'm going over the class schedule with Franco tomorrow morning."

Joe takes me by the arm and guides me to the dorm's back doors. There's a terrace that overlooks the campus, which is beautiful in the golden light of the setting sun. "I would have helped you with your schedule."

"I'll make one with him and then show it to you. My appointment with the advisor isn't until 9. There's something else though."

"No kidding?"

"It just happened. My wallet is gone."

"You left your wallet in your room? You need your driver's license for everything."

"Teri had me put it into my pocket."

"Well, that's a relief. But I thought WPC required students to be smart and honest? Haven't you freshmen met with the Chancellor yet to hear the Lecture of the Five Stars?"

"We haven't. Don't be so sarcastic. I live the Five Stars, or I wouldn't have come here. Who would take my wallet? My roommate? Great, just great."

And with that I launch into everything that has gone wrong since we got the truck going again. The whole thing with Shirley's leg, her bizarre friends, my mother, Norine. I leave out my visit to the R.A. I take up the entire walk to Al's spilling my guts to Joe. He's pretty patient actually, saying "uh huh" about thirty times.

We get to the student union, which is a modern building. The architecture doesn't fit in with the Rococo quad buildings.

"Don't go in through the student store. It's a mad house until everybody's bought their books." He guides me up the hill, and we go in through an entrance on the second floor. I can't believe it. There's a bowling alley in this place.

"Bowling alley," Joes inclines his head to the right. "Too bad Professor Pin isn't teaching it." He elbows me in the ribs.

"From what I remember, it's Professor Stu U."

We both crack up. Al's is noisy and dark. Bluesy jazz blares from a jukebox. I'm not into jazz, but it makes me feel collegiate. People yell back and forth across the noise, like a family in their own kitchen. Joe hands me a bowl to self-serve the soft ice cream. I get all vanilla. He goes for half chocolate and half vanilla. I douse mine with almonds, crushed graham crackers, and a flood of caramel syrup. He chooses hot fudge plus whipped cream and a cherry. He adds a cherry to the top of my sundae. He pays the lady at the register even though mine would be free with my meal card.

Guys wave us over to their table. Joe looks at me and asks, "Okay to join them?"

"Sure."

"Hey, buds. This is Carmen. She's from . . " he wrinkles his forehead and looks at me, "San Diego. Freshie."

They all say hello and go back to talking football. Their language is way crude, but it's a bunch of guys. I smile my sophisticated college girl patient-with-idiots smile, which I manage well until Joe points to my lip.

"What?" I touch my lip. There's a blob of caramel there. I try to lick it off with my tongue. It's a lot and really sticky. Conversation at the table stops as the guys watch my tongue reaching for the caramel.

Joe dips a napkin into his ice water. He reaches across and wipes my lip. "That better?" he asks, and my spirits soar.

The guys are members of Joe's frat. They're all wearing the same insignia on their sweatshirts. They tell Joe it's time to rock and roll, lifting their eyebrows over and over. "Little Sister night," Joe explains. "Girls from each sorority come by and we tell her all the things we like a Little Sister to do for the frat. It's strictly voluntary with lots of benefits."

"Yeah, I bet. Name one benefit."

"Hanging out with studs like us. Having one of us available as a date. Listen, Carmen, can you get back to the dorm okay? I should go with my brothers."

"Why not?" even though I have a sinking feeling about walking up the big hill to the dorm in the dark and the fog and alone.

Before he leaves, Joe gives me a hug. "I'm glad I met you. Even though you're such a newbie and a militant." He reaches down like he's going to pat my butt, but he slips something into the pocket. "You call me. Don't forget. Franco probably has no clue about what classes you should take. Pre-meds live in an alternate universe." For the last forty-five minutes, I had forgotten all about Franco and breakfast and making a class schedule.

"Bye." I watch the guys leave, like sparklers fizzing through the union, sparking with their energy. They each jump up to touch the upper threshold as they leave Al's, and they cheer Joe, who is shortest, when he taps it higher than the others.

I sit swirling the dregs of my sundae, trying to think of a non-confrontational opening line to use with Shirley about the missing wallet. This reminds me of the paper in my pocket. Not only has Joe left me his phone number, he put a twenty dollar bill inside it. I don't know whether to be glad or mad. I tune out all the noise around me, staring at the bill. Maybe I'll give it back to him. I don't want him to think he can buy me like, you know, a 'ho. I wonder if he was hinting that I should think about being a Little Sister. But he didn't insist that I come with him, now did he?

Out front of the student union there's a bus stop for the U-tram. It takes people up the hill to the dorms and the apartments across Arch Street. See, I learned about the tram, another positive thing today. So cool, I get on the tram and chill.

Chapter 7

I scoot into the middle seat. The driver turns back towards me, asking "Where to?" I want to say San Ysidro, but I tell him Ortega. He says okay, we have one more stop before heading up the hill. He guns it and stops at Crusader Way. Two girls in their classic sweater sets wear their sorority ribbons over their hearts. They step daintily into the back seat.

A guy hollers, "Wait up!" The tram stops with a clunk. The guy jumps in beside me. I have my sweatshirt's hood up, shielding my face. The guy nudges my shoulder, "Carmen. It's me, Franco." I push the hood back, and Franco gives me a toothy grin.

"I was up at Railey Library," he says, pointing to a stack of books.

"We're not even in class yet. What's up with that?"

"The Humanities courses are killer for pre-meds. I'm getting a head start on the reading list." He counts the books. "Five, for one class. Torture."

"You could use the notes."

"Never. Who wants a doctor who cheated his way through college?"

I pick up two of the books. "I'm not sure *Jude the Obscure* and *Catch-22* have much to do with your success as a doctor."

"How about as a literate human being? Doctors treat people, right? Books are about people." He shakes his head. "And the best prep for the MCAT is reading widely."

"You sound like a teacher. Is the MCAT like the SAT?" He nods. "You're right. Those stupid notes are nothing like reading the book." His face is serious. His eyes are big and brown and shining. His hair, still in its pony tail wrap, shines too. "How did you know what books to choose?"

"The Student Store has all the books by class. I usually use the library copies instead of buying them if I can. My science books cost a fortune."

"I pick up my scholarship money on Monday. Where should I open my checking account?"

"The closest bank. There are about ten of them. You can get cash at Berkebile's cashier. Which scholarship?"

I don't want to sound like a bragger. I have three. "One from my high school, one from the state, plus a grant, and a government loan, and a work-study job."

"Yeah, me too. I work in the chem lab. I distribute the chemicals people need for their lab experiments. Not much work and I can study."

"When will they tell me which job I'll have?"

"After you have a class schedule. The work-study office people are cool. Be sure to ask for Marlene. She'll call around until she can find something that works for you."

"Righteous."

"Carmen, nobody at the U says *righteous* anymore."

"I'm an old-fashioned girl."

The bus pulls into the dorm circle. The few of us riding grab our things to exit. People are waiting to get on, but the driver says this was his last trip.

"Franco, you'll still help me with my schedule in the morning?"

"Sure. I thought you'd forgotten. Are you going over to the frats tonight, the Little Sister thing?"

"Don't they only take sorority girls?"

"Not what I heard."

"That's not for me," I say even as I watch the two sorority girls fluffing their hair and checking their lipstick as they walk to the light on Arch.

"Righteous," says Franco with a big smile. "So goodnight. See you at breakfast."

"Deal," I say. I push the elevator button. Nobody is going upstairs with me. I hear the ping pong balls hitting the tables in the rec room, a television blares *Magnum, P.I.* I smell fresh popcorn. My pants feel tight in the waist. No popcorn after a sundae. I don't have to be an idiot about food, which reminds me I don't have any money for the machines anyway, just the bill Joe put into my pocket. For a first day at the university, I rate it a 50-50, half fun, half frustration.

When I get to my room, the door is open, but Shirley isn't there. If she's going to leave the door open for anybody in the world to walk in, I'm going to have to keep my money and my wallet in my backpack. I open my closet door to find where I stuffed my pj's, grab them and my bathroom kit, make sure I have my key, and zip up the hall to the bathroom. It's empty. I brush my teeth, tweeze my eyebrows, check my hair to see if I need to wash it in the morning. I sigh. Everything's done. I can go to bed now and see what tomorrow brings.

Outside the room when I return, Shirley is leaning against the wall. She has taken off her prosthetic leg, and is using her crutch for balance.

"Why'd you lock it? I didn't take my key." She says this in an annoyed voice.

"Sorry, I don't like having the door open when we're not there. Somebody took my wallet today."

Shirley doesn't blink. "Who would do that?"

"I don't know. I'm short of cash until I see the scholarship people on Monday."

"Sucks."

"So that's why I'm big on locking the door. Anybody could walk in and swipe whatever—our tapes, your tape deck, my record player.

"My leg."

This last is so ridiculous we both burst out laughing. "Yeah, your leg. They'd have to be complete losers to steal your leg."

"Somebody might do it as a joke."

"That is not even funny. So let's agree to lock the door and carry our keys?"

"It's hard for me to balance and get the key into the lock."

"We can't leave the door open all the time 'cause of money. . ."

"And a leg."

I unlock the door, and we both throw ourselves on our beds. We are laughing like I used to laugh with Ashley, sputtering words and laughing, snorting and laughing twice as hard. I say, "Goodnight, Shirley."

She snorts another laugh. I bury my head into my pillow. "Goodnight, Laverne," she says. "I'll turn out the light in a few minutes. I have to massage my stump, unless you want to." She unwraps an Ace bandage from the stump, rubbing an ointment into the calluses. The ointment gives off a lemony smell.

"Uh, no, but thanks for asking," I say, mashing a second pillow over my head, and pulling a little night mask over my eyes because I can't sleep if there is the least bit of light coming in. I really do not like seeing Shirley's leg stump. I imagine the doctors cutting through flesh and bone, Shirley waking up with one good leg and one amputated. I shiver.

The last thing I hear before I fall asleep is Shirley's crutch falling to the floor and the springs on her bed squeaking. I inhale the lemon scent and picture my house at home. WPC doesn't feel like home, not yet. I think about Mama turning the lights out, checking the doors, telling me not to stay up too late reading.

And then, in our room, it's dark, quiet, and sort of okay.

The fire alarm rings at 2 a.m. We shuffle down the stairs in a mob of grumbling, droopy, messy girls in long tee's, robes, or pj's. Shirley doesn't have her leg. She has to lean on me. People wake up enough as we wait in the cold and fog to huddle together. The pushy girls set themselves up in the middle of the circle so the boys can't see them at less than their best. They stare at Shirley like she's a freak.

"Get a life," I yell. People probably think it's the fire alarm that set me off.

Chapter 8

Somehow, I make it out of bed in the morning. Franco meets me outside the dorm caf. He scoops food onto two plates, fruit, eggs and bacon, a blueberry muffin. I choose cereal and coffee.

"Way to pile it on," I say as I pass him to sit at the nearest table. There's not one other person in the cafeteria yet.

"I'm a growing boy," he says to my back. When I return from the milk machine, he's pouring ketchup over the eggs and bacon. The smell makes me nauseated. I move around the table to sit by him so that I won't have to look at his plate full of ketchup and egg mash.

The schedule of classes is sitting between us by his right hand. He's left-handed. I start flipping the pages. Franco lets me start making a list on my note pad until he can't stand it anymore.

"Carmen, stop. Just stop."

"What?"

"That's not how you make a schedule. First things first. Did you test out of English 101?"

"I don't know."

"You'd know if you did. So that means you have to take the writing test before next quarter."

"So if I think I might major in English, I can't take an English class this quarter?"

"Basically."

"What about if I want to major in Art?"

"Do you have your portfolio together?"

I think of my pictures of Mama's piñatas. "Not completely."

"What kind of art?"

"Pottery?"

"Why bother coming here to learn pottery?"

"It sort of runs in our family. My mother is well known at home for her," I stop to swallow a gulp of coffee, "creations. I want to learn the art history of Mexican pottery."

"You can go undecided for two years, but that's not going to get you very far. Look. The schedule has this new department of Hispanic studies. I'm taking a class in that plus the Humanities class. Everything else is math and science. Pre-med, every quarter is laid out. Engineering too."

"Well, I hate math."

"Understandable. You artistes are big on the right-brain classes."

"I don't follow."

"Solution. Take Psych 10. Everybody takes it sooner or later. Take a required history class like History of the U.S. It's offered in two quarters and you can take either quarter first, A or B, they don't care which order. Listen, sooner or later, you're going to have to fulfill some science."

"History and psych. That sounds good. What's in Hispanic studies?"

He paws through the schedule until he reaches the department's offerings. He runs his finger down the list. His fingers are long, his nails are clipped to the quick, and he drums his right hand as he searches.

"How about 'Art of the Mayans'?"

"Are there field trips to Mexico?" I'm trying out Norine's flirty attitude.

Franco misses it or dismisses it, goes straight for the rules. "You have to be a grad student to enroll in the on-site digs. Plus you have to major in anthropology or archaeology. Anthro! That's a perfect class for you."He goes back to the first page of the schedule. "See, Anthro 1A, physical anthro. It's in Mead, which means they'll take about 500 people. You won't get shut out."

"Could we put that as a 'maybe'?" I don't even know what anthropology is.

"Let's work out the rest. Lots of people like classes on Tuesday-Thursday, so they can party the rest of the week. I'd rather go to class every day. Well, maybe not so much on Mondays."

"Is that when you turn into a party animal?"

"That's when I'm coming back from visiting family or studying for the MCAT."

"Franco, you are one serious dude."

"My roommate complains about that a lot."

"Not vice versa?"

"If he brings booze up or a girl to the room, I study in the lounge or the library. My family expects me to be a doctor, like my father wanted to be, and that's what I'm going to do. Some of the profs look at me like I'm the token Mexican, part of the affirmative action quota. They'll do that to you too. You have to be on top of all your reading and every assignment. Don't take any *mierda* from them. And don't give them any either. No matter who you were in high school, the U let you in, but they'll be happy to push you out."

"Maybe I should go home to San Ysidro and apprentice with my mom."

"That's not what I'm saying. *La Raza* needs educated Hispanics. You're here. Take advantage of everything. It's right in front of you."

We're quiet except for his drumming right hand. I bite my cheek and behind my lower lip. I know exactly what he means and since my high school was just okay, I'm getting worried about academics. In high school, it was all so easy. Franco sees the worry in my eyes and pats my hand.

"You can do this." He shows me how the classes meet at a certain time, like Monday, Wednesday, Friday at 10 a.m., but the big classes also have quiz sections where the T.A.s lead discussions and as Franco says "harass the hell out of everyone."

I breathe a big sigh of relief. The caf is filling up. Shirley, Norine, and two nuns are way back in line. Nuns? Clear proof there is a God since neither nun is Norine's roommate. How cosmically wrong would that be?

Franco hands me the schedule. "Keep this with you in case your advisor wants you to change something. I gotta go. I take a practice MCAT once a week with my study group."

"All right. I'll catch you later and tell you what happens. Thanks for helping me, Franco. Other people were suggesting a bunch of easy classes, what do you call them? Micks? Is that an insult to Irish people?"

Franco shakes his head, laughing. "No, Carmen. Mick stands for Mickey Mouse. Gets you credits, easy as shucking corn, but of absolutely no redeeming value. Who are these other people?"

I don't want to say it's Joe. Franco would start on a rant about the white-bread prejudice and trying to hold us back from our rights and our talents. "Some guy, maybe Shirley's friend, Salt."

"You know a guy named Salt?"

"His name is Morton. They call him Salt."

"Your name is Carmen. Should I call you Miranda?" He wiggles his slim hips and pretends he's holding a head dress up high.

"I thought you had places to go," I laugh.

"MCAT. Hey, my room number is 702. Call me later? Isn't today the Chancellor's Five Star talk with the freshmen?"

"It is. It's in Romans Hall. I'll call after I know the five secrets of WPC and which parts of our schedule are approved."

Franco backs out the door, snapping his fingers. He's spontaneously rapping loudly,

History's a mystery
Psych will get you psyched
Anthro is for the po'
So go girl go
Get in with *La Raza* and learn your traditions
Put yourself beyond Whitey's suspicions.
Go, girl, go, Go, girl, go.

I pick up my backpack, schedule tucked into the pocket where my financial aid contract is. The campus map I keep in my hands. All I know is go down the hill, walk up Founder's steps, and turn left at Founder's Rock. Bramble is the second building not the first. The professor's office is in the second level of the basement. I've hated basements since my cousins locked me in one when I was twelve. It was dark and creepy.

Chapter 9

Haze floats over campus. From the deck outside the cafeteria, the quad buildings float like a painting of Italy. I feel as if I am about to walk into a dream.

The ten-minute walk is five minutes downhill followed by five minutes uphill. I take the angled blacktop path, leaving the famous steps for another day. The sun has risen higher, and all of a sudden it's hot. I wish I had worn flip flops, a tee-shirt, and shorts instead of these sandals that are quickly giving me a blister on my right toe. My gingham sundress that Mama made and that I loved last summer now shouts scholarship student, poor kid. Everyone passes me in pairs or groups of three. Where are the other freshmen who haven't made friends yet?

I find the hall downstairs where my advisor has his office, and take a minute to stop in a bathroom to brush my hair and run a wet paper towel over my face, removing the sweat. I run a finger over each eyebrow. The bathroom is wonderful, a relief after the chaos of the dorm bathrooms, which get steamed up from showers and are under siege with chattering girls. This bathroom has the window thrown open, overlooking a sunken square edged by trees. That's where I'll study, I decide, out there under a tree.

Back into the gloomy hallway of the gloomy basement, I feel my stomach clenching. Stop, breathe, you're fine. There's a little museum exhibit of Mayan art behind glass-doored cupboards. I look at my watch, 8:45. No time for sightseeing right now although I note that this little museum wasn't on any of the campus tours I've attended.

When I turn the corner, a line of students sits against the wall. "Hispanic studies advisor?" I ask, hoping maybe I don't have to get into this line.

"Yep, late as usual," says the first girl in line, her hair block cut like Roseann Roseannadanna's on *Saturday Night Live*. She has on a poncho over a granny length dress and huarache sandals.

"You're sixth, sit here." The only boy in line points to the spot behind him. A nun lines up behind me. She is Hispanic, perhaps Mexican Indian. Her legs stick out from her blue serge skirt like mahogany in stockings. Her complexion is dark, but rosy and meek. I can't see her hair under her wimple-thing.

I offer to let her go ahead of me. She smiles and says it isn't important. Her English is heavily accented. She lives in Ortega with another nun on an educational respite. Her name is Sister Rosalie. Her roommate is Sister Octavia. This morning's riddle is answered, but a new one pops up. Why didn't I see them at the fire drill? They must sleep in pj's like the rest of us. I pity them the noise and idiocy of us all.

I show her and the guy in front of me my appointment card. He shrugs. "We all have the same time. Nothing to do but wait."

"They also serve who only stand and wait," says the nun.

"What book of the Bible is that?"

"Not the Bible. John Milton, English poet."

"Really? Guess I shouldn't major in English Lit. Could I see your schedule?" I ask them both to be friendly. The guy hands his paper over. He's taking calculus, biology, and one class in Hispanic Studies. He doesn't look Mexican or Latino. He looks like a white guy, like Joe.

"Mixed race parents. My last name is Guerra. Whatever works," he explains. "The last name opens doors for me. How 'bout you?"

Before I can answer, a dapper man with salt-and-pepper hair, dark skin, sunken, sad eyes and patrician cheekbones opens the door. He's been inside this whole time and made us wait?

"Phone call. Sorry. Who's first? You, Christabel?" He scans the rest of us. "Don't worry. This will go fast."

We all get to our feet. Christabel is in and out in about two minutes. Each person in front of me seems to take a little longer. Finally, it's my turn. Ten more students have lined up behind me.

"Welcome," says the professor. "Call me Jesus, please."

"Yes, sir. Here's my schedule for fall." I hand it over. He checks off classes and puts his initials on the bottom. He stamps a number on the paper.

"This is your call-in code. The classes I checked are the ones I encourage you to try to get into this fall, sort of test the waters. Pleasure to meet you," he looks at the paper again, "Carmen. Do you have any questions?"

"Only what my calling window is."

"Nobody told you in your admissions letter? You have open calling. You could call right now from this phone if I didn't have all those kids in line."

"Radical!" I could walk right out and use the pay phone.

"Come back in once the quarter is underway," he tells me, "and call the next person in, please." I send in the nun.

I walk outside to the little quad I saw to go over his suggestions. He's given me the go-ahead on everything Franco listed. I realize this advising thing is mostly a waste of time. Still debating whether to make my schedule top priority, I see a line forming outside the admin building. I know that's financial aid. Money or classes? I choose money since I have none.

More waiting. Hurry up and wait my Uncle Ernesto said was all he did in the army in Vietnam. WPC must follow the same procedures. I wish I had put a muffin in my backpack. My stomach is growling. Nobody in this line is wearing sorority pledge ribbons. I pull out my journal and start writing some ideas, but then a flood of emotions sinks my heart. I am absolutely drowning in homesickness. I take big, deep breaths and ask the person behind me to hold my place in line. I go to the drinking fountain and find a candy machine. Digging around in my backpack results in finding three dimes and three nickels. I buy M&M's.

The line has broken into two when I get back. The guy holding my place says a second window opened. Thank God. I give him three M&M's.

When I get up there, my driver's license and my signature are all I need for my money. The lady, who looks like an older version of Mallory in "Family Ties," tells me that I am in charge of paying everything from this check except fees which are paid automatically by the state.

"Budget your money," she warns. "Books and school supplies before tapes and meals out." I swallow an M&M, which catches in my guilty throat as I realize money for candy is not in the budget, at least not until I'm working.

"Could you point me to the work-study office, please?"

"Upstairs, double doors."

I thank her. Upstairs, the double doors open into a vast office space. There is no line. Maybe not as many qualify for work-study as for grants. Maybe everybody wants to put off working until they go to classes. I don't care. I ask for Marlene.

The student at the phone picks it up and tells me to have a seat in a row of chairs along the wall. "She'll be right out." It's like a doctor's office, very quiet except for typewriters. The room smells like paper and hums with the clacking of typewriter keys. I would love to work in an office like this.

The desk phone rings. "Marlene will see you now," says her clerk. "Down the hall on your right."

I'm not nervous about meeting Marlene. I'll tell her Franco sent me.

"Good morning, Carmen." She stands and holds out her hand. What did I think, that she would high five me? She has her hair up in a clip in back, curls cascading, and long, beaded earrings. Her smile is as white against her dark skin as Franco's except she's black and Franco is Latino.

"Franco told me to be sure to see you about my work-study."

"Oh, he did, did he?"

"Yes."

"Now, you're a freshman, so I hope you don't have your heart set on a job like Franco's. We take care of all of you, but especially the minority pre-meds."

"I see."

"We'll put you in the dorm caf, morning shift.

I don't answer. I want classes in the morning. I want time to study at my job. "Are there any jobs in the library?"

She yawns. "Oh, you freshmen. So much to learn. Those library jobs go to seniors. Don't worry. You'll make everything fit. Besides, you'll love it that morning shift workers get weekends off. If you have any questions, you come see me, Carmen." She stands. "Tell that devil Franco hello."

She says goodbye, sits down and flutters her fingers emphatically as she picks up her phone for her next candidate. I pass Norine in the hall. She gives me a hug and says, "Awesome to see you! Wouldn't it be fun to work together? What'd you take?"

"It's not like that. You go in, and the lady hands you an assignment." I cross my fingers that Norine is not on any shift I'm working.

Marlene steps into the hallway. I hurry away to pout about the crummy job. I wonder if maybe I can get along without working. My watch shows it's almost time to go to hear the Chancellor. I toss the last of my M&M's into my mouth, and my head starts pounding. Today is not a good day for a migraine.

Freshmen stand in groups outside the main auditorium. I check the doors, find them open, and walk in. I sit in front. The room is cool and dark, like the inside of a cave but with plush velvet seats. I slip my sandals off and rub my sore toe. A tech walks out on the stage and tests the microphone. He sees me and says "Welcome to WPC."

When the buzzer rings that ends class sessions, the herd of freshmen rush into the auditorium. A few venture forward to sit near me. One girl looks at me as she sits down. Then she changes her seat. I try not to be insulted. She probably knows someone behind us. Most everybody else sits farther back. I lean over to slip my sandals back on. Sister Rosalie taps me on the shoulder from behind. She's sitting with her nun roommate. Shirley waves to me from across the aisle. Salt waves too.

The buzz of conversation stops when a jaunty young man in blue beret comes out to the microphone. He introduces himself as the President of the Associated Students Systems. He writes, ASS in Berkebile 111 on the chalkboard. We laugh. "We could use your help," he says. "Join us. That's the main thing I want to get across. Your classes are why you're here, but your clubs and involvement will teach you too. Don't lose out on half of your education by holing up in your room. Get yourself a Crusader beret. Put your club pins on it. Everybody, Greeks or not, inhale life!" We laugh again. He erases the chalkboard before he turns the stage over to the Chancellor. The student body president motions that we should stand up and applaud. We do.

The Chancellor signals for quiet. He gazes at us. "Welcome freshmen and transfers to WPC. Freshmen, you will be the Class of 1988." Raucous applause begins again. "Let's keep this short. We are here today to say hello to you as our newest Crusaders. And with that hello come many responsibilities. Ushers are handing out our Code of Conduct." He pauses while pamphlets are passed across the rows. "The most important thing I can tell you is that you will always be on stage, maybe not one like this one, but wherever you are on campus, or wherever you go off campus with your Crusader wear on, you represent this university. You are not to take this privilege lightly."

He stops. A hand goes up. "I'll take questions at the end in person, young man. Be sure to attend our Chancellor's Tea. I hear the cookies are to die for."

We smile, clap, nudge one another. The Chancellor seems cool.

"Open your pamphlets please to page one, star one."

We dutifully follow along as he reminds us that WPC is a religion-based university. While not everyone is Catholic, all are expected to live the Five Star Code: Reverence for the Lord, reverence for our elders, reverence for ourselves, honesty, fair play.

"Now let's look at that third star again," he intones. The audience is getting restless. We've been sitting here underlining and repeating and being good little robots for half an hour.

"Reverence for yourselves covers many miles marked by crossroads. You will be making choices that are personal to you, and yet, those choices also are part of the larger body you are a part of, this student body. This is a reminder to honor your body and the University's body. Honor the gift of your sexuality by remaining chaste. Honor the words that come from your mouth by speaking without vulgarity. Honor yourself by the company you keep, making sure that you and your roommates stay true to the Crusader ideals.

"May I count on you?" We are quiet. "I couldn't hear your answer!"

"Yes!" a few hundred voices answer.

"I hope so," says a man's voice in the front. I look sideways to see none other than Salt with his arms out, his hands open in praise and prayer.

"We are here at many levels to support you in your Crusade. Together, please, the University's motto, "*Vivemus ad honorare et servire.*" We repeat after him.

"Let us begin by serving you. Lunch in the Commons begins now."

He walks off-stage and into the crowd of students, many reaching out to shake his hand or touch his coat. In the mobs, I lose track of Shirley and Salt. Norine probably didn't bother with a morals meeting. I take an extra pamphlet to pin to her door.

I lunch with Sister Rosalie and meet Sister Octavia. The nuns could be twins except Sister Octavia is more talkative and she has a Madonna-type upper lip mole. Some sorority pledges, who despite their universal stereotype of snootiness, join us. They are funny and kind. Actually, the nuns are pretty hilarious too describing how wonderful it is to have hot water and how hard it is to pack all their prayers into a day filled with classes. Sister Rosalie knows Franco. She wags her finger, informing us that he is a *muy inteligente mujeriego. Mujeriego* means ladies man or run-around, take your pick. Sister Octavia says there's a lot of things to like about being a nun. They don't ever have to worry about bed head or what to wear since it doesn't change day-to-day, wimple, white blouse, blue skirt, Doc Martens. I laugh like crazy, glad neither is going to have to put up with Norine even while wondering how Sister Rosalie knows Franco. She's probably from his home parish.

I slip a few extra chocolate chip cookies into my backpack to share back at the dorm like a welcome party.

When I return to my room, my wallet is lying on my bed. And my money is all there too.

Chapter 10

Sleep evades me. I am nervous about another fire drill, worried that the alarm will go off and wake up Shirley, afraid that I won't wake up or get to the kitchen on time.

Toss, turn, go to bathroom, avoid looking at my baggy eyelids and black circles. I'm 18. I look 92.

The kitchen crew wears regular clothes except for the hair nets --auuugh, ugly-- and the aprons. I have to quadruple fold the apron to keep it out of the way of my feet. Oh, another rule, no flip flops. I have on my plaid tennis shoes, which are totally cool and preppy and go with my first-day-of-classes blue plaid. But first I have three hours in the kitchen.

Head cook Mitchell weighs as much as a head cook should, meaning that he's over 300 pounds. The flab under his jaw tilts his head back so that he's always staring at me from a position exposing his nostril hairs. He laughs easily, especially because I fool with my hair net.

"It's hopeless," he says to me.

"What?"

"Trying to look charming in a hairnet. You're here to do a job, so do it. Forget who might see you. You're fine."

"Got it."

"Let's start easy. You open these cans," he points to mega-sized fruit cocktail barrels, "and you use this spoon to scoop a portion into each of these bowls. If you drop the spoon, get another. No dirty spoons from floor to bowl. OK? Fill ten trays with twelve bowls each."

"Sure." This is easy enough and there aren't that many people back here. Mitchell directs me, an Italian man at the griddle who says to call him Guido, and two other girls like myself, in the ugly hairnets. One has been dispatched to make toast, and the other is counting out cereal boxes, the individual portions, which I've wanted to try since I was a toddler, but Mama said I'd end up eating all the sugared stuff and never eat the plain ones. She was right. I wonder if there's an overload of Wheaties in the kitchen here?

Running the huge can opener scares me. We have on plastic gloves, which make everything feel slippery.

"Mitchell, do I open all the cans first, or do one at a time?"

He takes a big breath. "Right. Ask when you aren't sure. So one at a time until you know how many cans you need."

"I can do that." Immediately, I have a can opened and start scooping fruit cocktail into bowls. The bowls go on a tray. The tray is carried to the front by the cereal girl. The cereal girl says, "Hey" when she picks up the first tray from me. "I'm Penny." Penny could be Mitchell's daughter; she's so plain fat.

The first hour passes like a flash. Mitchell leans his head left and right to loosen the cricks. "We need to work faster. Early in the school year, breakfast is busy. By winter, they'll all sleep in—except you guys—and then we'll have it easier. As long as the admin doesn't notice at that point that we're overstaffed."

"I think they already know," I whisper to Penny. "Will any of us get kicked out of work study?"

Penny shrugs. "It's the U. They do whatever they want. We're just little dots they move around a board until eventually we pass go. What's your major?"

After my tussle with the computer and phoning in classes last night, my major is no where to be seen in my schedule. "Hispanic art emphasis," I say.

"So you're what. . .going to be an archeologist? Anthropologist?"

"I was thinking teacher."

"I wasn't thinking when I chose art history. What the hell does someone do with an art history major? How many museums are in big American cities? How many art history majors are graduating from just WPC? That's what my parents asked me. I didn't want to tell them they're right—too many grads, not enough jobs. So probably, I'll sell shoes after my four years here unless I go for the Master's and Ph.D. Then I could teach here or junior college. That would be cool."

She turns to take my last tray of fruit. As she pivots towards the serving counter, she slips, splat. The bowls scatter, clatter, and spill. Guido points to the corner where there's a mop and a broom.

Mitchell tears at his hair so that it stands up in spikes under his hair net.

"Who's at fault?"

Penny cocks her head towards me.

"Me? How did I make you fall?"

"Look at the floor! You're supposed to mop every time you spill."

"Nobody told me."

"Common sense," says Penny, handing me the mop. "Mitchell, I twisted my ankle. I'm out for today." She hobbles to the door. Guido hands her an ice pack. She waves goodbye. "Hey, new girl. Keep on truckin', baby."

Mitchell is grumbling about accident reports and his reputation. He squints his eyes in a mean way as if he's reassessing my ability in the kitchen. "Well, quit staring and get this cleaned up. We were cruising along, and now we're short-handed."

Scooping the fruit from the floor into the waste bin releases a sickening-sweet smell that wasn't there before. My throat closes off. I don't want to barf. The fruit is slippery, the floor is sticky, and the mop smells like sour milk. Nice wake-up call.

I finish the clean up and replace the missing bowls of fruit. The clock has inched by another thirty minutes. Maybe they'll let me go early, first day and all?

Guido says, "New girl. Over here. Change gloves. Crack eggs." The toast girl doesn't even look up, so he must mean me.

"Yes, sir." He shows me how he cracks eggs four at a time, two in each hand.

"That's a little advanced for me." I crack the eggs against a counter and slip them into bowls. I can't mess this up since these are for scrambled eggs. Every now and then I have to flick a bit of shell out of the amassing set of yolks. Guido is urging me to work faster because he wants to get the scrambles on and into the steam table. The sweat under my hair net trickles down the back of my neck. Crack, slop, crack, slop, when I could be writing in my journal at the library waiting for someone to need an assigned reading, which I imagine no one does until around mid-terms. Half the quarter getting paid for free writing instead of scooping, cracking, and mopping. Not a fair exchange. *Honore et sevire*? I get the honor part, but serve as in literally serving food, I don't see it as my holy mission.

With ten minutes to go in my shift, Mitchell walks by to survey my cracked eggs. "Holy Toledo. Girl, you are a snail, an anvil hanging around my neck. We need twice that many. Get moving or stay late. It's your choice." He goes back into his office. I hear him pounding away at the typewriter in there, probably writing a note to Marlene that I'm out of here, which would be fine if they'd like to reassign me to the library.

Guido chuckles. "You should learn the hand crack. Come early tomorrow. I'll show you." He has started scrambling a griddle-full of eggs, swooping across with salt and pepper when he turns the eggs. He tosses in a little cheese. He pulls bacon out of the oven. The bacon smells heavenly. He throws a crispy piece in his mouth and smiles like he's won some award.

"You have class today?" he asks.

I nod, miserably hot.

"You go. I'll tell Big Chef you finished. Here." He hands me a plate of bacon and scrambled eggs. "Eat fast." He points to some boxes. "Sit there. Put your dirty dishes into the sink."

"Coffee?"

"You have to go out to the counter for it."

So I open the kitchen door to walk out front. The clock is edging towards 7 when I'm off-shift. I grab two cups of coffee to save time. And who's first in line to see me in my hair-netted, plastic-gloved glory? Franco.

"Looking good, Carmenita," he says, as he slides his tray past me. "Get that kitchen gear off and come sit with me."

That's pretty presumptuous under the circumstances, but Franco's smile says he knows what I'm thinking.

"Let's go over your final schedule," he tosses back over his shoulder. The campus bell rings out the hour. I tear my gross net and apron off, wash my hands with about a quart of liquid soap, and take a swipe at my matted down hair. I shouldn't have cut it. I should have listened to Mama. It's a whole lot more fun playing with tissue paper and making piñatas than cleaning up squishy canned fruit and bobbing for egg shells. I always thought I was so very smart. Mama knew all along. She knows about hard, messy work. She knows about serving. She believes in all the honor stuff too, down to the letter.

There's Franco sitting with another guy. I'm not about to go sit with them. I hunker down on the boxes in the kitchen where I demolish my bacon and eggs washed down with the double cups of coffee. I thank Guido for being kind. If I can't get a shower before class I will smell like a garbage dump. Is there honor in that, Mr. Chancellor?

Chapter 11

Everybody knows that song, "It's Raining Men." It's raining kids. Students pour down the hill from the dorms, from the nearby frats, and the apartments. The sun isn't too high or too hot yet. Welcome splashes of shade cover the walkways, the trees blowing in the wind. My first class is at the top of the monster hill. Despite the hassles, I am way early instead of late.

I sit on a bench outside the lecture hall, breathing deeply to calm myself. You'd think I was the first person to struggle at the U, even when I'm surrounded by laughing girls with their pert little sorority ribbons above their hearts. All of them are in skirts. They are shrieking about a party and something called *Firstlings*. I am not in on it. I'm wearing jeans, my sweatshirt and a tee, having ditched the plaid.

Doors open, and the previous class exits in a flood of chattering students. I want to get in, but I can't maneuver through the mass of bodies coming my way. The flood lessens, and I squeeze into the lecture hall with the rest of what I assume to be freshmen, all of us with shining morning faces and eager eyes. My classmates choose one of two places, front row or back row. I sit in the front center of the section on the right-hand side. I've heard teachers teach towards their dominant hand. I want to be sure the prof sees me. The entire lecture hall is overwhelming with its stage for the prof, the pulldown screen and maps, the number of seats. Within ten minutes all the seats are filled, and kids sit in the aisle. The hum of conversation continues until a tall man with round black glasses and a pony tail bounds onto the stage, picks up the microphone, whacks it a couple of times (BLAM! BLAM!) and sits on the edge of the stage with his long legs hanging over.

"Welcome to Anthro 1A. First days are my favorite days, how 'bout you?" He turns the mike towards the audience, and we all yell, "Yeah!"

"Okay, so we'll keep this short. This is physical anthropology. Anybody in the wrong place?" There's some shuffling and quick exits. "Most of you have no clue about anthro, which is cool, neither did I when I came to college. You have one book to pick up at the book store, but you also have assigned readings for each quiz section. Those you get in the library. Try not to wait until the night before because everybody does that and then you'll be out of luck. Mid-term, a final, no papers."

Everybody cheers.

"Your participation in quiz sections will be assigned one third of your grade. That is completely between you and your T.A. Let me introduce them for you." He gestures stage right. Two young women come out. "Your TA's will be handing out the syllabus. That's it. Rock 'n roll, you guys." He pushes back and walks off. The TA's take his place. Immediately, students are shoving forward to get the syllabus. I hang back. People take off in a dozen directions, studying their syllabus. When I approach my TA she says, "Hello. Here you go," and beams a pretty smile. I scan the paper for the date of the midterm, clearly marked for mid-October, before Halloween. That's good because Mama might expect me home before the Day of the Dead.

My quiz section is tomorrow morning at 8. I'll have to be sure not to cause a mess in the kitchen. And I see there's a notation, "Quiz on Chapter One," in a book I haven't bought yet. The bookstore is going to be insane. What isn't?

I fold my syllabus and open my catalogue, which has a good map. My next class isn't until noon. Maybe I could buy my books now? But that's stupid because I shouldn't go without Franco or Joe to tell me which texts are unnecessary background reading that's available at the library. I don't want to spend extra money. I'll catch a meal at the Stu U and explore a little.

The cafeteria there is broken into stations. I pick up soup and a chicken salad sandwich. I don't know why I'm starving all the time. The cashier asks, "Student?" That seems like a stupid question, but hand her my meal card, have it stamped, and take my tray to the outdoor tables. It's quiet in the morning light even with all the activity on the walkway below me.

I'm thinking about a million things. The chicken salad is really good; the soup too. Just when I've made my next plan to move on to explore campus and find my way around, somebody pulls my hood up over my hair.

"Hey!" I yell, sort of annoyed.

"You looked cold," says a guy. I push the hood down and he moves across from me. It's Joe.

"Well, I'm not," I tell Joe.

"Let's see your schedule."

"I thought you didn't have morning classes?"

"Are you kidding?

"Obviously not," I smile.

"My major's undeclared so I sample a lot of lower division stuff. I was in Anthro 1. Those TA's, I got the hippie lady. She'll give everybody an A."

"You think? I was in there too. I thought the little one looked nicer."

"I didn't see you in there."

"Front row."

"I was against the wall. I hope a ton of people drop. That prof, he's cool. I like the jeans and the boots and the no class bit. You'll see. Some of the profs take off lecturing and keep people late the first day to get them to drop."

"Thanks for clueing me in. I have another class at noon over in Bramble."

He checks his watch. "I'm trying to get into a math class where I'm on the waiting list and then I have swim practice."

"You're on the team?"

"Sort of. I'm a diver. So I practice alone or with the one other diver. The team thinks diving is like ballet. They treat us like, you know, like we're in water ballet."

"Don't they think it's scary, jumping off platforms and doing somersaults.

"No respect. Know what's worse? Ear pressure. How about you?"

"My nightmare is my job."

"Gotta run. Catch you tomorrow or Wednesday? Tell me if you survive your job until then." He gives me a noogie as he leaves, loping over to a bunch of muscular guys in tight tee-shirts and tight jeans. I catch some girls staring at me in amazement, as if this little Chicana has no right to talk to a Big Man on Campus.

"To hell with you," I say under my breath and go into my personal pep talk. "I have every right to everything offered at this campus, same as all of you prissy, preppy girls, with your skirts and matching cardigans." I am fired up and ready for my next class. My next class, crap, forgot what it is. I have to stop and dig my schedule out of my backpack.

Hispanic Studies, 12-2 p.m. I'm glad I ate lunch even if it was a tad bit early. I repack everything and wander over to Bramble. This class is one floor up from my advisor's office.

Nobody's in there yet. I sit down in the front row. I hear the end-of-class buzzer go off. Feet tromp up and down the stairs. The door squeaks open. A dozen students come in, all Hispanic. They sprawl into the desks near the back, except for one beautiful girl, who looks like Dolly Parton in *9 to 5*, except this girl's black hair comes down to her waist and she's wearing Catholic school plaid. She does have Dolly boobs. She sits by me, says her name is Maria. Then the nun, Sister Rosalie, comes in and sits at the end of my row.

Christabel, the girl in front of the line yesterday, walks in with an armload of papers. She writes her name on the chalkboard parentheses TA in bright pink chalk.

Seriously, I thought she was a freshman like me. I am about to be enlightened about this whole Hispanic Studies thing.

Chapter 12

Campus bells ring out from the Campanile. They are deep and resounding, making my bones quiver. Scanning the room to my left and right, I see only Hispanic faces.

Most of us are wearing tee's and jeans, except the nun of course. The girl with long, curly hair streaming down her back in her plaid outfit looks too old-fashioned, and I smile about my good sense, just saying no to plaid. We settle back in our desks, notebooks out, as Christabel writes stuff on the board. We can't copy through her, so we have to wait until she finishes.

She turns to the class with a stern frown. She counts us. "Welcome to all of you. Welcome to Sister Rosalie from Los Angelitos, the Orphanage of Blessed Children in Tijuana. I see we have a few students missing. Does anyone know who they might be? Friends or roommates who've sent you to scout the class?" She takes roll. Five students don't answer.

We look at one another, shake our heads no. Christabel gestures towards a pile of books on the teacher's desk. "These are for this class. I'll talk about each one. First thing this quarter, you'll do a paper, okay?"

Why bother asking *okay* if we're not going to vote?

She lifts *Bad Boys*. "This book is extraordinary in its realism. Parents complain about it. I find those people hilarious. The book is. . . ."

Before she can finish her sentence, the classroom door opens. A deep male voice hollers, "Hispanic Studies?"

Christabel gives him the mad-teacher stare. "Yes, you're late. Come in, sit down."

Joe Sneed walks in and takes the seat on the other side of me.

"Young man, are you sure you're in the right class?"

"Hispanic Studies, right? Sorry I'm a late add. My math class was overenrolled."

"Yes. All right, fine. Now as I was saying, each of these books will give you a different perspective on the Hispanic experience. Your job throughout the semester will be to measure what you know and what you have left to learn. Have you delved into Hispanic culture deeply? Are you trying to pass as White Bread?"

Joe raises his hand. "I've been told I'm the White Bread. Is that a problem?"

Christabel stands up straighter. "Of course not. The curriculum is designed to be inclusive. Your journal for the books will definitely reflect a new awareness of the Hispanics who share your university world. Might be refreshing."

"Good. I'm looking forward to learning about Mexican customs."

"Hispanic."

"That's what I said," says Joe. "Isn't it?

"Anyone else want to answer?"

I raise my hand. I want to soften the image Joe has thrown out there, as if he's mocking the whole program by just being himself.

"Yes, you are?"

"Carmen Principia."

"From?"

"San Ysidro, down by the border."

"Great. So, Carmen Principia from San Ysidro down by the border, how can you clarify for this student," she points at Joe and asks, "Name?" the misuse of the word *Mexican* in his last statement?

"Joe Sneed," he says, his cheeks flaming red. Christabel writes in his name in a roll book.

I turn to Joe. I'm glad to see him discomfited, shifting in his seat, flushed, flustered.

"*Mexican* means from Mexico, with cultural roots in the country to a particular city or region. Many Mexicans have native Indian ancestors. Hispanic covers a lot more people. The countries in Latin America and their people are mostly Hispanic."

"Fine, Carmen. Just a little something missing."

Maria speaks up. "She forgot Central America. My parents are from El Salvador. Central America is part of Hispanic culture too."

"What about in the United States?" asks Joe. "You mean the guys who mow our lawn aren't Mexicans? I shouldn't speak Spanish to them? They are Hispanic and might be from anywhere?"

"Exactly," pronounces Christabel with a nod.

"Who knew?" Joe whispers to me.

"Mr. Sneed, you have more opinions?"

"No, no, sorry." He leans back in his chair.

Christabel picks up another of the books and as the period stretches on, she gives her opinion on each of them. She hands us a syllabus showing the weeks of the quarter, which books are to be read by when, the dates of two midterms and the final, the date of a paper due (next week?), and a mysterious group presentation. She promises this last assignment will be fun.

Joe raises his hand. "Isn't this a lower division class?"

"We wouldn't want anyone to call our classes or our whole department unnecessary fluff, what is the campus parlance, Micks?"

"No worries there," says Joe. "Carmen here will tutor me."

Christabel has put all her books and papers into her striped raffia tote. She erases the chalkboard. "Adios," she says. "Class dismissed. Please come prepared to discuss the first book on Wednesday."

Joe turns to me. "Which one?" I point to *Bad Boys*, which is clear as day on his syllabus.

"Figures."

"Poor men. They don't get enough respect. Just read it."

"I'd rather interview you," he jokes. "Over sundaes at Al's."

"Okay, at Al's, and you still have to read the book."

"All right, Caramel. I have swim practice and books to buy."

"Me too about the books. Want to help me?"

"I'm sending one of our pledges to the book store. I'll give him cash, so it's a no-go on the help."

"Fine. I have other offers. My books are going to weigh a ton."

Joe either doesn't hear me or doesn't care. He doesn't react to my insinuation that there are more men on earth than just him, at least in my world. "I'll be back," he says like Arnold in *The Terminator.*

"You better be, and with that book read. I'll quiz you before class Wednesday."

"Over a sundae."

"Done deal."

The class that follows ours is pushing through the doorway. I lose track of Joe among the crush of students. I don't have a way to call Franco for his help with my books.

But class today was sort of fun. I'm totally psyched about my classes and classmates, how free we are to come and go, nothing like my little high school at home with dress codes and drama over who's dating who. San Ysidro seems very far away.

Chapter 13

The sun is hot, our dorm room is stuffy, the floor is quiet. When I look out the window, I see the rec center pool, which is different from the on-campus team pool. I've read my assignment. I've taken a nap. What the heck. I grab my beach towel, sun screen, a visor, and throw on my bathing suit. That's how I notice the first appearance of the freshman fifteen, already showing up. No more chocolate, I swear.

Swimming is my favorite exercise. It's a ten-minute walk up more stairs to get to the rec center. No one is swimming. The grass area is covered by bronzed bodies sheened with tanning oil. The smell intoxicates me, and for just a moment, I am home with Mama, lying on towels in our dusty backyard, drinking lemonade.

Dropping my junk, I don't allow myself time to think. I stride over to the pool's edge and dive in. I start swimming laps. This is the biggest pool I've ever seen, and by the end of two laps I'm hanging off the side, gasping for breath.

Like a seal, a head pops up next to me, shaking his hair. Do I know this guy? Franco.

"How's the water?" he asks, smiling.

"Purrrr-fect!" I roll my *r's* because that's what Ashley and I did when something was extra good.

"I like it that you're not afraid to mess up your hair."

"As if it makes any difference." I run my hands through my short 'do.

"Race to the far end?"

"Not a chance. I'm not race-ready. And all these people, wouldn't they be watching?"

"Right. Look at them. Half are asleep, a quarter of them are pretending to study with their backs to the sun, and the others are probably stoned. Sister Rosalie is splashing her feet over there with her nun gear on. Is she stopped by those ugly boots beside her? Don't go around not doing stuff because you're afraid of what people might say. That should be rule #1 taught here. I guess it is, if you think about the First Star. You've had the Five Stars lecture, right?"

"The Chancellor was cool. WPC is good, not like my high school. It's so random here. I have that nun in Hispanic Studies with me. How do you know her anyway?"

"Summer volunteer work."

"That's what I was guessing. Anyway, I like flying under the radar this year."

"Is that why you chose WPC?"

"Partly. I like the anonymous vibe."

"What else?"

"Prestige."

"That's honest."

"I wanted a name school. Stuck up, I know."

"Big deal. I came for the money. I had some other offers, but the transportation costs to get back East would've put me into debt. So here I am."

I glance up at him, give him my best flirtatious eye lash batting. "Here we are!"

He pulls himself up to sit on the side of the pool. His muscles are toned, his chest has a scattering of black hair, and again, he shakes his head, first left, then right. "Water in my ears."

He reaches out as I put my hands on the edge. He pulls me up to sit by him. I shake my head, water flying.

I remember flab on my stomach, and I stand up and stretch. "I need my towel."

Franco follows me. He dives onto the grass, sits up, Indian style. "How go your classes?" he asks me.

"Good. I love anthro. And my Hispanic Studies class, it might be okay. The teacher's weird, that Christabel."

"You have her? Good luck. She's crazy about giving C's to everybody."

"Why would she do that?"

"So no one calls our department a fake, stuffed with a bunch of mick classes. Our department and Black Studies and Women's Studies, all the new stuff, the gender issues and the racial issues, we have to keep the bar high. Fat-cat alum aren't too happy with new ideas about curriculum."

"Politics."

"Yep, that's why you need to get yourself involved. You can't assume someone else will do your part."

"I hate clubs. I want to concentrate on my classes."

"Pretty selfish."

"Not. I'm here to get my degree. My mother, my friends, nobody thinks I'll make it here except one aunt."

"Making it here is more than straight A's. When you get out of college, who is going to ask you about your grades?"

"My mother."

"She won't understand what the U means either way."

"You don't even know her."

"Carmen, I have a mother. Mexican mothers are mostly the same, family, religion, and food."

"My mom has her art too."

"Does that make her interested in your degree?"

"No." Franco's right. I won't win over my mother to the idea of the U no matter what grades I get. She might like it if I brought home some Mexican friends, not just Franco, who she'd be asking how soon he's going to marry me. Not Joe, though she seemed to like the Little Hulk. Little Hulk is a good one that I hope I remember for next time he teases me.

Franco gets up. "Time for me to get some work in at the chem lab. I'm lucky they're letting me put in hours already. Marlene knows experiments start the third week or so. She puts us first. I love that woman."

"I don't." I gather my things. "She gave me the worst job ever, in the cafeteria.

"Yeah, I saw. Stay on Mitchell's good side."

"He has one?" I try to joke about it. "Guido helps me. Mitchell sits in his office. I'm fine except the hair nets and the stink, the grease, the burned toast. I don't want to be 'the smelly girl' in all my classes. How do you say that in Spanish"

Franco dips his nose against my neck. "*Foetid puella.* That's not you. *Sabroso,*" he says. "Coconut."

I giggle. "Coconut at the pool, but *foetid puella* in class."

"You'll work it out, Carmen."

"I'm glad you were here. All I wanted was to cool off and chill out. You schooled me, in a good way. Thank you." I try to kiss his cheek, but I miss and kiss his shoulder.

"Ah," he says. "Come with me to *La Raza* tonight?"

"What time?"

"Seven-thirty."

"Casual?"

"Of course, we're not on Frat Row holding some Greek ceremony. Just the homies getting ideas together, Homecoming float, recruiting more members."

"I'd be good at helping with the float. Recruiting, uh, no."

"Carmen. What's your middle name, anyway?"

"Carmen is my middle name. First name, Josephine, gag me.

"All right, Josephine Carmen Principia. Think back ten minutes. Remember what I told you about the U? Try everything. It's like vegetables. The dorm does something to all our vegetables, like overcook them, but we still should eat them. Put ketchup on them if you have to. What I am saying is let go of the old you, find a new way."

"You're so confident in me." I suddenly feel shy, like he doesn't know the real me.

"The U is confident in you." He grins, back-pedaling and I follow along.

What cha gonna do
If the big old U
Thinks more of you
Than you do of you.
Jump into the stew,
No melting pot fondue,
Be the spice, the cilantro,
In this white bread goo,
Get a clue,
Mexican true.
Up to you,
Watcha gonna do?"

He's bopping his fists left over right. He's pulled his tee-shirt over his head and waves bye, takes off jogging. I should jog back to the dorm so that next week my swimsuit fits like it used to. Instead, I walk to the beat of Franco's new rap. I love the way the words come to him, out of the blue. Mexican true, out of the blue. Good rhyme! I'll tell him tonight.

Chapter 14

My alarm goes off, which I hadn't expected to need when I set it, assuming that reading *Bad Boys* would be a page counter. But the book makes me cringe, I love it, and it's 7 p.m., I've missed dinner, and I get to go out sort of with Franco, if clubs count as going out. My shower takes all of two minutes. I use a light vanilla-scented cologne, drag a brush through my hair, and throw on my same jeans with a new red tee-shirt. I add huge hoop earrings because I love to see my face framed by their dangly faux gold. Maybe Franco will compliment me on the ethnic look. Shirley's not around, dinner probably, so I lock the door and take the stairs to the lobby.

Franco's sitting on the couch sharing a book with Shirley. He's wearing a red beret. I sit down across from him, he glances at me, and his face lights up.

"Hey. I met your roommate. You're on time! I like that."

"Shirley, I wondered where you were. Good to see you. Franco, is it time to go?"

"He's going to tutor me in math. Isn't that lucky?"

"It is. He has a way of explaining complicated things. Anyway, where's our meeting?"

"Dorm basement."

"Ours?"

"No. I'll show you. I'm ready. Want to come, Shirley?" She doesn't, thank God. He slings his backpack on, tucks the book away in the outer pocket, and lets the door slam before I'm through it. I take that as a sign that he believes in women's lib.

We don't talk outside because there's a stereo war going on between the dorms, with music blasting from the top floors of each residence hall. I hadn't even noticed it inside. Now it makes my ears hurt.

The path through the hedges is a short cut, we enter Marshall, and take the first elevator down. It's weird because this dorm has no wings, just floor upon floor, no division between girls and guys, totally coed. I'm not sure how I'd like men in our bathroom.

In the basement, the light is low, and the smell is damp. Franco leads me past storage closets and a room marked "Professor in residence."

"That guy must be majorly weird to live here."

"Wouldn't know. Bet it's cheap or free. Housing is free for the nuns."

"Really?"

"Yeah. The U thinks they'll be a good influence on our naughty impulses."

"I barely see them on the floor."

"Go knock on their door. They're normal people."

"Why aren't they coming to *La Raza*?"

"Low profile. The Church insists no politics during educational sabbaticals."

We've arrived at our meeting. Someone has hung a *La Raza* flag. When we walk in, my TA Christabel turns from the tray of cookies she has laid out. "Welcome! Franco, I hope everybody else completed their mission to bring one guest. How are you, Carmen from San Ysidro?"

"Surprised you remember me." And annoyed that Franco had an order to bring some new person to the meeting, that he didn't choose me because I'm so cute.

"I have an unfortunate habit of remembering people's names and faces. It's good when I like them and bad when I don't. Like that Joe guy in our class. He's going to be a problem."

I feel as if I should defend Joe, but I don't.

Four more members come in, all wearing different colors of berets. They look a little gangsta, but I know that's not *La Raza's* agenda.

"Welcome," says Christabel. "Grab a cookie, have a seat, and let's do introductions."

Each of the members presents the person they've brought and takes a minute to say where the visitor is from and where they themselves are from. Franco introduces me. I am the only one from south of here. The rest of the club members come from the Los Angeles area.

"Good, great. Next time, let's see if we can spread out our geographical memberships. Now let's move on." Christabel walks to an easel holding newsprint where she has listed our activities, all two of them, Intros and Decide. She crosses the first one off.

Franco stands up. "For anyone who's new, I'd like to add my welcome, and let you know that we are a non-violent group seeking ways to make the Hispanic presence at this university stronger. We should not be a silent minority, or worse, the invisible minority. We're going to have to make some noise."

"When do we get *La Raza* pins for our berets?" asks the boy next to me. He's dressed in a white tee and baggy pants.

"Later with the beret pins. We'll put that on next week's agenda though," answers Christabel, making a note in her notebook.

I hesitantly raise my hand.

"We don't go with the classroom thing here, Carmen. Just speak."

"Fine. What are we deciding?"

The members all start talking at once. I catch little pieces of conversation, some of which is in Spanish. Christabel claps her hands.

"Hey, you guys. Come on. We want to keep this short and decide tonight. Could someone please make a motion or whatever?"

Franco nods. "I move that we discuss Homecoming."

"I second it," I say to get Franco's approval.

Christabel flips the paper tablet on the easel. She writes HC in big graphic letters that resemble freeway graffiti.

Franco goes up to the tablet. He writes, *Firstlings demo* and a question mark and hands the pen to the green beret guy, who writes, *Float.*

"More ideas?" he asks before placing the felt pen on the desk and sitting down. Another buzz of conversation breaks out. Christabel thumps the cookie tray against the desk. It makes that whoooonnnggg noise of aluminum.

"Let's get this done. We have two ideas. Participate in the usual Homecoming float to build and ride in the traditional parade or a demonstration at the Sorority *Firstlings* night. Now you know those sorority girls are not going to be at all happy if we disrupt their ceremonial rites." She smiles with a devilish quirk.

"Why can't we do both?" asks beret wannabe boy.

"Too close together and not enough members. We need to recruit more. First, let's vote."

"Maybe we should know more before we vote." I surprise myself by speaking up.

"It's two sides of the same coin," Franco tells me. "One is traditional and one is not. So tonight we decide whose rules do we want to play by? Go with the old and honored or make a statement like 'Hey! Dude! Times have changed!'"

Everybody claps, even Christabel. Franco pumps his fist in the air. "*Viva La Raza*! The people UNITED will never be defeated."

We go through three of these chants, having fun making noise.

"Just think, if we brought maybe a mariachi horn, a drum, and every new member had one more person with them. All those pretty little sorority songs and the candelight walk and all that bullshit, they would be so freaked." Christabel sniggers.

"Ya think?" Franco turns his head to assess her feisty willingness to go into something big and new. He stares at the rest of us to see how the group itself responds.

"What say you?" he asks. "Vote now. All those for a Homecoming float raise their hand."

I raise mine. No one else does. "It would be fun to do the parade thing," I offer.

"All those for having a little mariachi party in the lot where the buses turn around that just happens to be across from the sororities?"

Eleven hands go up.

"*Gracias, mis amigos,*" says Franco. He flips the page of the newsprint, scribbles out committees: posters, music, recruitment.

"Shouldn't we all participate in every step, Franco? If we end up with too many people, then we can go into separate committees. We have five weeks until the snots get together for *Firstlings.* And you know what's even better? That moves our demo right into the Day of the Dead." Christabel mimes a surprised open mouth. "Oh no, Mr. Bill!"

Everybody laughs except me. "What if we are supposed to be home for *El Dia*?" I can picture Mama's sadness if I'm not there with her.

Christabel frowns. "What if we all grow up? What if you try something out of your comfort zone, Carmen? What if you use the U to learn that it's a big world and that our families are just one part of the big world? Our Mexican mommies have to cut that cord sooner or later. Fall is a good time, wouldn't you agree?"

I feel pressure on my heart. I've fought so hard against Mama to get here, and the one thing I can do to show her I'm still her Carmenita is be there for *El Dia de los Muertos.* But here's Franco and here's Christabel and these other people telling me I'm acting like a baby.

Franco raises my hand in his. "Carmen gets it. She's with us."

"Meeting adjourned," says Christabel. "See you next week, *compadres.*" She puts the newsprint tablet under her arm, the cookie tray she hands to Franco, and announces, "Executive board, please wait. Five minutes. Everybody else, thank you for coming."

"Franco? Should I wait?"

"No. Christabel's five minutes always come out to thirty. See you at breakfast, Carmen."

The club members pile into the elevator. I take the stairs. It seems like a long walk back in the dark alone. Bumping into a couple making out in the hedges doesn't help. "Sorry," I say to them, realizing that it's some random girl playing kissy face with Joe Sneed.

And I wonder how sorry I may be in a few weeks. Maybe this ethnic bonding isn't the best idea for me. I whack my head with my hand. I forgot to tell Franco my new rap rhyme, "Mexican True/Out of the blue," which I thought was clever for a minute. His raps, good. Mine? Eh. Joe's sex appeal, obvious. Mine, in need of improvement. Franco told me to spend time with the Sisters Rosalie and Octavia. Norine could teach me more and a lot faster about what I'm interested in, hooking up with the campus foxes.

Chapter 15

The door to our room is thrown open, so I promise myself not to blab about *La Raza.* Shirley would never understand. Music echoes off the hallway walls, a mix of Metallica and Michael Jackson. Here's to Michael Jackson, please God, at that volume.

Shirley in red and purple pajamas and a white plush robe is rocking out on her bed. The pj's have the Stones tongue caricature spotted all over them. Shirley's eyes are closed, and she's mouthing the words to "Bad." I turn the music lower, and she opens her eyes.

"Hey, why didn't you come with us?"

"Math is crazy. I wanted to finish the homework while I still remembered the stuff Franco showed me. And I've got a secret just like you."

"Me? Shut up! I have no secrets. Now, you, are you engaged?"

She collapses back on the bed, laughing. "Sort of."

"I give."

"Well, after Botany I walked out to catch the bus around to the dorms. What with my leg and all. And across the street, these girls were like waving. I said, 'Me?' and they were like 'Yes, come over.' So I did. And it was a sorority and some pledges had dropped out and they wanted a few more girls who fit their house so I had dinner there and then they voted while I was out of the room, and TA DA!"

She pulls her robe back to show me a lime green bow on her pajamas over her heart.

"You pledged a sorority?"

"Tri Chi! It's going to be so fun, and they don't care about my leg, or maybe they do care and they gave me the handicapped person pity vote, whatever. I have all these sisters, and now I can be a frat's Little Sister, and I can buy a formal for our big night, which is called *Frattlings*."

"*Firstlings*?"

"Yeah, that. This is the best thing that ever happened to me. I can't even believe it."

I don't want to be rude, and now I really don't want to tell more about *La Raza*, so I say, "Cool. Are you moving into the sorority house?"

"Yeah. That's where your secret comes in. Salt and Norine saw you coming out from the RA's office. So, see, now you don't have to change roommates if you can stand me for one quarter. My grandma said she paid the dorm in full for this quarter." Shirley pauses to pat her pledge ribbon with a faraway look in her eyes. "Living there, I can't even believe it. They have all these dinners and dances and songs and traditions. And I won't be around to bother you with my smelly, weird leg."

"Stop one second, Shirley. Salt doesn't know what I was doing at the RA's. Why would you think I went there for a new roommate? I had some money issues if you must know. Tell both those rat-finks to shove it. Are we cool again?" She shrugs. "All right, so listen, I have a paper due next week. Need to get on it." I pull my anthro book towards me from the shelf, checking how many pages are left in the assignment. I feel behind, and it's only the first week of class.

"Salt said he saw you over at Marshall Dorm too. Thinking about going full-on coed dorm?"

"What is he, your secret agent? Are you smoking too much weed? Remember, Franco and I had a meeting. We invited you. I wasn't over there scoping out a new room or a new roommate." Shirley's already hopped over to turn the music back up.

"Do you mind? I really need to study." That's my cranky voice. I slap the book against my thigh. "Please."

"You could go to the floor lounge."

"It's noisy there too, and I wanted to chill here. Compromise? Finish this side of the tape and then music off?"

Shirley turns it down. "Never compromise." She slouches into full-on pout mode.

I pop the tape out and hand it to Shirley. She throws it into a pile of tapes on her desk, rummages around, and finds a textbook.

Our official study session begins. The room is so quiet we can hear my clock ticking. With a highlighter, Shirley starts flying through the pages. If you're going to highlight everything in the chapter, what good is that? I could make a suggestion, but her new sorority sisters can teach her how to study.

One hour passes. Shirley throws the book on the floor. As she stands, she slips. Before I can catch her, she crashes backwards against the bed frame. "OW!" she yells. I give her a hand up.

"I broke my butt." She has tears in her eyes.

"Want ice?"

"No, just check it."

I look at her butt. Bruises are forming. Otherwise, it's just a butt.

"Did I break it in two?"

"Well, um, Shirley, you do have two cheeks here. I think most people have two cheeks, yeah? So, no, you didn't break it in two."

Now she's laughing. "Oh, my God, Carmen, stop. You are crazy, girl. I'm out of here." She grabs her crutch and turns back to me. "Good thing I'm such a hard ass." She clumps off to the bathroom.

Relieved the big tension has passed, I pull out a notebook and outline my paper. It's not even a hard topic and now that I know Christabel better, she will probably help me some. She already doesn't like Joe. I hope he's a good writer 'cause as the White Bread in the room, he's going to need help around the radicals. This leads to thinking about *La Raza* and the demonstration on *Firstlings*. With Shirley there, I'll feel more like a traitor. How to get out of it without setting off Franco?

That's a stupid thought because I'd lose total cred with my people. Closing my eyes, I try to focus on disguises or excuses, which is not very mature. Who's Shirley anyway? Like she's some big deal, now that's she's the token cripple in Tri Chi.

She's put a giant calendar of the academic year on the wall, one of those boring ones without pictures, the weeks long ribbons of dates. *Firstlings* is marked in lime green.

A thought hits me. It's close to *El Dia de los Muertos*. I'll suggest that we paint our faces like *calacas*, skeletons. With the white make-up and black outlines, it's a disguise with Hispanic roots, totally *incognito*, I stifle a snort. At the U, I'm smarter and sneakier and more flirtatious and all the good stuff in less than a week. We go with lights out at 11. I'm wiped out. My paper is outlined, and I can whip it out tomorrow for sure.

I'm dreaming of running on the beach, running and laughing and looking over my shoulder. Somebody wonderful is chasing me, and ringing a bell, like the bell chorus in Church. I can't tell who's running, if it's Mama or my cousin or Joe or Franco, only that my body feels light and warm and lovely.

Shirley erupts in a loud yell that pulls me from my dream. "Carmen, get the damn phone."

"What?" Then I hear the ringing. My dream evaporates like fog. "I got it." My stomach drops. What if there's trouble at home?

"Hello?"

"Carmen?"

"Yeah. It's past midnight. Who calls past midnight?"

"I do, Joe."

"Rude, totally rude."

"You were sleeping?"

I want to say something ridiculous. My brain isn't working fast enough. "Yeah, sleeping, the real thing, REM sleep, the whole deal."

"Was I in your dreams?"

"That would be a nightmare."

Joe laughs. "You are quickly picking up a bad attitude."

"Good role models."

Joe laughs again. "Yeah, anyway, could you meet me downstairs? I need to ask about that paper."

"Are you crazy or just an ass?"

"Both. C'mon, Carmen, I want to talk about your people. Aren't you happy that I'm interested in making the world a better place through interracial understanding?"

I blow air out in a huge sigh. "Joe, stop the crap. No, I won't come downstairs, no, I don't want to help you with your paper, and no, I don't believe you. Goodnight, idiot." I slam the phone down to break the connection. I pick up the receiver and leave it off the hook so it can't ring again. I shut the stupid thing in a drawer with a pillow over it, so we don't have to listen to it buzz all night.

"Good job," mumbles Shirley. She turns over with a moan.

I slip back into my bed. Then I get up and kneel, whisper my rosary and add an extra prayer for Mama since I haven't given her a second thought recently. The phone call scared me into remembering Mama alone at home.

After prayers, my heart feels better. A pain begins behind my right eye, signaling a migraine. Crap, shoot, shit. I get up again to take my migraine meds, hoping to prevent a full-blown three-day event. Lights burst in the corners of my vision. Crap, shoot, shit. I fumble around and find a tube of Ben Gay, take a wash cloth to the bathroom, run the water as hot as it gets, and return to my bed. Two dabs of Ben Gay to the temples and the hot wash cloth to soothe my aching eyes. Finally, I fall asleep.

The morning light streams into our room. Shirley has pulled the drapes wide open. I didn't even hear her get up. The clock says 9. Oh my God, I missed morning shift in the kitchen. My job is toast. Please, please, Mitchell, don't have already fired me.

My head begins to pound again. Fear propels the migraine despite last night's remedies. I take two more tablets of my prescription, get dressed, and hope I worm my way out of trouble in the kitchen.

On our door board, Shirley has her arrow set to *out*. A paper is pinned under my name. The paper is definitely for me, probably my pink slip from Mitchell. I unfold it.

I hold it at arm's length and then close to my eyes. I cock my head this way and that. Someone has xeroxed a hairy butt. I would laugh if I felt better. Plus, there's an arrow drawn from the outside corner to the middle of the butt where one would find the anus. Along the arrow, the word *YOU* in all caps. I look up and down the hall, a few girls migrating towards the bathroom, a few spilling out of the elevator with coffee mugs in hand. Who are the major suspects? Salt under Shirl's directions because of the hairy butt, Joe for the midnight phone call, someone random. I decide on Joe.

I fold the paper like a high school note, the little triangle, and jam it into my jeans. My heads throbs. I try more Ben Gay. It smells like it smells, minty and mediciney, and the heat helps with the pain. If I hurry, I won't be late to class.

"Just you wait, Joe White Bread Sneed, Mr. Ego of the World. You'll get yours. Nobody calls me asshole." My revenge plot doesn't get very far as I plod miserably to class.

Chapter 16

Berkebile for a coffee is medically necessary to treat the migraine. The guy in front of me is ordering some concoction of medium roast decaf, soy milk, and no whip. My order must seem really boring: "Large, fresh-brewed. "The clerk gives me a smile, "Everybody should be so easy to please." I smile back and throw a quarter into the tip jar.

Halfway to class, the caffeine hits my brain. My migraine diminishes to barely there. I feel awake and ready. The classroom is empty. I choose a desk towards the back so Sneed-head will either have to make a scene or sit where I'm not.

Classmates wander in, most of them, like me, with a cup of coffee and the post-weekend droop. Christabel strides through the door. She starts taking roll before the bell even rings. Funny. Sneed's not here yet.

She finishes roll and throws a question on the overhead projector. "Pop quiz, 5 minutes," she says. She winds a kitchen timer. "Define *Hispanic*." A collective gasp ensues. With all that breath in-taken at once, I can't believe she wasn't inhaled.

"Get going. Four minutes, ninety seconds."

A mad scramble for paper, pencils, pens. The clock is ticking too loud so I plug one ear with a hand to concentrate.

"Three minutes."

I have written two sentences. For a five-minute quiz, she probably expects five sentences so I force my pen to add three more ideas. The question is not hard. It could have been a lot more random. We've already talked about the subject forever.

The clock dings. "Pens, down; pass those papers forward," Christabel says with a pretty smile.

Joe pops through the door. "*Buenos tardes*," he says, "*Tardes* means *tardy, si*? He scans the room. I look down at my desk. He takes a seat front and center.

"You've missed the quiz," Christabel tells him.

"Oh." His shoulders slump. "May I make it up?"

"That wouldn't be fair. It would no longer be a pop quiz. It would be a prepared quiz. Get it?"

"I would like to make up the prepared quiz at your convenience."

"Fine." Christabel shifts the papers she has collected, and opens the door for Joe. "Mr. Sneed, if you would wait outside for a few minutes, please?" He exits. He shadows the frosted glass in the doorway with both hands up like a kid peeking into a pet store window. "Let's break into groups and rate these." She counts out four-member groups. "Discuss the papers I give you and rank them as *poor, good, better*, and *best*."

In my group is Maria of the plaid outfits. That's when I notice the lime green pledge ribbon that matches Shirley's. Tri Chi actually takes Hispanics? I should get the 411 on that.

The groups read aloud all at the same time, which makes for a friendly buzz in the room. We finish our grading. Christabel has Joe return while one member of each group reads the best ones, which are to be marked with *A*'s (not mine), read the worst ones, which are to be marked with *D*'s (not mine, whew), and Christabel gives us the evil eye.

"Fine, now all the rest of you mark *C* on the paper you're holding and pass them in. We have established a standard for excellence and a standard for barely above failing. Do you hear the difference among them?"

"Yes," we answer.

. "So go back to your studies, come more prepared next time, and those papers you are writing had better be both fully researched and well documented. Class is dismissed." She stuffs the quizzes into her woven bag. Maria sidles up to complain about how her paper was scored. Christabel listens for a couple of minutes and says, "College. It's not high school. Work harder." They both leave, Maria still yammering about her grade.

Joe gets up to follow them, probably about his make-up quiz. He stops and turns to the back of the classroom where I am heaving my backpack on.

"Caramel. Which one was yours?"

"*Nada.* Not read."

"See, it's your karma for not being nice last night."

"Whatever. Peer opinions on writing don't bother me. Oh, by the way, here's a little something for you." I hand him the triangle-folded note, the one of the xeroxed butt. He'll know I caught him.

He opens it. His eyes kind of bug out, and he blushes. I'm nearly through the door when I hear him yell, "Wait! Caramel, where'd you get this?"

"Off my door where you put it."

"I didn't do this."

"Who else would?"

"Your roommate? One of the people in the cafeteria? Maybe it was random?"

I walk faster before I turn back to him, "Random? I wish. Don't mess with me, okay, Joe? You know I saw you last night."

"And?"

"And if you're going lip lock with someone, have a little dignity. Maybe think about the girl." I don't tell him I wish he would think about me.

"Are you from Mars?"

"No, but you seem to be from the planet Venus, lover boy." I stop. "You do have a cute butt though."

He looks down at the paper. "Yeah, I do."

Chapter 17

So I almost laugh when Joe says that *yeah I do* remark. Instead, I walk away. For such an immature boy, Joe is also funny and sweet. If I could take his silliness and pour it into Franco, mmmm, that's what I'm talking about, a smart, sexy Latino man with a sense of humor.

Back at the dorm, I jump to check my mail box, expecting the usual pile of dust in there. Wrong. A pink slip sits waiting. My stomach drops and twists. Pink slip. As in lost job? Please, please, please, I pray as I turn the combination. I pull the slip out, expecting the worst, a big "See Me" from Mitchell.

It's a phone call message. All the calls go through the main switchboard and sometimes the desk clerk leaves a written message. "Carmen," it says, "call home." Then it lists the phone number as if I don't know my own phone number, which we've had for ten years except when the state changed our area code.

What would my mom want? Oh God, what if she's sick? Or she thinks I should come home because my last letter home was full of complaining?

I take the stairs to give myself longer to compose my thoughts. I call home. The phone rings and rings. I know to wait because if Mama is talking to the neighbors or she's busy with a piñata, it's hard to answer the phone. I lean towards the windows and watch the tennis team practice. I rearrange my bulletin board. Fifty is a good number. If she doesn't answer after the fiftieth ring, I'll call back.

I start flipping the pages of my psych book, close it, open my notebook. Doodling is good. I make hash marks for every ten rings. I'm up to thirty-three, when Mama, out of breath, yells, "Who is it?"

"Me."

"You know to call at night. My fingers are sticking together. Wait." I hear a faucet. "I can't get paste off so fast."

"Yeah, I took a chance. It was weird you'd leave a message, and I got scared. So what's happening, you're okay, right? You're not having a heart attack? Nobody stole your purse? Did President Reagan call because he wants a piñata for Nancy?"

She laughs. "You are such a silly child. I thought the University would make you grow up too fast. You sound like a ten-year-old."

"Well, isn't that wonderful?"

"Yes, it is wonderful."

"Okay, Mom, let's have it because I have a paper due tomorrow and a boss to talk to this afternoon." And some men to think about and a roommate who's sort of crazy.

"Hold your horses."

"Mother, no one says that."

"Slow down."

"Better."

"Good, I'm so glad my college girl approves of her ignorant mother's language."

I count to ten. "Mama, what's the news? Why did you call?"

"I need some ideas for *El Dia* altars."

"And?"

"And I thought since you are seeing so many new things and talking to so many new people, especially new men, maybe you could give me some ideas."

"Mother! Sit down in a chair. Grab a piece of paper. Think of the person. Start making a list of qualities. It's the same way every year. You are afraid you won't do the right thing and then everyone in town comes to you at the festival and asks for your help the next year."

"I know. It's this year. All I can think about are your new friends and all those new books you're reading and what if my daughter is not the same daughter when she comes home?"

"I won't be."

"See."

"But even if I still slept in my own bed and was still in high school, or I had gone to junior college with Gayla, I would be changing. It's called growing up."

"Moving makes more changes," she says, and I hear a little *eerk*.

"Don't cry, Mama."

"I'm not, *eerk*, crying, *snuffle*, I'm fine."

"When I get home, I'll show you my new books. I'll send you a long letter tonight once I finish my paper for Hispanic Studies."

"Hispanic Studies? You study yourself?"

"Myself in the context of my American social norms and my Hispanic family customs."

"Speak English. I am not understanding you, Carmenita. You gave me a good idea though! I am going to make the altar for Hector. He died in Vietnam. But he had been a college student before he was drafted. I'll have a huge open book, with the pages underlined and a pair of glasses, and. . . ."

"See, there you go, Mama! Believe in yourself. Now, I'm going to get to work here, and you go work on the altar, just a sketch and then send me a sketch too, okay?"

"All right, *mi hija*. I miss you so much. You are so smart." She stops. She blows her nose. "*Eerk*."

"Don't cry, Mama. I'll be home for break soon. It's not a problem for you to call me. We're a good team, huh?"

"*Snuffle*."

"I love you, Mama. Go draw, and I'll study. I love you. Bye." I hang up the phone before she has a chance to start the conversation over again. I love my mother, who doesn't? but I don't have time for these phone calls. Since when has my mother become so emotionally needy? I used to be an extra pair of hands. Anymore, I am an extra heart.

I rush off to the kitchen to see if I can explain myself to Mitchell. It's prep time, the cafeteria doors are open. A folding gate has been pulled across the serving area. Pots and pans clanging and knives chopping tell me a crew is at work. I holler through the cage, "Hey, hellooooooo?"

More crashing follows. Guido is swinging a mop, laughing and singing. I bang on the cage again so that he looks up.

"What, Carmen? You work mornings."

"I know, usually. I need to talk to Mitch."

Guido unlocks the gate. "Come on in. And good luck. He was pretty mad this morning. He had a few choice words for workers who don't show up the second day."

"Yeah, I. . . "

"Tell it to the man, Carmen. I just work here."

"How do I handle Mitchell?"

"Truth."

"Good one."

"Truth."

I knock on Mitchell's door though I can see through his little window he's shouting into a phone. He doesn't turn around but reaches behind him and opens the door. He's still yelling about the price of bread. I sit down in a chair by the door.

He sets the phone down. He turns to me and immediately swipes his big paw across his face. He reaches into his white coveralls and pulls out a hankie the size of a pillow case and swirls it in a pan on his desk. Vinegar permeates the air. He wrings out the hankie, leans back in his chair, and spreads the cloth across his face.

"Okay, loser, talk to me. Make it fast, make it good, and make it true."

I explain to him about my migraines and my meds and how yesterday was a bad day and today was even worse. The smell of the vinegar makes me start sneezing.

He hands me a tissue.

"So you're not sick are you?"

"No, like I said, the headaches come and go, and the medicine makes me sleepy."

"Maybe you shouldn't be working around knives and certain, shall we say, aromas?"

"That's not the problem, Sir."

"Call me Chef or Mitchell."

"Yes, Sir."

He sighs heavily and picks up a small chalkboard. He studies the chart on it while I sit there sweating.

"Can you work this evening?"

I want to say no, no way. "Sure."

"All right. Do your studying and all that stuff this afternoon before dinner because you're going to do clean up after dinner, so probably 8 p.m. to midnight. Will that work or not?"

"Absolutely. Sure, thank you, um, Chef."

"And don't miss another day unless you call me first."

"Absolutely. I won't do that again. I can handle whatever you need me to do."

"I'll believe it when I see it. You're on probation, you know that, right?"

My hands are sweating. I stick one out anyway. "Shake on it. I won't disappoint you again, Sir." He ignores my hand sticking out so I give my hair the fake-fluff.

"Okay, we're done." Mitchell picks up the phone. "Close the door when you leave."

I do that. Guido gives me a thumb's up. "Not so bad, huh, Carmen?"

"I'll let you know tomorrow after I work tonight and get in on time for breakfast."

"Mitchell, that's his favorite test. Come early for both shifts. Plus, he's going to keep you past midnight, probably scrubbing the floorboards with a toothbrush." Guido starts laughing.

"Whatever he needs me to do, I'm ready."

"You're a good one. See you in the morning."

I pulled some all nighters in high school. I have a feeling this one is going to be much worse. When I get to my room, Shirley's not there, I plug in my earphones and start banging out my paper from the outline I wrote. I don't have time for two drafts. I type the last three words of "Why *La Raza* Matters" at 7:30 p.m. I pet my soft pj's with longing, change into my work clothes and go on downstairs.

Chapter 18

Shirley exits the elevator. "You're up?" she asks. She wiggles her eyebrows up and down. "Going to get lucky? Which guy? Or do I even know him?"

"Long story," I answer and bash the down button. Let her feed on that since I'm prepping breakfast or cleaning up dinner. The elevator goes up two floors before it settles back to five where Shirley is still leaning against the wall.

"Have fun," she smirks.

I hit the down button again, and for my efforts, I receive a non-stop ride to the lobby. Loving how I look in my work clothes, (not), I pull the hairnet from my pocket. The net adds just the right touch of old lady to humiliate me more. A group of guys is standing by the xerox machine in the lounge, backs to me. Their barking laughter suggests they're copying private parts again. I analyze their backs and decide nobody over there is as cute as Joe.

Franco is chatting up the clerk at the front desk. I'm hopeful I can slide right by, but without even turning around he greets me, "Carmen! The hair! What have you done?"

"Make-up shift tonight."

"That's good. I thought you cut your hair or something. I love your hair."

I blush. "Cool, thanks. Listen, I can't be late tonight."

"When do you get off?"

"Midnight?"

"See you then? I'm tutoring Shirley late."

"No. Shower, crash, work, class. That's my schedule."

"I hear you." He slips his backpack off his shoulders and takes the couch in the lobby for himself.

When I get to the kitchen, at least the mesh doors are open. Mitchell is ordering around a bunch of people I don't know. He points to me. "You, Carmen, do what Anaissa says."

He points at a Hispanic girl. Her skin is darker than mine, she has make-up on like a girl from the 'hood, and let's just say she doesn't look happy to see me.

She hands me a wire brush. "You scrub the grill. When you're done, empty the grease vats. After that, check with me."

"I'm Carmen," I say to her retreating back.

"So I've heard."

I start scrubbing with the steel brush. The grill is nasty with bits of bacon, hamburger, and some unnamable substance sticking in the edges closest to the tiles.

"Lift it, *stupido*," orders Anaissa.

"Right." I try to keep a pleasant demeanor. I don't need anyone else to argue with, especially when I'm so tired. I scrub away with one hand, holding the grill up with the other.

"It has a rod to prop it open, like the hood of a car." Anaissa pulls up the rod and latches it to the top of the grill. "See?"

"Thank you. That helps." I'm making progress. The grill starts to look shiny instead of crummy. Ha! I wonder if I can use that as a joke with Guido in the morning, you know, crummy versus crumby.

"Grease vats next. Over there."

"Is that a one-person job?"

"Usually."

So I go over to the vats. I can barely lift one to tip it toward the drainage pipe. The old grease stinks like the pig farms of Otay Mesa north of our house. I get the dry heaves.

"Anaissa," I croak, "Isn't there a better way?"

"Vicks under your nose like in bio lab dissections."

"Sure, I carry Vicks on me at all times."

"Don't be rude," she says, and she pushes me, and I slip into the grease that has slopped over.

"You're the one being rude. Help me up." I extend my hand, but before I get up, I puke right there behind the drain. Mitchell comes running in with a mop.

"You spill it, you clean it," he tells me, handing me the mop. He reaches into his pocket and pulls out a jar of Vicks VapoRub. "A gift for you, newbie." He pats me on the back.

"You're not the first one to lose her lunch at the grease bombs."

I wash my face at the sink. The cool water helps bring my balance back. I slide a finger in and out of the Vapo Rub and draw it across my lip. With the menthol sizzling up my nostrils, I'm good to go. "How many more?" I ask the room.

"Two," smiles Anaissa. "It appears you've passed the night-shift test. Why don't you transfer to our shift so you can sleep late?"

"Early classes. Might as well work first."

"Are you taking Hispanic Studies?"

"What was your first clue?"

We both laugh. Mitchell peeks out of his office, frowning as if laughter is indefensible. He wags his finger back and forth. "Cut the chatter."

Anaissa salutes him. "Yes, sir. On with our business at hand, sir. Anything you say, sir." This seems pretty rude, but Mitchell actually laughs.

"You're something else, Anaissa."

"Aren't I now?" she answers in a flirty way. I stare at her to see if this is a serious flirtation or an act. I can't really tell.

Mitchell eases back into his office, Anaissa hums some song my mother likes, *Querida*. She adds lyrics. She pulls the stinky mop I used towards her to use the handle like a microphone, belting out the song like a pop star. Her voice is rich and throaty. She's not even embarrassed.

I clap.

"Thank you, thank you very much," she says in a husky Elvis voice. "Your turn."

"I don't sing."

"Then whistle."

"I don't whistle."

"Then hum."

I start humming the fight song that we learned at UR-U. Anaissa rolls her eyes. "What are you, some wanna be cheerleader, song girl, sorority sister?"

"Surely, you jest."

"About which one? And don't call me Shirley." She cracks herself up to the point that she has to sit down. Tears roll down her cheeks. "If I pee my pants, you've had it."

"Christ, Anaissa. You started it. And besides," but I only get that far before I start laughing too, "and besides, my roommate's name is Shirley."

"The crip?"

"What?"

"The cancer crip?"

"That's mean, she's nice. Well sort of. She's pledged Tri Chi."

"Yeah, they're not into competition from the Latina beauties on campus."

"I saw one! Maria, in my Hispanic Studies class, she's wearing a pledge ribbon."

"No way."

"Yes, way." We've stopped laughing. Anaissa gets up and has started putting polish on all the chrome in the kitchen.

"Last chore of the night. Why don't you finish? I think I'm going to take a powder room break and trek on back."

"You don't live here in this dorm?"

"No, an apartment with three roommates. They're all crazy. I'm the normal one."

I blink my eyes. She's the normal one? God help the landlord. "Do you like it?"

"It's cool. Not so many rules as dorms. But the oldest roommate, Christabel? She's this hot head radical. She's always trying to get me to join the *La Raza* cause. All I want is my degree, and I'm out of here. No time for politics."

"People in *La Raza* make me feel important," I say, and I realize it's true.

"Dandy. Go ahead and get all tied up in that stuff. Me, I need good grades, enough sleep, and money. So *adios, amiga.* You should be done in half an hour. Catch some z's before class."

"Here's hoping."

She pulls off her hair net. She bends at the waist and shakes her hair out. She puts her dirtied kitchen jacket in the laundry bin, revealing her outfit, a tight blue tank top, which clings to her large boobs and cut-off jeans. She does a little shimmy-shimmy-coco-bop. Her boobs bob. "Was Franco out there studying?" she asks me.

Franco? She knows Franco? Great, who doesn't? More competition for somebody I like. "Uh, yeah, he's tutoring my roommate, or so he says. He was in the lobby."

She applies lipstick in a shade of orange pop, checks the effect in the now shining freezer. She runs her fingers through her hair and kisses the 'fridge. "Little smudge here, Carmen."

I spray the chrome cleaner on the spot and rub it until it feels like I have pushed the two-ton freezer off its pad.

Chapter 19

The days fly by. Our papers are due. Christabel counts them. "Five are missing. Spread the word that they are to be delivered to the Hispanic Studies office by noon."

Then she dismisses class, saying "No use talking to people who've been up all night."

Ever since my double shift at work, I'm too tired to think straight. Is today Shirley's long day or is today Shirley's no class day? My thoughts are like sludge in my brain, slogging around randomly. I buy a coffee at the kiosk, too lazy to wait in line at Berkebile. Gross, it's a watery brew. I dump it in the trash can and sit on the lawn in the sun, reading the student newspaper. The headlines are about the Italian Department and allegations of inappropriate sexual contact between T.A.'s and female students.

The campus bells ring out. Students swarm down the hill from the upper campus. A number sit on the grass where I am. Who called a party?

It's not random though. This is the Free Speech area. People come here to talk about campus issues, world issues, gender issues, and race. Some guy with a beard takes his place behind an improvised green podium. He starts rambling on about *the man* and the way even our college education has been influenced by *the man*. I want to yell at him to can it, but I could simply leave. All I have to do is move. The sun is warm on my back, and it's easier to go away in my head.

The next speaker gets my attention. Franco jumps up on the brick wall along the planter. He stands still. He puts a bull horn to his mouth. "Hey! Time to listen!" The buzz of conversation dies down. "Thank you." He dips his chin like a bow. "My issue today is discrimination."

"Oh shut up," yells a voice from the back. "You've done this same speech for at least two years, Franco." The crowd and I turn to the interrupter, Joe Sneed.

"Yeah, I've discussed discrimination since I've come here, and every day, every week goes by the same way. On this campus, we are not all treated equally."

A few minority students, a black couple and some Latina girls, shout, "Yeah."

Somebody adds, "You got that right."

"Let the man speak, White Bread," says a Latino guy.

Joe sits down. He doesn't leave. His cheeks are red, like his head is going to explode.

Franco talks for another five minutes. He explains the ratio of Latinos in California, especially Southern California, to the ratio of Latinos enrolled at the U. "Are we all stupid? Or is it a choice? Should the U do more outreach? What are you doing in your volunteer hours to make this university a better place? And how about your clubs? How racially diverse are they? Talk to somebody near you about that for a minute." Nobody moves, nobody talks. We sit in the sun.

Franco's shoulders slump. "I'll leave you with a final thought: Change is slow,/ Until you know,/ What the change could do,/ It starts with YOU!" He moves towards the crowd, repeating, "You! You! You!" as he points people out. He has pointed at Joe. He has pointed at me. "Anybody else want to speak?" he asks. Nobody moves, nobody talks. He takes the bull horn that he has been extending toward his listeners and marches away into Berkebile.

I yank dandelions out of the grass, blowing the fluff away. Our words are like that, so much fluff, blowing in the wind. I wonder if that's what the song means. The world is a confusing place. The U makes me question so much more than anything that happened to me before this time in my life. Maybe Franco has something in his radicalism. *Firstlings* is two weeks away.

I pull out my date book. Nothing stands between me and the demonstration at *Firstlings*. There's a meeting tomorrow night to finalize our roles, timing, and all that. Seeing Franco so passionate about something besides his studies or a girl lights a fire in me. I'll find him inside, I hope, and talk to him a little more about his philosophy. I brush the grass off my jeans, and a familiar voice says, "Allow me."

"Uh, no thanks, Joe."

He grins. "I was just offering."

"Sure. Play grab ass. It's all the rage."

"Caramel, I'm beyond insulted."

"Good." I should get moving, but Joe is like a magnet to me. "Why were you rude to Franco?"

"Sick of him, sick of whiners, sick of all these little groups. We all have problems. Get over it. Get to work."

"You should talk about work.'

"I turned my paper in."

"But didn't go to class?"

"Right. True. But I'm not out here saying the world is unfair, which it is. That Christabel and half the class think their class should have exclusive enrollment. Exclusive as in excluding white boys."

"Poor, powerless Joey White Bread," I say. I rub his back. "All these new movements and people disrespecting the white elite." Now I sound like Franco. "I'm out. Gotta go."

"Cool. See you, Caramel. Maybe you could finish the back rub at the Frat House some night?"

"Not a chance."

He picks up his books and jogs away, stopping to talk to a covey of sorority girls in their pastel sweater/skirt sets. Their pledge ribbons flutter in the breeze. They burst out in little puppy squeals at something Joe has said to them. He laughs and joins the frat guys sitting near the straw-covered hill where skiing is taught. He throws himself sideways on the hill and rolls down it. At the bottom, he picks straw out of his hair. The frat boys clap. The sorority girls arrive and cheer. Joe puts a piece of straw into his mouth. He looks like Huck Finn in a letter jacket. One of the girls, the one with the longest blond pony tail, steals the straw from his mouth and runs off shrieking. Joe tackles her. They're both laughing. Actually, everybody watching is laughing.

"Nothing like a little roll in the hay," shouts Joe. He pins her hands to the ground up by her head and kisses her.

I've seen enough. They live in a very different world than I do, and it's not one I expect to enter, ever. I walk into Berkebile to seek out Franco. It's dark in the building after the blinding sunlight outside. My eyes are slow to adjust. The hall is noisy with students working in every office. Nameplates identify the *Daily Pilgrimage* (newspaper); the *Full Pilgrimage* (yearbook); and ASS (Associated Society of Students). On and on they go all the way around the central study-meeting area with leather couches.

"Hey, Carmen!" Across the hall, Franco is gesturing for me to come in.

"Hi. Nice speech."

"Can't wait for you to make one."

"Give me three years?"

"You'd be surprised. I bet by spring quarter."

"We'll see how *Firstlings* goes. What's new with that?"

"Tonight's agenda. I'm typing committee summaries. Want to help?"

I know I should. I've had my consciousness raised. "Tonight? What happened to tomorrow?"

"Strategizing about apathy."

I'm embarrassed. "Well, I should help my mom."

"Your mom's in town?"

"No, home, but I should be home to help her with her El Dia altars. I'm embarrassed. After Christabel's rant about letting go, I don't know what to do."

"That's college. Solving problems, making choices. I'd love to see your mom's work. It's authentic, right?"

"Mostly."

Franco gives me a long look. "See you at the meeting tonight?"

"Wouldn't miss it."

"Excellent." He turns back to the typewriter.

I didn't handle this right. "I can help here for a bit." I concede.

Franco shrugs. "Never mind. Bye, Carmen. Don't go out and get radical or anything."

Chapter 20

Pushing my way through the coffee line to get outside, something doesn't feel right. What am I forgetting? The steps are frat boy territory. I don't want to walk through them, especially today after the free speech rally. The inside of Berkebile feels safer.

Eyes closed, Franco's on the phone, leaving a message about tonight's meeting. I gaze at him, his shiny hair, his long eyelashes. Maybe he's what I was forgetting.

"Hey," I say.

He opens his eyes, brown, luminous, deep.

"I could do those phone calls if you want me to."

"That would help. Here's the script." He hands me notebook paper with a short paragraph.

"What if they won't listen?"

"Now why would you think that?" He's already on his feet, unrolling poster paper and laying each tear-off on the floor. "If they won't listen, tell them thank you and goodbye. We're not going to hassle people. We're raising their consciousness."

"Pop psych?"

"Whatever works. Guilt never works."

"You definitely need to meet my mother."

"Latina mothers are born knowing every guilt line ever deployed against children."

We laugh. I dial. I like it best when no one answers, and I can leave a message.

Franco assembles kits of poster paints and brushes in Coke cartons. He has chosen green, red, black, the colors of Mexico's flag.

"Last call," I tell him.

"Check the name."

"Christabel. She doesn't need me to call her, right?"

"Correct, my sweet-rabble-rouser. We are finished here. I thank you." He drops the list into a desk drawer, and lifts my hand off the phone. He pushes my hair back behind my ears. I'm still sitting down, and I can't decide if I should stand. I wish I had remembered earrings.

Franco leans in to kiss me. His lips are soft and warm. I kiss him back. We move to the couch where we sit close enough that he can pull me into an embrace, kissing me again, more deeply. I am melting.

Voices from the hallway pull me back to myself. "Franco, not here, okay?"

"Not here, what?"

"Not here make-out session. It's so public."

"Carmen, you're very uptight. We should work on that."

"Sure, just not here."

"One more kiss," he says and then we're kissing again as if we are starving for kisses. I swing around to sit on his lap, which is strangely comfortable, especially the pressure below his belt. His fingers trail along the buttons of my blouse.

A knock on the office door. Franco's eyes are langurous. I glance over my shoulder and use the twist of my shoulders to escape and stand up, moving away against my desire.

"Caramel! I guess I don't know you as well as I thought I did," says Joe.

He's going to call me on some kissing after what I've seen him up to? "What's it to you, Joe?"

"A big *nada.* You're absolutely right."

"So why are you here? Are you stalking me?"

Joe squints his face into a pained expression. "Puh-lease."

Franco has recovered from our kiss. He stands next to me, an arm across my shoulders.

"So what's the deal, Sneed?"

"I came by to say sorry. About the rally. I"ve been thinking about what you said."

"Right," says Franco. "Good."

"Right," I say. "Did you get the brainstorm before or after the roll in the hay?"

Joe doesn't flinch. "Probably after, you know, turning it around in my brain like that so that I could see things from a new point of view."

"Interesting. Maybe I should try your method." I make eyes at Franco. He pulls me closer. One thing Mama taught me is to always keep men guessing, so I slip out from under Franco's arm even though I'd like to stay longer. "See you guys later. Franco, we're on for tonight, right?" I say this just to get under Joe's skin. Joe's cheeks bloom with red spots. Good.

"Carmenita, 7 p.m. I'll walk you over like last time."

"What last time?" asks Joe.

"Our secret," I taunt. "Bye now."

The two of them watch me leave. I feel their eyes on my back, laser beams. How fun is that to have two guys looking at me as if I am something special? I'm so caught up in my fantasy that I'm some hot chick, I'm not looking where I'm going, completely spaced out. I bounce off a body, who yelps as hot coffee splatters us both.

"Sorry, sorry, sorry," I tell her. She hands me the coffee cup while she wipes off her hand with a napkin. "Oh, Lord, hi Anaissa. I'm so sorry."

"Your blouse is unbuttoned," she points out. "Must have been over at the *La Raza* office with Franco."

"That's rude."

"That's plain as day. Why do you think I don't get myself involved with the politics around here? Let me give you a piece of advice, Chiquita. You're at the University, not high school. The guys see freshmen as opportunities. So you need to take care of you. Franco, he's a major player. He's no better and no worse than other guys. The only reason girls outnumber guys in La Raza is Franco. He's the only one who could get me to even think about a beret and a pin. So you know. Take your time. Show respect for yourself." She walks away.

I had been so happy and now I'm not. My heart, throbbing like a balloon, shrivels up into a tight coil. I look down and button my blouse, chastened and guilty and trying not to think about what Joe saw when he came to the door. I don't want him assuming I'm slutty. Who can I talk to about this stuff? The boys can act any way they want and that makes them big man on campus. A girl kisses a guy and suddenly she's got a sleazy reputation? This has been my mother's advice since I was twelve. I thought the U would be different. Maybe it is, and maybe it isn't. Maybe Anaissa's just jealous.

I'll talk to Norine. She doesn't give a rat's ass about reputation. She's having fun. She's a liberated woman. We're not the Age of Aquarius and free love and hippie love fests, but we are free to be our body, ourselves. Wait, wrong analogy because that book was all about respect for ourselves like WPC's last star, and what I'm looking for is freedom, freedom for girls to be women if they want to, if they're ready. Why wouldn't I be ready? Why would I accept the impossible double standard, play boys and chaste girls?

Franco called me uptight. He's one Hispanic man who knows his women. At least he seems to know me.

Chapter 21

Our door is open. Shirley's grandmother sits at my desk. "Hello, Carmen," she says, which shocks me that she remembers my name. I don't think my mother would know Shirley's name. My letters and phone calls aren't ever about Shirley.

What do you say to someone else's grandmother when you want to eat your sack lunch and take a nap and she's just sitting there at your desk? "Hi, Mrs. Wooster. Where's Shirley?" I ask to be polite.

"She's taking a shower. We bought her a dress for *Firstlings*. It's so beautiful! It's right here." She gets up to lift a dress bag off Shirley's bed. "I won't show it to you yet. Shirley wants to try it on again to see if we need to adjust it at all. It's the most wonderful dress." When she smiles, her wrinkles turn her face into a younger version of herself. Her eyes sparkle.

Shirley arrives in her robe. "Hey! You're here for the great unveiling?"

"I'm here for lunch and a nap, but sure, I'd love to see your dress."

"I don't like the white rule for pledges. This dress is pretty, but sort of wedding dressy. Next year, I'll be done with initiation, and I can wear my sorority colors. I love lime green."

"Now Shirley," her grandmother begins, pulling the garment bag off something white, long, and sheer.

First, Shirl puts on her leg. She wriggles herself into a strapless bra and pulls on a girdle with a flat pane of elastic across the front. Shirley sits a moment on her bed, her grandmother drops the dress over her head, and with Shirley standing, they pull the dress down from her shoulders to her feet.

"Wow! Shirley, you look amazing." I gawk at the transformation of my roommate from regular college freshman to ethereal and pretty. The dress is a shiny fabric like satin everywhere except for sheer sleeves and a sheer fabric above her boobs to her neckline.

Her grandmother opens her closet door where there's a full-length mirror. Shirley turns sideways and pats her flat stomach. She turns to the back. Her grandmother holds a hand mirror so that she can see the back better.

The dress does seem sort of wedding dress to me too, but it is also the prettiest dress I've ever seen on Shirley. It would definitely be better in a bright color.

"I like the sheer top and sleeves. It's sexy without being bare. What did the salesgirl call it, Grammie?"

"A sweetheart neckline with illusion sleeves and bodice."

"Yeah. It's good to have the sheer plus this satin binding to set it off. I like that the skirt's not too full." She smoothes the satin and shakes the skirt, an A-line. She pinches the neckline to see if a tuck would show off her boobs more. She extends her arms to check the sleeve length.

"Should we hem these sleeves, Carmen?"

"No way. You look perfect."

"I do, don't I?" She grins and hugs her grandmother. "Thank you, Grammie," she says.

Her grandmother is sniffling. "You'll take lots of pictures at *Firstlings*, won't you?"

"Don't worry. The Greek Council hired a photographer. Carmen will take some pictures before I leave, won't you, Carm?"

For a moment, I'm caught up in the romantic vision of a few hundred girls singing songs by candlelight, all of them dressed in white, with their sorority sisters dressed in gowns in the colors of their chapter. A little stab of jealousy screws into my heart that I have shrugged off about this glamorous night. And I picture our demonstration, the promise I made to participate, to be a nuisance at *Firstlings*.

"Sure, before you leave, I'll try to take pictures. I have something going that night too."

Mrs. Wooster claps her hands. "Maybe Grandpa and I can stand across the street just to see you?"

Shirley sucks in her breath. "Not the best idea, okay, please, Grammie? We'll make sure you have pictures. No big scene out there, please, okay? With this dress, people won't even think about my leg, will they?"

"Who cares if they do?" I ask, unwrapping my sandwich. I stuff my face with bites of sandwich and bites of apples. "I'm going for water," I tell them, grabbing my toothbrush cup. "You are *muy buena*, Shirley."

She cracks up. As I leave, they fuss a little more with the sleeves.

I stall in the bathroom. I get back to find the dress hanging in its garment bag and the room empty. I'd like to try on Shirley's dress, just to see what I'd look like if I didn't look like everyday me. The dress slips over my head and shoulders. It's tight in the bodice so I won't try to zip it. I tug at the skirt to make it lie flat. The fabric feels like those nightgowns at Victoria's Secret, soft and shiny and clingy. Clingy is bad though when I turn to the mirror and see my stomach outline, Carmen Big Belly, too stupid to quit eating sweets or at least put on Shirley's girdle.What kind of roommate would borrow your girdle?

My bare feet poke out from under the hem. This dress that looked beautiful on Shirley feels great on me. It looks so-so. I like the whatmacallit, illusion sleeves and bodice. I trace along the neckline. I sweep my hair back and up in a clip like an updo. Much, much better. Whatever. Not for me, not this time, maybe in ten years when I get married. I bend to my toes and pull the whole thing off, replace it on the hanger.

I throw myself on my bed, kicking my books onto the floor. The phone rings. I don't answer. It could be Franco, Joe, or Shirley. It could be Mitchell wanting me to work more hours. I realize it could be Mama, and I grab the receiver, but only a click comes from the other end. Too late. I want to sleep. My brain is buzzing with questions and conflicts over *La Raza* and *Firstlings*, over Franco and Joe.

When in doubt, pray, I tell myself. The click of rosary beads is strangely soothing even if I'm lying on my back and holding the loop above my eyes. Click, click, click, clack. I search for a novena in my Bible for the first time since I arrived here. I choose the novena of St. Luke, patron saint of artists. If I read this for nine days, I should remember my goals, to become a Latina artist, quit fantasizing that I will fall in love or become this great leader in the protest movement when I can't even stand up for Franco. I wonder if there is a patron saint of protest? I'll ask the Sisters. One more novena falls out of my Bible when I pick it up to replace St. Luke. Perfect, the novena for Procrastinators: St. Expedite. Mama put that one into my Bible. May it come to my rescue.

Chapter 22

The phone is in my hand to call Franco and back out of *Firstlings* when Shirley comes back into the room. She hangs the dress in the closet without another word about her grand sorority debut and all that bull.

"Wrong number," I say when she raises an eyebrow about the phone. "I have a meeting tonight. You going to be in?"

"Nope. I have a meeting too, at the sorority house. Something about afternoon tea for the mothers the day after *Firstlings*. Maybe the tea will make Grammie happy except she's so old, it's embarrassing. My sisters probably have movie star moms."

"What's the deal with your own mom, Shirley?"

She frowns. "Not a good day for that story."

I shrug. "Okay, when you're ready. Too bad you didn't meet my mom when you checked in."

"What's she like?"

"My mom, I guess she's a typical Mexican mom, except she likes weird music, wants me to get married and forget college, and gets herself all wrapped up in her art."

"So she gets a cool for the music and the art, and a 'no-way' for the married thing."

"You wouldn't believe how hard I fought to come here instead of junior college."

"Way weird. Way no way."

"If she comes up parents' weekend, I'll introduce you."

"Right. How about your dad?"

"Raincheck. The day you tell me about your mother, I'll tell you about my father."

"Deal."

Shirley puts in a Michael Jackson tape. I put in my ear plugs. She's working math problems at her desk, alternating with moments of dancing behind her chair. I'm supposedly studying physical anthro. I grab a sweatshirt and leave for the meeting. Norine meets me in the hall, half-hysterical because she's met some new guy who stood her up for a beach run date. The U is one big party for Norine. "I have a club meeting," I tell her.

"Can I come?"

Now, that's a hard one. Christabel and Franco both want more members. It's pretty obvious that they assume we'll bring another Latino. So maybe I can shake them up, get their focus refocused. "Sure, c'mon. Norine, here's the deal. You are new, so they will introduce you and then you should probably listen and see if it's a club you want to be part of. Don't try to vote or throw in comments."

"I can do that." She slows down, peering into the rec room. "Uh, maybe I'll go with you next time. Does that look like Salt over there?"

"Something going on with you and Salt?"

"Are you kidding? He's hilarious, fun to hang with," she says, walking away.

What a relief! I have to learn to say no to people who are imposing their agendas on me. She didn't care about my club. She was bored. Franco would be so pissed if I brought a bubble head like her. Besides, he might walk me home tonight. What would I have done with Norine with me? Awkward, to say the least, so yeah, good, she's not my problem.

I'm a little bit late for the meeting. People are divided into two's, making posters. Christabel waves me over as I come in. She hands me a paint kit. "What's the message?" I ask, so I won't paint something stupid.

"Franco can tell you. I have papers to grade." She flips through them. "God, these are terrible."

Has she forgotten I'm in that class? I wander over to where Franco is crouched on the edge of a poster, sketching out fat letters in pencil. Anaissa is there with him. Anaissa! I thought she had no use for clubs, oh yeah, except for Franco's magnetic hunkiness.

"Hi," I say and they both glance up.

"Late, Carmen."

"I know. Roommate stuff," which is sort of true. "What goes on the posters?"

"Something positive, not anti-anybody. No hate speech."

"Makes sense"

"If you can put a little pun in there about *Firstlings* or the Greek system, all the better, but nothing straight out bashing them."

Anaissa leans backwards for a better view of Franco's lettering. She falls back completely, knocking him off balance, so that she's lying on top of him. He pushes them both upright. "Watch it, Anaissa," he says, and breaks into song. "Your Spanish eyes, your glossy hair, your wicked ways, Might take me. . . THERE." He points towards the sky.

She chuckles. "I wish."

"Do I detect liquor on your breath? Let's stick to posters."

"Liquor? Me? See," she puts her hand in a pie plate of green paint, "I'm sticking to the poster." She leaves a trail of small handprints, each one lighter than the last around the corners of the poster.

"You're very handy to have around, Anaissa," I tell her in a snit.

She giggles some more. "Yeah, that's what all the guys say, that I'm good with my hands." Franco backs up before she can put one of her handprints on his zipper.

"Whoa, baby. This is a business meeting."

"That's me, all business! I'd like to make you my business, Franco."

He stands up. "What is with you tonight, Anaissa? Get ahold of yourself. I'm going to help Carmen get started. See if you can fill in the letters so they're like graffiti."

Anaissa sticks her lower lip out. "Whatever you say, gorgeous."

Franco sends out air kisses to her.

"What was that all about?"

"What that?"

"The rhyme, the bootie boogie lap dance?"

"College, liquor, life, hormones, *de nada.* You've got a lot to learn, kid."

"Yup. Here I am, a sponge for knowledge." This gives me an idea. I find a sponge in a cupboard. "Let's do this one with a sponge instead of brushes! But what to say?

"Start with a Mexican flag. While you do that, I'll think of a saying."

"I can do that." Tearing the sponge into three smaller pieces, I paint two vertical stripes, the first edge red, the far edge green. The middle is white. I drop the sponges in with the paint brushes and start penciling in the symbol of the eagle and the snake.

"How about using an American saying in Spanish?" I ask Franco.

"Such as?"

"Don't tread on me. Or a government for the people. Or something about the pursuit of happiness?"

"Possible. Those don't insult anybody."

"Good luck. Like nobody's insulted with us mocking their big night."

"Carmen, you want out? Go ahead. Drop."

"Arguing for the sake of argument." I stop. "Franco, my roommate is a pledge. She bought her dress. *Firstlings* is a big deal to her."

"You worry too much. We're doing the *calacas* face paint you suggested. And we're planning a legal march."

"Okay."

"So maybe something on here about brotherhood? Sisterhood?"

"He ain't heavy, he's my brother?"

"For one:. Have you seen a frat boy lately? Four-ton men. For two: In *Espanol*, totally lost on them."

"One earth, one people?"

"Corny. Environmental."

"We are all brothers and sisters?"

"I like it."

"Should we put it in Spanish anyway?"

"Maybe we should write it in Greek." Franco made a joke? It's a first.

"Along one side in English, and along the other in Spanish?" I have solved the problem. I paint carefully after Franco does his graffiti writing on the right-hand side, using Spanish, "*Todos somos hermanos y hermanas*." He moves over to the left-hand side, making his letters look straight and restricted.

"Christabel! How about this one?" he calls out.

We hold our poster up. There's a round of applause. "I think we need more of those. That's a play on their system of brothers and sisters and still gets our message out there. You are too brilliant, Franco."

"Carmen's idea," he says, pushing me forward. I blush, but I love it. I am so proud. It's a good thing I don't have on the blouse from the other morning, the one Franco unbuttoned because if I did, those buttons would be popping right off my prideful chest, synonym for bodice, which dumps my spirit right back into a blob of kitchen grease until Franco pecks my ear. At that point, we start cleaning up the room, and the only grease I have in mind is the lubricant that comes on a condom. Carmen, Carmen, I think, you have become such a red-hot little devil. Franco's eyes take on that dreamy softness. He ushers me to the door, leaving Anaissa behind.

Christabel jumps from her chair and bars the doorway with her arms against the door frame. "What are you thinking? Skipping out on the clean up?"

Franco puts his hands in his front pockets. "I set it up. When did set up/clean up become one committee?"

"You can go, but not her. We should talk." She inclines her head in my direction.

"Carmen came up with the slogan all of us should be using. Taste the irony? We are all brothers and sisters. Sorority, sister. Fraternity, brother. But they set up their Greek system to leave out anyone they decide doesn't fit their definition of brother or sister. It's so succinct. We need to put that on sweatshirts." Franco hits his head with his hand. "Genius, pure genius. I'll fax the order to PrimePrint."

"Money?"

"The owner is Mexican. He'll cover us."

"Vote?"

"Sometimes perfection doesn't require a vote, Christabel. And whatever 'issue' you have with Carmen can wait until office hours." He pulls me by the hand out the door. On the windy walk back to Oretga, we huddle together. Inside, he leads me around the corner where the phones are. Nobody else is in the narrow hallway. He bumps me up to the wall and kisses me. I kiss him back.

"Is your roommate home?" he asks between kisses.

"Probably. Yours?"

"Always."

We are breathing like the weather in Mexico before a storm, hot, heavy, wet. I really do not want this to end.

"Wheels?"

"*Nada.*"

I hug him, my head buried into his shoulder, standing on tip-toe to take nibbles of his ear. I pull the leather thong out of his pony tail so that his hair falls loose to his shoulders. He slides his hands up my sweatshirt as if he's had plenty of experience with the mechanics of bra removal.

"Franco, not here."

"You're with me, you're safe."

"I don't trust myself."

He tilts my chin towards him. "But you trust me? You shouldn't."

I sigh and shake my arms out. I try to get the adrenalin rush in my heart to slow down. I shove Franco lightly to back him up while I reposition my bra.

"Let's think about it."

"It?"

"As in the S word."

"What would you like to think about the S word?"

"Hook up with you somewhere wonderful, not in the lobby of the dorm."

"Technically, this is an alcove of the lobby of the dorm."

"Not in the alcove either."

"And so we let this passionate interlude fizzle? Tease."

"You started it."

"You did."

"Me? Me? Exactly how did I come on to you?"

He pushes his hair away from his face. "If I had a mirror, I bet I could show you teeth marks on my ears." I hand him his hair elastic. He reties his hair. He glowers with frustration.

"Don't be mad."

"Don't be sexy. Go back to cute. Whew, I'm going up for a cold shower."

"Just like that?"

"Yes, my sweet. Flip the switch. Turn off the hormones. Take your time and think before you heat up some guy who isn't the gentleman I am."

"So now you're my big brother with advice?" I reach up to fasten my bra, which flashes my tits, but just for a second.

"See, that last move? With some other guys, it would be a come on. Next time don't expose the goods, and say good night."

"Other guys?"

"Reminder. This is college, Carmen. You're going to know a lot of men the way I know a lot of women. Big deal. No one's planning weddings. We spend our free time examining our souls."

This last statement is a long way from making out, and we both laugh. "Save your sermon on chastity for the Church of Franco," I tell him and ask, "Is there a saint of choosing?"

"Probably. Ask your mama. I'll walk you to the elevator and bid you good night. I have work to do, and you have morning shift."

"Exactly right." I pull my sweatshirt as low as it will go around my jeans, breathe deeply, and offer him my arm. "Would you escort me to the lift, kind sir?" My British accent is terrible.

"But of course, *mon amie*," he says like a Frenchman. We walk back around the corner where Anaissa and Christabel are deep in conversation on the lobby couch. They seem shocked to see me with Franco coming from the make-out alcove.

"Good night, one and all," says Franco when the elevator doors open. I step in and just before the doors close, he gives me a little kiss. "Until next time, Carmen," he whispers.

"We are all brothers and sisters," I tell him solemnly.

"As if," says Franco with a smile.

The elevator takes me upstairs. My heart is racing again. Boys aren't the only ones who need the occasional cold shower. Maybe the nuns shower in cold water because of their vows of chastity, and cold water works to lower their lust levels?

Chapter 23

First midterm scores are posted in the hallway we are told at the end of anthro. The mad scramble, moans, and yells make it impossible to hear anything. A mob pushes.

I stay in my seat, waiting for things to clear up. By the time I find my grade (90%), my TA stands next to me. "Good job, Carmen," she says. "You should change your major to anthro."

In Hispanic Studies, Christabel offsets my success by calling my name at the end of class. "You too, Mr. Sneed," she says. "Meet me at my office in ten minutes."

Joe's cheeks flame red. "What do you think she wants, Caramel?"

I shrug my shoulders. "Dunno. We know we didn't copy papers."

"Good point. I hate getting called out anyway," he says.

We move downstairs, swimming against the stream of students climbing up to exit. Joe slides downward along the wall until he's sitting. He pats a place next to him.

"If we stand up, it would feel like a firing squad."

"That's pretty negative."

"You didn't read my paper. Remember I asked you for help and you declined."

"Sorry, I was having a bad day."

"This one might be worse."

"I wrote a good paper," I tell him.

Christabel arrives. She leans to use the key hanging around her neck to open the door. The string reminds me of Franco. I shake my head. This is not the time to think about Franco. I must focus.

"Have a seat, please."

Joe pulls a chair out and gestures for me to sit. He sits by my side. Christabel opens a manila folder on her desk, pulling two papers from it. Each is creased vertically in the way of college papers. Our names are on the outside, showing.

"Your first papers."

We grab at them. Joe scratches his chin, fakes he's crossing himself, and unfolds his. He places it flat on the desk, running his finger across each typed line. From where I sit, I see lots and lots of writing and circled words in green felt pen and a happy face. I open mine. There's tons of miniscule writing and a bunch of circled words. At the top, an unhappy face with the letter *F*.

Christabel leans back in her chair. It squeaks. "What we have here is the best paper and the worst." Joe pats my hand with his. I blink, worried and embarrassed. What's she up to?

"In the spirit of *La Raza*, I am assigning the two of you as study partners. When we do the projects in November, you will have had a head start. I can't overemphasize how important the project is, especially if you intend to pass, Ms. Principia."

"But, maybe Carmen doesn't want to work with me."

"It's fine," I say. All I want is to get out of the office.

"You have work and that club with Franco; I have swimming and the frat. How can we work together?"

I wonder if he already knows that Franco is more my style and has given up on me. "It's fine," I say again. "We'll manage. Let's try it."

"Great." Christabel hands us the project sheet. It's an oral report. We have to create a facsimile of a Latino artifact and talk about its history. "That's all for now unless you have questions? We'll be going over the project guidelines in class soon. As you can imagine, I am being zealous in my efforts to see excellent work, Carmen, to offset the dismal performance on your paper."

"Thank you, Ma'am. I won't disappoint you again." I shove the paper in my book bag. "Could I come in later to talk about this?"

"*Cada loco con su tema*, Each madman on his high horse." Christabel smiles like a Cheshire cat and opens her office door. "Read the comments. You'll find the problems."

We leave.

"What was that about?" asks Joe.

"She means I was talking around the subject instead of sticking to the main points, in other words, I wrote a bunch of bull."

"Most TA's are quick to spot a runaround."

"Wouldn't that be you?"

"See, off topic already."

"So now what?"

"Your mom, the artisan?"

"She's really busy right now." I don't want to go into all the Day of the Dead stuff. Someone in class will pick that anyway.

"Okay, suggestion?"

"Library? Librarian? Somebody can help us choose."

"When?"

"Now."

"I have practice."

"So go, I'll brainstorm. Call me later?"

Joe points to his head and runs his finger in a circle. "*Loco,* this whole thing, totally *loco*."

"Try being me."

"What's that saying she threw at us?"

"*Cada loco con su tema--Each madman on his high horse.*"

"She got that right." He jogs away, stuffing our project sheet into his backpack.

I follow him until I have to turn at the library and climb the marble stairs to the main reading room. I find Mexican art in the library's huge card catalogue, ask the reference person where those numbers are shelved, and follow a map with colored arrows down, down, down into the catacombs. Nobody else is working at this level of the stacks. I pull as many books as I can carry over to a study carrel. Starting with the index of each book, I make a list of possible projects. Murals, paintings and painters, piñatas, pottery. Sculpture, stonework, tiles. I start over, adding dolls, flutes, frescoes and weavings. Everything marked Day of the Dead, for which there is a ton of information, I skip as too easy.

Sitting in the study carrel, I zone in on the lists. Somewhere here is our golden ticket. The art books capture me. Time goes away. My list has been pared down to three choices: dolls (easy to make but probably not a Joe-choice); weaving, which would be original but a hassle, and tiles. We could go to East LA and pick up tiles. I flip a few pages to see how much is in this book about tiles. It falls open to a page about piñatas. Piñatas! Hello! Whose brain shut off at the sight of an F? I am a piñata-maker's daughter

Piñatas. I'll call home and see if I can bring Joe down to the house in November after *El Dia de los Muertos*. Mama gets a break then before the Christmas orders come in. Joe and I can make our piñata. I won't ask Mama to make one for us, just to critique it.

In my mind I'm already in Joe's Miata speeding south on a sunny day with my hair flying in the wind, his arm across my seat. We're singing Phil Collins and Madonna and Wham! Once I've restacked the books, I fly out of the library like a happy hummingbird. I hope Gayla is right. She says guys like a damsel in distress.

Chapter 24

Along the campus pool fence, the levered slats give me the best chance to catch a glimpse of Joe. The piñata idea rockets around my mind, and I want to share with him right now. The pool is filled with thrashing arms and fluttering feet churning up white water. The air smells heavily of chlorine. Laid out perpendicularly to the lanes of the swimming pool, a smaller pool with deep blue water lies quiet. I lean in and close one eye to see if Joe is diving as someone bursts from the high dive in a backward somersault. The guy punches the water when he erupts from his dive. He glides to the side and climbs out. Nearby, a man with a clipboard waves him over.

I'm about to turn away when Joe emerges from a hot tub behind the diving platform. He scrambles up the steps with the same enthusiasm he uses for everything. I watch him walk to the end of the platform, positioning his toes at the final inch, balancing his body with only his toes gripping the final half inch of the board. Seconds pass. He breathes deeply, his chest muscles rippling. The coach blows a whistle. Joe counts aloud, "One, two, three." He sails through the air in a series of twists, cutting through the water. The water moves in the smallest of ripples. The coach applauds. In my head, I'm yelling "Yeah!" Joe confers with the coach and the other diver.

Joe the diver is different than Joe the campus frat man. He is elegant and serious. I wonder if there is a way to get him to show this side of himself to me? I wonder how to get a better look at his amazing toes. Carrying my backpack, I zip over to the gym doors to see if I can find a swim meet schedule, like I have enough extra time in my life to attend swim meets to watch Joe's toes.

I make notes anyway. The schedule is for next quarter. By next quarter, I should have better classes, better working hours, and better knowledge of one Joe Sneed. The thought makes me smile. He said he'd call tonight. I can't wait to tell him about the piñata project, which reminds me of Christabel, which reminds me I have a campus meeting tonight. Now I'm torn. After *Firstlings*, Joe could be pinned; he could also be pissed. The whole *Firstlings* idea that I have worked on with Franco reflects so much negativity. Life is hard here. So many decisions, so many people. I want to go back to the day I arrived and change my whole approach. I thought it would be like high school: find your group, go to class, hang out. Instead it's a barrage of thoughts, pages to read, and huge new decisions about morals and status.

I struggle through the afternoon hours, pulled by the piñata book instead of anthro or psych. Salt calls. Shirley calls to find out if Salt called. I'm not going to get any studying done in the room. Against my will, I abandon waiting for Joe's call and go to the dorm library, which is miraculously empty. I assign myself the next hour to read my psych book. The prof makes it all funny, but the text is like reading a foreign language. I'm not that interested in the theories of Carl Jung and the collective unconscious. Introvert, extrovert, I understand. These other theories sound like Shirley trying to explain how her disease could have been worse if she had had less karma. Since I'm not a big believer in karma, it's so much psychobabble. Shirley says Catholicism is the same as karma. That's one I have to think about. I pull my rosary out of my pocket, and say a penitential prayer to St. Bede. I only know him because he pulled me through my SATs.

Finally it's time to get ready for the meeting and Franco. I consider telling him I think our idea for *Firstlings* is self-centered, but then he'll counter that my non-participation is totally self-centered. True and true.

Aunt Ines gave me an aqua sweater for my birthday last year. It's cashmere, soft as my *abuela's* lullabies. I put it on with a turtleneck underneath to match the stripes around the sweater's cuffs. The only undies I have are red, but I like the color of temptation. My unpainted toenails stare up at me from my flip flops, but no time to paint them red.

The phone rings.

"I'll be right down," I say without even a hello.

"Oh, I'm not there. Wanted to check on our project."

It's Joe. The song Guido was singing this morning, "Torn Between Two Lovers," jangles around in my head. "Yeah, Joe. I've got something cool. I'm late. Talk to you in class? Can you come early?"

"What's the hurry tonight?"

"Mind your own business."

"Our project ties to my grades, so my business."

"Right. Hang on for Friday's class. Bye now."

"Caramel, you're killing me."

"Good. Bye." I drop the phone into its cradle. One quick swipe through my hair, a dot of Obsession perfume, and I'm out the door. Franco is lounging in the lobby, eyes closed. He's stroking Christabel's hair. Christabel is curled into his lap, a sight not good for my sore eyes-brain-soul. Christabel's faraway smile pinches my jealousy neurons.

They stare at me, seemingly arriving from some other point in the universe via Franco Love Trek transporter.

"Here I am," I announce.

"So you are," winks Franco. "Let's get this meeting started. Get the troops fired up!" He nudges Christabel out of his lap. She stretches, yawns, and stands up. Once on her feet, she leans back in a limber, sexy backbend I can only do in my dreams.

We hurry off to the meeting where we find the rest of the club assessing posters on the wall.

Christabel takes her spot up front. Franco sits in a chair next to her. I sit down with the rest of the group. Christabel looks to Franco, who begins writing a timeline on the chalkboard.

"Here's the schedule for our *Firstlings* presentation, make that demonstration." He laughs. Someone yells out, "Good one, Franco."

"Carmen, the *calacas* make-up. Is this enough time?"

"An hour should do if everybody is on time to begin with."

"No brainer. We'll be there. Won't we?"

"Sure."

"Yes."

"*Si.*"

"Okay, so we get on our make-up, we're all wearing black sweats. Question: Do we keep the posters under wraps or march with them over to Sorority Row?"

Christabel stands up. "We don't want trouble. Let's walk as a group with the posters rolled, unfurl them when we get there. Too early, and somebody, some WP-UniCop, is bound to stop us."

"Agreed."

"Do we have the instruments? Who's on drums? Flute? Maracas?"

Three people I don't know well raise their hands.

"Do we need more musicians?" Franco asks Christabel.

"No, we have our voices. We have our chant, thanks to Carmen."

"Do we need to practice?"

A groan ripples through the room. No one has time for more practice with midterms, papers, *El Dia*, Halloween, other clubs and Homecoming, all this stuff coming up.

"I take that as a no. Fine. Let me read you the University policy on demonstrations."

Another groan en masse, but Franco goes forward with the reading of what we can and cannot do, what we can and cannot say, where we can and cannot stand.

"That's it. See you Friday, right here in black sweats, Here are the sweatshirts with our slogan. Carmen will bring the make-up and help anybody who needs help. We march at six to arrive in our spot along the Row by 6:15. We position ourselves before all the girls are outside and the frat boys begin their stroll. Any questions?"

Somebody asks, "Who has money for bail?"

We laugh.

"Don't even go there," says Franco. "This whole thing is a reminder that we are all brothers and sisters. If the Greeks can sing their exclusionary songs, we Latinos can certainly sing our inclusionary songs. *Todos somos hermanos y hermanas.*" He raises his fist over his head and pops it to the beat: *Todos somos hermanos y hermanas.* He chants it in English next: WE are All brothers and sisters. Let me leave you with this *mis amigos:*

> Together we are one, unstoppable
> Together we are strong, undoubtable,
> Together we stand
> For our place in this land,
> We claim our right,
> We honor this night.

Chapter 25

Anaissa shouts the slogan again and again. "Come on. Let's say it together. Let your voice be heard." She's trying way too hard to be the radical.

Franco puts a finger over his lips. "Too many spies out there. Let's keep this quiet. When we assemble, that's the time to chant."

Our group dismantles in a rush of backpacks, notebooks, and chairs clattering as they are stacked back against the wall. Each of us exits, passing Christabel on one side and Franco on the other. I wait until last, putting a sweatshirt over my perfect-for-seduction outfit.

"Franco, any more details, call me?" asks Christabel, focusing above my head to see Franco.

"Got it. I'm going to walk Ms. Carmen back to the dorm."

"Sure, I believe that."

"Me? You would doubt me?" Franco winks at me or Christabel, maybe both of us. He grabs my hand to hold. I glance down at our intertwined fingers. His are long, made for playing a guitar or a piano. Or a girl. I blush. My libido is out of control.

We stop outside Ortega. "I don't want to go in," I say. "I love walking with you. Wish we had some music."

"Wish we had an apartment."

"You do? Like me and you?"

"Not that, Carmen. I wish I had an apartment where you and I could get to know each other. I'm not monogamous, not interested in shacking up, you know what I mean?"

I try not to feel hurt. It's my words that were wrong, not Franco's. I try to make a joke of it, "Like a sugar shack?" I fake nonchalance by singing, "There's a crazy little shack beyond the tracks."

Franco covers his ears. "You're not a voice major, right?"

"Ha ha, big funny." I pull his hands down and hold them in front of me, not thinking how they're at crotch level until Franco's hand wanders there.

"That's tempting." He kisses my neck. "No one will be in the office. C'mon."

Ten-second delay. That's what Ashley said about making sexual decisions. You don't just go with it. You process the situation. That was about ten seconds, I think.

"Okay."

We fly to Berkebile. Franco unlocks the office door. He hangs a couple of posters across the lower part of the windows. I watch. If I want out, now is the time to say so. I pull off my sweatshirt. Beer materializes from the corner 'fridge. Girls must be fairly predictable when it comes to Franco. We swig one beer, then chug them.

He tugs me to the couch, encountering no resistance from me. We kiss. We kiss with tongues. He leans over me, so that I'm lying down. He rubs his cheek against the cashmere, saying "so soft, soft and fuzzy." He puts his hands under it, rubbing my breasts, unfastening my bra, saying "beautiful, perfect." I'm on fire with desire. What could I say sexy back to him? I settle for "yes, perfect."

His hand is on my jeans. "Take them off."

"What if someone?"

"They won't. I work here most nights. No visitors. Ever."

I tug off my jeans. My panties rip at the waist. I'm mortified.

"These go too," he says, lifting my hips to slip the panties off. He doesn't fling them. "Sexy! Rojo!" He places them on top of my jeans. He stands to unzip his jeans.

"Franco?"

"It's okay," he soothes me with kisses. "Are you a virgin?"

I want to tell him yes. "I'm not. But inexperienced."

"Shhhh." He kisses me and lies on top of me. He's so slender. I run my hands across his back. He runs his hands and then his lips across my breasts. Everything in me feels liquid, melted, hot. There is no pain when he enters me, there is no pain as he rocks and bucks and thrusts. This is nothing like what happened prom night.

When he finishes with a groan, I cry out too, to suggest that I've experienced what I should have, according to Gayla's books anyway.

He holds me, spooning against my back. From his regular breathing, I can tell he has fallen asleep. How can he sleep? My heart beats like a wild thing. I reach to touch his neck. His pulse point is slow and regular.

When I roll out of his arms, he rolls towards the edge of the couch. I don't want to wake him. I want to escape. I cover his butt with his shirt. I need a shower. I pick up my undies and stash them in the front pouch of my sweatshirt as I pull it on. I zip my jeans and whisper, "Good night. I wish I meant more than sex to you."

Outside, the wind is blowing. I pull my hood up. I stop by a trash can to deposit the panties, change my mind, stuff them back into the pouch.

I'm too restless to try to sleep and fake everything is okay for Shirley, so I walk to the library. It's open practically all night. My footsteps echo on the metal stairways of the stacks. I find my way to the Mexican art section.

Rather than searching for project information, I pull huge art print books. I study the women of Diego Rivera. He painted them subservient, rounded, full. I study *Nude with Calla Lillies* and wonder about the juxtaposition. Is this woman like Eve, all innocence? *The Flower Carrier, The Flower Seller, The Grinder.* Mexican people, strong people, all with work to do. Work and flowers. I turn the page. *La Noche de Los Pobres*, a mother asleep with her children

Franco is supposed to be my bridge into a deeper understanding of my culture. He is the brains behind what I learn, he and Christabel. Is sex on a couch a way to learn about my culture? I am such a phony. I squeeze my legs tight where they are sticky with Franco. At least the book helps distract me from the smell of Franco on my skin. I hold the book closer to my face. A painting called *Mother and Children* appears on the next page. The baby is awake. Though I see only his back, he reaches out, exuding curiosity. The mother is sleeping. A sister looks on in with big eyes, quietly touching the baby to allow her mother a moment.

I was that girl. I was the one who worked for Mama, who sat with a*buela*, who helped to ease the load. I turn the page. A full frontal nude, the hair on her head spread past her shoulders, framing her. The hair creates an upside down V, with the point on her pubic hair. Did Franco see me this way? This girl sits nude, unafraid, eyes wide, her private self on view. What I just did with Franco, this sex, was not beautiful like this painting. What was it?

Sitting in the stacks, I cry. I lift my sweatshirt up to cover my face, crying for the lack of beauty in my life, crying about giving away my most private self. I think about Sister Rosalie, how she has married Christ, accepted a life of poverty and chastity.

College is all about learning. Diego Rivera has tutored me tonight; Franco tutored me tonight. He told me straight out where he stands on sex. I am the one who made up the romance to assuage the guilt, a lifetime of lessons from my aunt, my mother, my *abuela*, Gayla.

Gathering my things, I re-shelve the Rivera book. I know where to find it when I need it. I wish I knew where to find the real me.

Chapter 26

Tents line the courtyard in front of the arena, basketball nuts already lining up for the big scrimmage tomorrow night. I don't get the fanatic attitude about our basketball team's "Midnight Madness." It's not even the first game of the season, it's not our big rivals from St. Luke's, it's an intra-squad scrimmage for God's sake. Big whoop.

Careful where I put my feet with tents and ice chests and chairs everywhere, I try some yoga breathing. Tape decks blare rival music, *Madonna* versus *Depeche Mode*. A guy and a girl share a blanket around their shoulders, playing guitars.

I'm almost out of the crazy zone when I stumble and fall. That's not exactly true. I didn't stumble. Somebody tripped me. I lift my head, expecting Salt or Shirley. It's Joe.

"Hey, Baby! Stay over with me!" he says as he pulls me to my feet.

"Are you crazy?"

"We could talk about our project. I called again. Nobody home, and I had to stake out the tent until the plebes arrive."

"Like I want to be awakened by horny frat boys after midnight?"

"They're not coming until morning. C'mon, Caramel, it's a chance to spend some quality time on the project. Between your job and my sport, when are we going to have a chance like this again?"

"Maybe. Let me see how you have things set up." I peek into the tent. Two sleeping bags are rolled up in one corner. Two low beach chairs face one another. Joe has a cardboard box holding bottles of beer and bags of chips. "Healthy eating guaranteed, I see."

"Whatever. I was in a hurry. Say you'll stay, Caramel."

"What time is the next shift coming?"

"Six."

"I can't be late for work."

"You won't be."

"Study session, no benefits."

His chipper attitude slips, "Your call."

"Bathroom?"

"The arena is open."

I pee the beer, wash my face in the sink, and wet a towel to clean up quickly elsewhere.

Joe's waiting outside the door. "I wanted to be sure you were safe. You shoudn't walk around at night alone. Call for an escort. Or call me."

"Right. You have time for that."

Joe throws my backpack into the tent. We scoot in after it and wiggle into the beach chairs. We take off our shoes. Our socks are touching. I want to see his amazing toes, the ones that hold him to a diving platform. Toes seem safe enough, cozy in a way. The arena's lights dot the canvas. "It's dark in here, Joe."

He turns on a flashlight. "Super batteries, good for an hour at least." He opens two beers and hands me one. "Let's hear about the Christabel project ideas."

"These are my best choices: dolls, tiles, or piñatas."

"Piñatas! I love those! We could buy one at the party store."

"No, we have to make one, that's part of the project."

Joe's big smile droops. "Make one? I can't draw anything except a turtle."

"I can. I have some insider knowledge on piñatas, a family thing."

"You mean we could interview somebody?"

"Maybe. It would cost you a weekend in San Diego."

"Can we go to the zoo?" He puts his arm up to simulate a trunk and makes a god-awful snorting sound. "Snuffle, snuff, eeeoooooooooow!"

"As much as I'd like to help you with your anteater imitation, there's no time for the zoo."

"Anybody could tell that was my elephant call."

"Anybody but me." I drain the beer. "I was parched! Listen, Joe, elephants go like this." I put my arm out and sway it. "Booooo-oooong!"

"Is that its death call?"

"Cruel. Listen again." I produce a better-sounding trumpet with a convincing flap of my arm-trunk.

"Ah!" Joe yanks me out of my chair by my extended arm trunk. I'm suddenly in his arms. "I do believe that was the elephant's mating call."

"Are you crazy?"

He holds my hands down and kisses me. "Are you?"

"Remember no benefits?"

"No," he kisses my ears. "Do you?"

I giggle. I want to stay focused on the project, what was it, to build a piñata like an elephant? I can't remember. "Did you slip something into my beer?"

"Caramel, you watch too many hours of Lifetime movies."

"We don't get cable. Plus, name one day of the week I have time to watch TV."

"Friday nights?"

"You are so bad." I push him back, but that results in him hovering over me. His arms ripple with muscles. His teeth are shiny white when he smiles, and as he leans in to kiss me again, his brush cut hair tickles my neck.

"I'm not bad," he assures me. He works his hands down under my sweatshirt and my cashmere sweater. His hands are warm. He slips his hands to my jeans. I hear the jeans unzip. "Holy shit, Sherlock," he says, finding I have no underwear on.

Oh, my God. I try to sit up, but I'm wasted. My undies are a red flag in my sweatshirt. What if he finds them? I try to enunciate. "Hello! Ran out of quarters. Laundromat."

"Say no more, baby." He has pulled my jeans off and unzips his. I reach for him, pull him into my arms.

"Let's get this sweater off too. Put it under your head. It's so soft." No hesitation, he makes a pillow for me of my sweater. He slips his jeans and briefs down. His butt cheeks are firm, tight, smooth. Like an athlete, he moves from one tactic to another. He's murmuring wordless compliments, "mmm. .

mmmm….mmm." By this time, I'm breathing heavily and my body is screaming.

"Carmen, are you sure?" He's poised on his hands above me. "Remember, it's your call."

"So gallant," I murmur. To prove no further words are necessary, I touch him and guide him. His skin breaks into goose bumps when he comes. He doesn't stop with that though, applying himself to me until I am in some new pleasure zone.

"Oh, baby," I whisper.

"Sweet, huh?"

"Totally, absolutely, fabuloso."

"Don't start talking to me in Spanish now."

"*Mi querido.*" I trace his profile.

"Meaning?"

"Darling."

Joe rests his head on my breasts. "And how do I say it back?"

"*Mi querida.*"

"What's this 'do/da' stuff?"

"The *a* and *o* rule in Spanish."

"Oh yeah, I was lost for a minute." He squirms around to find his pants, throws mine to me.

"Wait!"

"What?"

I don't want him to throw my sweatshirt. He'll find my undies and then what? "Could we chill like a minute?"

He lies down beside me. "I could look at you forever. Isn't there some poem everybody reads in high school about how a guy could look at his lady for ages and eons for this part and that part of her body?"

"Yeah. I didn't get it until now."

"And he tells her to make hay while the sun is shining?"

"Not exactly. The guy says they can't make the sun stand still, but they can make him run."

"I don't get that."

"*Carpe diem.* Seize the day."

"How about seize the titties?" He swirls his tongue around each nipple.

"Whoa, whoa, whoa. Joe, I'd better get dressed or we're not going to get any sleep and then I'll get fired and I'll have to leave you all alone at the U."

"I'd be like Romeo or somebody. I'd die if you weren't here. Hold me tight."

And even though I know that's not true, I like hearing it. We zip the two sleeping bags together, and I cuddle him close, skin against skin. He sets the alarm on his watch.

"Good night, *mi querido*."

He's almost asleep. He mumbles, "Night, Caramel. *Carpe Caramel*."

Chapter 27

Can't sleep, need a shower, need my bed, need to clear my brain. In the past twenty-four hours, I have acted as some other me. Joe has kicked out of the sleeping bag.

He shifts and mumbles when I get up, but he doesn't awaken. In the dark, I find my clothes. I lie down to scrim the jeans up my legs, suck in my gut, and zip them. The tent is low, and the whole structure wobbles when I knock into it. Hood up over my head, I kiss Joe's cheek. He smiles in his sleep.

Fog has settled over campus. Outside the arena, the tents huddle together. A girl walks, swaying drunkenly, on her way out of the bathrooms in the arena. She slips into a tent, and I'm alone again.

I take off my flip-flops. They're so noisy. I want to glide through the fog into my room and snooze in my own my bed for a few hours. I definitely do not want to talk to anyone. Think, think, think.

Opening the door, I sneak like a thief to my closet for my bathroom kit and clean clothes. As I edge away, Shirley whispers, "Hey." It's completely dark, but I wave. I don't turn around.

The hot shower pounds my sore back and neck. I create a foam with my Ivory soap, choking back a sob, Ivory, the purest soap. Will it purify me, Carmen, who has slept with two different guys on the same night? My body aches, my head aches, my heart aches. Under the shower, as I stretch my neck, I wash my mouth and cheeks and ears. I open my mouth to rinse it of the taste of beer, the taste of Franco, and the taste of Joe. I sit in the corner of the shower, letting the water pelt my thighs, all the places I've let go of tonight, handed over to men, not out of love. I'm not going to kid myself. This is not love. It is sex. Lust. Sin.

In the shower, I say a rosary. I ask for forgiveness. I will go to mass on Sunday if I can find time for confession today. A day ago, I felt filled with joy and adventure. Today I feel low and cold, sore and used.

Once I'm toweled off and dressed in clean clothes, it's too late to sleep. I return to my room to leave my dirty clothes and wet towels. I am about to throw them on the bed when I realize it's occupied. Who the hell is that? I lift the coverlet. Salt. Why is Salt sleeping in my bed? I'm late, but it's my bed. I'm ready to explode with a few choice words when Shirley yanks my tee-shirt.

"Shhh, I'll explain," she assures me.

"Out of bounds, over the line. Of all the gross things you could do, this is the grossest. Never mind." I self-righteously slam the door.

Nothing goes right in my kitchen shift. I am slow and clumsy. Guido pats my back.

"We all have bad days, no worries," he says. "Mitchell is out with the flu. Lucky girl!"

At least that's a relief. Penny and I get enough done to leave early. Still, it's insufficient time to sleep. I order a double coffee at Berkebile, glancing at the door down the hallway. The blinds are closed. Franco is undoubtedly sleeping like a worn-out dog. I'd say baby, but there's nothing babyish about Franco. And I know all about babies. My cousins scream half the night every night when we visit.

The coffee is too hot. It burns the roof of my mouth. I'm glad for the pain. I swallow another scorching mouthful, and my mind loses some of its fuzz.

I sit through Psych, forcing myself to take notes. The prof is going over mathematical tables of trials. He announces that we'll get our psych trial experiment hours from our TA's this week. Lovely. Someone is going to use me as a test subject. I hope they aren't trying to see how many WPC freshmen are normal since I'm one who has proven she's not. How many Crusader girls sleep with two men in one night? The answer makes me sick. I imagine the answer is one. Maybe two. There's always Norine.

The bell rings. We shuffle to the door. I scan the room, hoping Joe has come to meet me. No Joe. Either his frat buddies didn't show up to take tent duty or his watch alarm didn't work. He's probably back at the frat house buried in clean sheets, flannel blankets, one pillow under his head and one over it to keep out the noise. The frat has a maid. I'm envious thinking how pampered some of my classmates are.

It's finally time for Hispanic Studies. Christabel leans against the doorway, waiting for the class.

"What did you choose, Carmen?"

For a moment, my gut aches, thinking she knows about Joe and Franco. "Choose?"

"The project?"

"Oh, right. I researched it and talked it over with Joe. We decided on the *pinata*."

Christabel smiles. "Good idea! Your classmates will enjoy that."

"Right." I take my seat.

"Here's the sign-up list." She hands me a sheet with dates and numbers.

"Do we have to go first?"

"You should, for your sake."

I flick my pen in my fingers back and forth, deciding. "How will it help me?"

"If it's not good enough, you can do an extra report at the end."

"Great. It will be good enough." I sign *Carmen Principia* and *Joe Sneed* on the first spot, parentheses *piñata*, and hand it back. She tucks it into her bag

"Carmen, since you know about the project, you don't have to stay today."

"Really?" I'm kind of stalling. I want to see Joe.

"Go. You look completely beaten down." She says this with a smile even though there's something bitter in her eyes. Joe walks in as she guesses, "Too much Franco?"

Joe winks at me. "Latin lover boy?" he asks in his joke voice.

"What's the dif? Latino, white? Playboys of the college world," I say. "Is the free pass still on, Christabel? Does it apply to Joe?"

"It shouldn't."

"Harassment! Prejudice!" accuses Joe. He is grinning.

"Sure, Sneed, people in this class are out for your blood."

"Don't I know it," he says, pushing me towards the door.

"Catch you next week. Is there reading assigned? Pop quiz next time?"

"Reading yes, quiz, who knows? Good idea though." She turns away.

The bell rings. The last of the stragglers enter classrooms. The hall is empty except for us.

Joe closes his eyes and opens them. "You're still here?"

"Yep."

"Want to come to my room?"

"Nope.'

"Carmen, what's with you?"

"Tired."

"I suppose you are, considering."

"Considering?"

He pulls my red panties out of his pocket. "These seem to have dropped under the sleeping bags. So I'm thinking you were two steps ahead of me on our liaison, coming to my tent with your panties off."

"Um, no, Like I told you, laundry problems."

"So you carry your dirty laundry and leave it in my sleeping bag? Is that like a test to see if another girl would find them? You must think I'm a scumbag."

"Think what you want." I walk away, totally humiliated.

He rushes after me, yanking me by my backpack. "I don't get it. I thought you were going to be my girl."

"Not ready for commitment. We'll do the report. Be classmates. The other—that just happened. It's not like it's going to happen again."

"Carmen, it was so special with you." Joe stops when he sees my scowl. "I guess you didn't feel it back. *Buenos adios, senorita.*"

He takes two steps and turns, throwing my wadded up panties at me. "You must think about me a lot because your panties tell a tale. You arrived amazingly lubricious, unless that's for all

the guys. See you, Spankie. Maybe that should be Skankie."
Mortified, I watch him walk away.

Chapter 28

Messages in my mail box: Franco, don't be late for *Firstlings*. Franco, Bring *Dia* make-up. Franco, After party? Nothing from Joe. Time has moved on even when every hour drags me drooping from one chore to the next. Neither one would miss a beat if I disappeared.

Disappear. That sounds tempting. Miss *Firstlings,* miss the rebellion, miss the confrontation, miss the guilt every time I see Joe or Franco. Beam me up, Scottie.

I get to our room and pick up the phone to call Aunt Ines. Her phone rings and rings. No answer, no answering machine. I call home next. Mama answers as if she knew I needed to hear her voice.

"Maybe I could come home this weekend? Help you some?"

"I've been using Gayla's help. I'm caught up. Do you believe that? If you come home, you can help me shop in Tijuana. Okay?"

"Gross, I want to sleep in my own bed, chill with you."

"Chill?"

"Hang out."

"I'd be gone most of the day. You want my company, you come shopping."

I chew my lip. I pick my hangnails. "Never mind. I'll come in two weeks. Is it okay if I bring a friend?"

"I would love to meet your roommate!" I picture Mama writing down the things she will cook just for us, albondigas soup, chili verde.

"Not my roommate, a classmate. We have a project on piñatas."

"Praise God! You are learning something about piñatas?"

"My Hispanic Studies class project."

"Two weeks then. I love you, my daughter."

"I can bring the classmate, yes?"

"Yes." Click.

Did I or did I not mention Joe's name? Does she know or care that I am bringing a man into the house? If he can sleep in a tent for a basketball game, he can survive a night on our couch. Unbidden, the aromas of the house come to me, chilis and frying oil, the musty couch and stiff, cheap towels that smell of bleach.

I collapse on my bed, head-first into the pillow. It smells funky, and I remember Salt was staying over for some weird reason. I strip the linens off and march them to the coin laundry on our floor. I double the soap to erase the Salt-stink. When I get back to the room, I pull a blanket over me. The blanket whiffs too. I study in my blanket cave until midnight, turn off the lights, fall asleep.

Somebody shakes me.

"Don't," I snap without opening my eyes.

"I have to start getting ready for *Firstlings*. Would you do my make up?"

"You'd be very sorry, Shirley, if I did your make-up."

"Who then?"

"Norine? She wears enough."

"I'll go find her." She exits. The clock says I've slept for twelve hours. It's noon, Friday. Thank the Lord I have this Fall Break day off. The big day for Shirley and the sorority snobs; the day for me and Franco and our statement to the world. I really want to catch a southbound bus all the way home.

Shirley returns with Norine. Norine has her hair extra poofed. She's wearing a pink dressy suit with big shoulders. Under the suit jacket, a low-cut camisole, apple green and lacey, flaunts her cleavage.

"Nice outfit," I say.

Norine turns to the mirror, pulling the camisole tighter by reaching under her skirt. "Jennifer lets me borrow clothes any time. Do you think I should dye my hair red like hers? Anyway, Little Sisters have greeting duties today." She preens again at the mirror.

"But you can help Shirley?"

"Half hour tops. I wouldn't want to miss any greetings." She licks her lips.

"Aren't you greeting parents?"

"Only at tomorrow's brunch. Might miss that one, it's so early and tonight is going to be a late, late night for some of us." She smiles like she has hot connections.

"Thanks, Norine. If you handle the eye make-up and get my hair in a French braid, Carmen will do up my dress and take the pictures my grandmother wants."

I'm suddenly aware that my schedule is tight. "We better get a move on 'cause I have a meeting of *La Raza* to prepare for."

"What's the big?"

"I told you, Shirley. We're practicing a play for the Day of the Dead." This seems to be a good enough lie.

"What time are you leaving?"

"Two."

"But the pictures?"

"Raincheck? Your sorority sisters?"

"You promised. You're a snake, Carmen."

"La di da. Scheduling conflict. Oh, no! I didn't put sweet sorority lady Shirley ahead of everything else in the world."

"Get out, okay?" Shirley rubs at her nose with her bathrobe. Norine puts her arm around her.

"You're just one big mess, Shirley. Everything's going to be okay. Today is a huge day for you. I know it. You know it. Carmen doesn't know anything about the Greeks since she's Mexican and all. See you, Carmen." She pushes me out the door.

"Fine!" I yell. Racist pigs. Franco's right. We may all be brothers and sisters, but some of the human family thinks it's so completely in command. I'm fired up.

In our *La Raza* meeting room, I set up stations for people to get their *calaca* face on. White paint, station one; black paint, station two. an array of colors to paint flowers and symbols at station three.

The others arrive one by one.

I begin doing my face so that people can copy my technique. I lose myself in visions of *calaca* masks, obliterating my brown face with white paint, smooth as Noxema skin cream. I add black hollows around my eyes, and a design on my forehead. I color in my nose, all black like a puppy's. Etching in big teeth makes the face appear more death-like, like stitches across. For color, some hearts in red on the forehead design and ruby red lips just in the center as if death has not quite finished with my body. I am leaning toward my make-up mirror when Christabel appears behind me.

"Devastating, my pretty," she says. "I love *El Dia.*"

"I always have too, except it was so busy at my mom's shop."

"Does she sell flowers?"

"Piñatas."

"Ah ha! Your report with Joe!"

"I don't know anything about piñatas except how to make them. I have to do the research anyway."

"Be sure he does his share."

"Of course."

Franco interrupts us. "Everybody, get your sweatshirt on before you do make up!" He has painted his face already, half him, half calaca. Nothing, not even *El Dia* paint, makes him less attractive. "No kissing until after the parade," he whispers into my ear. How can I fizz with desire at his words, knowing what I know? "Christabel, Carmen, my two favorite *calacas*!"

I pull *La Raza*'s black sweatshirt carefully over my head, trying not to smear my make-up. Franco, Christabel, and I have to dash from station to station, trying to paint each arriving member in an original design. Franco stares at the clock, stands at the door, jitters his shoes.

"Five minutes and we march," he yells. He gathers the posters from the corner, hands them out. "When we get there, two to a poster. On the way, we walk mute as ghosts. Once we reach the row, we sing. Do you have your instruments?"

A chorus of twangs and rattles and tambourines assures him the instruments are present. We line up. Franco and Christabel are at the front.

I'm next in line with Anaissa. She's sweating.

"No fear," I tell her. We leave together in silence.

Chapter 29

Streets hum with student activity, buses, cars, groups walking. Frat boys are dressed in their tuxes with cumberbunds that match their frat's colors. Well, guess what frat boys? We're in our colors too.

Stopped at the light, Franco leads a first chant, "We are all brothers and sisters. We are all one world." The *calacas* behind me pick it up in monotones. No one is shouting.

We get some funny looks. One guy flips us off. Another yells, "Go home to your brothers and sisters!"

Franco hands the poster to Christabel. "Raise it high," he tells her. To us behind him, he says, "Time for the posters. Walk with your heads and posters high. Don't get caught in crossfire talk. We'll have our say when we get to our corner."

We forge ahead as a group. I'm up front so I can't see if anybody is wimping out. Sweat forms at my hairline and on my neck. The evening is much too warm for these outfits. If I wipe my brow, I'll smear my make-up. If it drips, it will look like the track of a tear. That could be a symbol of our struggle for equality, the tear. I wish I had painted one on every face.

Before we reach Sorority Row, a burst of song hovers in the night. Franco walks faster. "We're late. They've started," he tells Christabel.

At the top of the hill, we have a view of the Row. The *Firstlings* girls dressed in white formals, all holding candles. Their sisters stand to the side in colored dresses: orange and blue; yellow and red; maroon and blue; more colors, more houses, more girls. It is the inductees who hold my attention as I search for Shirley and Maria in the *Firstlings* line next to Tri Chi's lime greens. I catch sight of my roommate, the candlelight on her face, excited and proud. I wish I were taking pictures as I promised Shirley.

Our group slithers down the wet grass, doing what we can not to fall. In the center of the block, we form a single-file semi-circle. Franco steps to the front. "No talking, signs higher." We obey.

The Greeks stop singing, and there is a rising murmur. The next house sings louder. Frat boys turn away from us, shielding the *Firstlings* girls with their own group. The boys' voices are low, but loud, singing homage to the initiates.

Franco speaks to our musicians. He gives them the signal to begin. The tambourine, the guitar, the maracas, a steady beat of a drum. Franco, Christabel, Anaissa, and I know the lyrics of our opening anthem. "The Revolution Will Not Be Televised." We sing one verse, allow the instruments to take it from there.

The sororities and the fraternities sing louder. Our band plays louder. We begin our chant, "We are all brothers and sisters. We are all one world."

"Stick it up your ass," yells a stocky frat boy.

"*Uno mundo*!" Franco yells.

"Yeah, say it in English, wetback.

"Together," Franco tell us. "*Uno mundo, Todos somos hermanos y hermanas*." Our voices grow raucus, urgent.

Firstlings stops. The frat boys converge from places along the street to gather at the house across from us.

"Stand your ground. We have the right to be here," Franco exhorts us. I hear someone sniffling behind me. "If you want to leave, leave now." A ripple of paper as a poster is folded. We have lost one or two. "No problem. Stand firm. Our motto, in English: "We are all brothers and sisters/One world."

"One world, one world, one world, one world." The adrenaline shoots into my heart and up through my throat. My voice is already hoarse. I feel the justice of our cause, the injustice of their secret exclusionary society.

Like ravens, the frat boys turn in a flock, their tuxes morphing into a multicolored blob of danger. They rush the street. An ox of a guy throws a punch. We are outnumbered. The boys strip our posters from our hands, shred them, crumple them. The guitar is bashed against the sidewalk. The maracas are thrown into the gutter. A frat boy beats a wild rhythm on the drum befote he lifts it overhead and tosses the drum into the street.

Franco's nose is bleeding. He wipes the blood on his sweatshirt. His *calaca* paint smears with red. Christabel is pushed back and forth between two guys. They call her "whore" and "donkey."

Anaissa and I move in to protect her. "Stop," I shout. "Stop it. Boys against girls? That's real manly."

They shove her to the ground and slap me.

"Go home, all the way to Mexico!"

My cheek stings. I strike outward, wishing I had long nails to claw a mark down their smirking faces. I hear screaming, high girlish voices from across the street. I start to cross.

"Carmen, no," says Franco. He pulls me back.

Sirens blare and police car lights flash as WP Uni-cops pull up. Two cars skid to a stop. Four cops emerge. They have Billy clubs out. Pepper spray bottles are clipped to their belts.

"Good," says Franco. "Everybody, stand your ground. We have our rights. Our cause is right. By law, they must leave us alone."

The guy who threw the first punch gestures as he talks to the cop. He keeps pointing at us, pointing at the sorority houses, pointing at the now-broken lines of girls in white. Their candles have gone out. I can't find Shirley.

The cop, listening, scribbles in his notebook. He picks up a bullhorn from the squad car.

"This assembly is no longer a legal assembly. Everyone, move on." We don't move. The frat boys re-cross the street. The girls surround them. They re-form into groups by house colors.

"I gave an order to disburse," yells the cop at us.

We look to Franco. He shakes his head. "We are not wrong." The Unicop stands in front of Franco, hitting his baton against his hand. His partner walks along the line of us shining a flashlight into our faces.

"Remove your disguise," he orders.

"What statute is that?" Franco counters.

"How about the one called disobeying an officer. I am warning you."

We sit. Franco picks up our chant, and our voices join his, "We are all brothers and sisters. We are all one world." Our diminished group roars with energy and belief.

"Now see here," the boss cop tries a new strategy. "These men and women," he points across the street, "have a right to their ceremony."

"They can have their ceremony. We can have ours. There is no law against expressing opposing beliefs," says Franco.

The policeman takes his arm and calls to a colleague. "Officer, escort this young man to the station if you would, please."

"Will you take all of us?" asks Christabel. "If not, you are guilty of harassment."

An officer leans into his patrol car and speaks into the radio. "Assistance needed on Sorority Row. Send a paddy wagon."

"You're making a mistake. We'll sue for false arrest."

"Boo hoo. Last chance. Disperse now."

With our group quiet, the street again resounds with harmonies, songs of call and answer between the low bass voices of the men, the high sopranos of the girls.

All of the cops stand in position to use their pepper spray. "A little hot sauce before you go?" one asks me.

I am about to give him an argument when I am tugged from behind. I lose my balance on the curb and fall back. I am staring into Joe's eyes. He's wearing his tux, which is rumpled, his white shirt unbuttoned and untucked.

"Caramel," he says, "I'd know you anywhere. What are you doing? I thought you believed in fairness and equality?"

I sit up and turn to him. "I do believe that."

"And does it apply only to minorities?"

"Of course not."

"May I take you home?"

Franco is watching us, his mouth a grim line of discontent. The paddy wagon pulls up in front of the two police cars. Doors swing open.

"Last chance," says the sergeant. "Disburse or step into the wagon."

Franco holds Christabel's hand. Christabel holds Anaissa's hand. They throw their fists into the air. "One world." The Latino officer yanks the hands down, cuffs them, holds them by the elbow at they climb in.

Joe takes me by the upper arm. "You're not going there, are you, Carmen? Really?"

I try to shake free."I must go."

Joe drops my arm. He puts both hands on my shoulders. "Look at me, Carmen."

My chin is down. I lift it with defiance.

"We are one world. Don't divide us into two." He slides my hair behind my ears. "Come with me."

There's nothing I want more, but I bite the inside of my cheeks. I shake my head no. The Latino officer puts handcuffs on my wrists, too tight. I bite harder on my cheek. Joe stands watching. I cock my head to see around the arresting officer. "One world," I mouth to Joe.

"Anyone else want to join the party on the bus?" snarls the sergeant. He slams the left door.

Joe calls to him. "Hey, cop!" He gives him the finger. "One more," says Joe, turning to be cuffed. He is pushed face-first into the dirty floor of the bus.

Face to face with tennis shoes, old gum, and disgusting stains, he turns his head and winks at me. All my anger at him melts away.

Chapter 30

Girls are separated from boys. We have been washed of our *calacas* paint. My cheeks are sore outside from the rough scrubbing and inside from biting on them. Our holding cells are small. The cells have toilets and white tile. A cement bench runs the length of the walls. A heavy mesh separates us from the hall way. We can't see the clock or the front door. It must be near midnight. I am exhausted.

Christabel and Anaissa have fallen asleep, Anaissa's head pillowed on Christabel's lap. Funny, I think, it should be the other way around. Anaissa would be much more comfortable than skinny Christabel. I pace. I hear Joe and Franco arguing in low voices.

The University's Chancellor and a man with a briefcase arrive together under the bored eyes of a guard. The Chancellor's face is creased and wrinkled. His back is straight, his expression solemn. He whispers in the aide's ear. The aide shakes his head. He whispers again. The aide agrees.

"I am Peter DeMott, attorney for the Chancellor's office," he begins. "The incident this evening, an unfortunate gathering of opposing forces, is not, technically, illegal." We cheer and high five. "You will be released soon, but because you have signed our university's Oath of Conduct upon entry, we will be meeting with you to discuss repercussions."

Christabel speaks out. "These repercussions, they cannot be academic or in any way impede our completion of courses."

The attorney swipes at his greasy black hair. One lock falls forward out of place. "Correct."

We cheer and high five again.

"You will meet the board of conduct next week. Repercussions usually take the form of apology and community service."

"Rock on," blurts Joe.

"The University van is here to transport you back to your dorms," the Chancellor tells us. His face is grayish white, and he's sweating. "I cannot describe to you how your childish and embarrassing actions will be portrayed in the media. You have put our credo as a Christian university at risk. I am ashamed of each and every one of you, and I will be, until you make good on whatever punishment is meted out."

No cheering follows this remark.

"It is hard to be sorry for standing up for equality," Franco says evenly.

The attorney steps forward. "We aren't here to debate your case. We are here to escort you back to campus with the clear understanding that the fraternities and sororities will not be harassed further during any of their rites, including their games during Greek Week. Do you understand me?"

I guess we have all agreed because the guard unlocks our cell. "Single file, hands behind backs," he orders. "You are in our custody until you walk out that door."

Our high spirits sink, and we appropriately shuffle through the door where we embrace one another before boarding the van. Christabel sits by Anaissa. Franco sits alone. He glares at me. I decide to sit alone too. Joe hesitates by the driver after stepping into the bus. He takes the seat in front of me.

The bus stops in front of Ortega. We all get out, even Joe. Franco says we'll meet again, normal place, normal time.

Joe asks, "Me too?"

Franco raises his eyebrows. "If you wish." Is Franco really so altruistic?

"Cool."

"Joe, wait," I call to him after Franco enters the dorm. "Is your frat going to throw you out for coming with us?"

"I doubt it. They don't know why the cops picked me up. It's all good. I don't feel like a big fancy party tonight though." He checks his watch. "It's winding down now anyway.

"What about your date?"

"What about her?"

"Won't she be mad?"

"Nah. It was like a lottery. You get whoever. So somebody would have stepped in to be her escort."

"That's good. I'm sorry we messed up something so beautiful."

"Really?"

"Yeah. One world is one thing, but everybody has rights."

"Even the right to exclude people?"

"I guess so."

"Want to go for a drive and talk some more?"

"If we went driving, I'd fall asleep. I haven't been sleeping well." This is a major admission for me.

"Me either. Listen, I'm going to go get my car. You go up and pack for a one-day trip."

"What?"

"But you have to stay awake part of the time."

"Because?"

"We're going to your house to work on our project. What time does your mom get up in the morning?"

"Early."

"So I'll take you to downtown LA where we'll have the world's best pancakes at The Pantry, and drive south from there. By the time we get to San Diego, your mom should be up."

"Should I call her?"

"You decide. I'll be back in fifteen minutes. Don't make me come upstairs to get you, Caramel."

I don't call Mama, and the next thing I know we're in this deserted block of downtown L.A. with a line along the wall near The Pantry and a line of homeless people, sleeping under their blankets. Even with a wrapping, the sour smell of urine and dirty bodies hovers over them.

The door guy calls "Joe" and seats us in a booth. He says, "Hey, buddy!" to Joe and then loud enough that I can hear, "New girl?"

I seat myself and don't bother with Joe's answer. He has already demonstrated that I'm his new girl. At least I think he has.

Our massive pancakes are served. The round balls of butter on top of them melt in streams down the side. We soak each stack in syrup. The waiter refills our coffee over and over, and finally I am awake and stuffed.

"Restroom?" I ask Joe.

"In back. You're the one with the skirt, Caramel."

"Uh, yeah, that would be true." I tromp off, use the toilet, and try to do something with my hair. Lipstick or no? Not necessary for Joe.

I open the women's bathroom door just as Joe comes out of the men's room. He's jangling his car keys. "Let's get this show on the road. Your house today, my house tomorrow."

"Your house?"

"Don't you want to meet my folks?"

"I didn't bring anything fancy to wear."

"You think my parents care about fancy? We live at the beach, Carmen. My mother runs around in her bathing suit and flip flops and a sarong. Her hair is bleached out, and she wears it short and straight. You'll be fine."

"What about your father?"

He hesitates. "I'm anxious for you to meet him. If he's not surfing, he'll be fishing. If he's not fishing, he'll be taking the boat's motor apart with grease up to his elbows. We are, shall I say, not a family that stands on much ceremony."

"But I'm Mexican."

"True, that will be a new one. I don't see a problem. They like our maid and our gardener a lot. They're Mexicans."

Great, I think.

Joe kisses me. "It's not like we're getting married, Carmen."

"Oh, yeah, I forgot that part. WPC is all about screwing. Marriage is a dirty word."

"I didn't say that. Don't be that way. It's going to be a fun day, especially after the whole deal tonight. Don't start looking for trouble where there is none. Please."

"Not yet, anyway."

"Exactly."

"We've had enough trouble tonight to cover a whole year."

"You got that right." He kisses me again. "*Mi querida*, let's *hasta luego* ourselves on out of here."

He opens the car door for me. I check my backpack for breath mints while he comes around to the driver's side. I toss a Tic-Tac at him which hits his nose. He opens his mouth wide. "Three points if you can put one in there." I sink it.

"Now you." I open my mouth as wide as I can, but it's hard because I'm laughing.

"Score!" he says as the mint lands on my tongue.

"Scoring is for later, bad boy." We laugh together as Joe takes the freeway on-ramp south.

Chapter 31

I awaken when Joe pulls into a rest stop on Interstate 5. Joe has covered me with his lettermen's jacket.

"Nice to see you, Carmen," he says, kissing my cheek.

"Wow, you must drive fast!"

"No, but you slept a couple of hours. What's your exit? Please say it's coming soon."

"Relative to how far we've traveled, yeah, soon. Keep going south until you see the signs about buying Mexican car insurance."

"Is that before or after the yellow sign that warns people may be running across the freeway. Cracks me up, the kid doesn't even have her feet on the ground."

"Don't be an ogre."

"A what?"

"After the sign. Our exit is one before the border."

"Were you a TJ party girl in high school?"

"Absolutely not." Rude remark, but I let it pass. "Do you want a Coke?" I point to the machine next to the bathrooms.

"I'm coming with you."

"What?"

"Bad stuff happens at rest stops."

"I don't even want to know. You can wait right here. I promise, I'll be fine." Even with this said, I peek under the stall doors to see if anybody's in the bathroom with me. When I exit, Joe takes my hand. Dawn is breaking to the east over the mountains. We join a group of tourists taking pictures of the Pacific. Sea birds ride the swells. Clumps of seaweed wash ashore.

"I used to come down and surf Trestles," says Joe.

"And then?"

"And then I decided I'd rather go north. I almost chose UC Santa Cruz for the surfing. I still might transfer there."

"What?"

"WPC, the frat scene, the Five Stars, the rules. Might be time for a change."

"Would Santa Cruz put you on the diving team?"

"I don't think so. Their mascot is the banana slug. Not exactly a big sports school."

"You could afford it without your sports scholarship?"

"Never thought about that."

And there's the difference between us. I'm counting every penny that comes my way, deciding on the cheapest shampoos and wearing the same jeans half the time. Joe doesn't worry about money. Joe doesn't worry about much. Except that he does worry about me. That's cool. I feel safe with him. Franco, I shake my head to get rid of Franco thoughts. I was out of my mind to have sex with him.

"What, Carmen?"

"Thinking. I'd miss you if you transferred."

"Nah. With your looks, a few hundred guys must be waiting to date you."

"You are so full of it." I punch his arm and run.

He chases me, which is not much of a chase. "I'd tackle you except the grass is wet."

"Considerate man."

"Have I ever been otherwise?"

I put my knuckles under my chin like the famous statue, furrow my brow. "Yes, once or twice. Like the xeroxed butt."

"Oh yeah. That. Silly stuff. Forgive me?"

"Maybe."

"Ah, the coy Ms. Caramel slays her love once again."

I burst out laughing. Joe hugs me. We jump back into his car. He hits the button in the car so that the top comes up.

"Heater too, please," I say.

"It's not cold."

"It is. I'm cold."

"Yes, ma'am. You can be one cold, hard-assed woman."

"Such a romantic."

"Learning to be a realist at the U."

"Survival 101."

"I suppose that's true." He adjusts the heater knob. "You warm enough?"

"Perfect."

He tilts his head, assessing me. "Yep," he kisses me, "Perfect."

He puts the car into gear, and we're on our way south. I gaze out the window at these places I've driven by on so many past trips. I wonder how I missed the expanse of Pacific, ocean meeting sky, the sailboats like birds at sea, the flowers blooming on the center island between the lanes.

As we pass Mission Bay, I sit up straighter. We are twenty minutes from my house. Traffic is still light, even in downtown San Diego. My watch says 7:45 a.m. I haven't had too many all-night adventures in my life except for Prom, and that wasn't even fun, just a rite of passage to which everybody goes, everybody parties, everybody scores.

Past downtown San Diego, the Coronado Bridge sweeps to the west.

"We'll take that coming home, okay?" asks Joe.

"As long as you're driving. I get scared, like I'm going to drive off the edge. I never take the bridge around through Coronado and Imperial Beach."

"That beach has rad waves at the river mouth! I wish I had my board."

"Next time," I say, hoping.

"Exactly. Maybe Thanksgiving, just you and me, at my parents' condo in Coronado?" Joe takes it as a given that we'll be back here together. My heart beats accelerate.

"I'd like that a lot."

"Which off ramp?"

"Dairy Mart Road."

Joe snorts. "Your family owns a dairy?"

I try not to sound defensive. "I told you, my mom is an artisan. The dairy is near us, the pig farms too."

We pass all the exits to Chula Vista. We pass the exit to Imperial Beach.

"There it is," Joe crows, pointing. "Mex-Insure your car!"

"Now we're close. See there's Dairy Mart Road, in two exits. Get off there and turn left, then left at Tequila Way."

"You're shitting me. Tequila Way?"

"I know. Wait until you hear the next one."

"Hoochie Coochie Dancer Drive?"

"You are totally Mr. Stereotype."

"Tequila Way, c'mon. You know that's hilarious."

He stops at the light, Dairy Mart Road and Tequila Way.

"Okay, you go down three streets. Just continue where it says "Isla."

"Isla."

The road swings left. "We're the corner house." I wish the front yard had some grass and flowers. Mama's truck is in the drive way. "Right there, 301 Isla."

"That sign says Isla de something." Joe parks the car at the curb and walks to the corner where the sign is. "Isla de Carmen?"

"Yep. My name is Josephina Carmen Principia. When we moved here, I thought it would help kids get to know me if I went by Carmen."

"Tequila and Caramel, gotta love that combination!"

We pull our overnight bags out of the backseat.

The door opens, Mama runs out in her blue flannel shirt, cut-off jeans dusty with papier mache, and barefooted. "Carmenita! Carmenita! I've missed you." I am swamped by her hug. Joe stands back.

"Missed you too, Mama. Remember Joe?" He steps forward. "The guy who helped us on the freeway?"

She stands on her tiptoes to hug him. "Of course, I would never forget how St. Jude sent someone to help us. Mr. Joe, it is good to see you again. Are you coming with us to Tijuana for shopping?"

Joe gives me a sideways glance.

"No shopping trip. I told you, Mama. We have a piñata project. Where better for us to work on it than here?"

"Good! Come in, are you starving? I have fresh tamales and menudo." She bustles in front of us, "Back bedroom for you, Mr. Joe. Carmen, you put your things in my room."

"Mrs. Gracia, I don't want to be a bother. I can sleep on this couch just fine," says Joe, moving aside three piñatas.

"I think you will sleep better in Carmen's room. She's okay sleeping with her mama."

My mother is not well educated or Miss Manners, but she suddenly seems to know about hormones. Did my red cheeks give it all away? Can she feel the electricity between us?

She has ladled out two bowls of *menudo* and placed a platter of *tamales* on the table. Joe and I sit. He eats like he's been fasting. How can he eat like that after pancakes two hours ago? We do not talk. He is too busy saying, "Mmmm, mmmmm, mmmm," a lot like he sounds when he's having sex. Men and food.

"What's in this soup?"

"Ox tails," I say with a straight face.

"No, Carmen. You know *menudo* is not that soup, no bones in the broth. Tripe, the stomach of the cow," says Mama.

Joe stops chewing, then swallows. "Well, let's hear it for cow's stomach." He ladles out another portion.

Chapter 32

Mama opens and shuts drawers noisily in the kitchen. "Hsst, Carmen. Come in here. I need your help for a minute."

I cut my eyes toward Joe like *big surprise*, but I go in. Sunlight dapples the walls. Pots clutter the stove. Dishes overflow the sink. Same old kitchen, same Mama, except with more worry lines.

"The shopping trip today? I promised Ernesto." Mama unties her apron and hangs it from a nail.

"We have research and writing. It's okay, Mama. There's plenty for lunch."

"It's not okay leaving you two in the house alone all day."

"Oh, Mama. I told you I can't go shopping."

"And I'm telling you that you can't stay here alone with a man."

"You used to trust me."

"Yes, but you are changing."

That's for sure, I think, remembering Friday night. "No worries. Joe is a gentleman. Gayla can come over."

"Gayla is busy. I asked her to come shopping for some fun. You and Joe, come with me."

"And get an *F* on our project? We came all the way here, Mama. Couldn't you go shopping tomorrow?" I throw my arms around her neck. I'm taller than she is. She smells like tortillas and cinnamon, chilis and body odor. "Did you make *churros*?"

"Yes, *churros,* for a party, not for daughters who show up as a heart-attack surprise to their mama." Mama's eyes twinkle, and I know I've won. "You and Joe start your work. I will call Ernesto to go instead of me."

"You really could go." I try not to sound exasperated or otherwise guilty.

Joe leans his head into the kitchen. "Carmen, can we get started? We'll need to leave early tomorrow if we're going to drop in on my folks."

"What?" asks Mama.

"Time for Carmen to meet my mom and dad."

"Oh!" says Mama, raising her eyebrows. "Your mother and your father? Won't that be a surprise?"

"I bring home girls all the time."

Mama wrinkles her brow, and I do too. "All the time? Glad I'm so special"

"That's not what I meant. In high school everybody came over to swim and dance. The house has a recreation room."

Mama's eyebrows swoop up in alarm. "Recreation room? A room for kids to play in? A room for" she stumbles to say it, "privacy? For teenagers?"

"A room to keep my parents from going deaf. They like the oldies. We play metal rock. A room to keep my parents sane. My friends are way loud when the party gets going."

"I cannot imagine such a thing, a recreation room. Leave the dishes. Go start your project, but be careful of the piñatas and the *Dia* sculptures."

"Could we have one piñata?" I ask, hoping that maybe we can skip a few steps.

"No traditional ones, but I broke a silly cartoon. Take the broken dog and see if you can fix it. If you can't, you'll have to start over. I'll be right back." She hurries into her bedroom to call Ernesto. She speaks to him in Spanish, saying "boy" and "alone" and "no, no, no."

Joe and I walk into the living room, which is a mess of white paste and shreds of tissues in the brightest shades of orange, pink, blue, yellow, purple, and red. Joe lifts a piñata.

"Is this the dog one?"

I get the giggles. "Joe, that's a cat."

"How can you tell?"

"Ears, whiskers?"

"I thought maybe its snout broke off." He gently returns it to the drying rack. "Where's our broken dog?"

"Look in the corner where all that stuff is piled up."

He gingerly pokes into newspapers, cracked pots, empty paste jars. "Got it," he says, turning to me with a blob of red tissue stuck to his forehead.

"Yes, you have certainly got it," I say, trying to sound seductive while keeping a straight face. I pull the red tissue from his forehead, form a mustache with it under his nose.

"You're going to get it."

"Promise?"

He closes his eyes and puckers his lips. Mama comes barreling in. We jump apart. "Ernesto says okay. So I'll help you. What do you need?"

Joe fake-stretches his arms above his head. He asks, "May I interview you about piñata making, Mrs. Gracia? I'll take notes while Carmen fixes the dog"

Mama sits on the hip-slung couch. The springs groan. "Ask away." She smiles. "Sit right here," patting the place next to her. "Are you going to make me famous?"

I shoot her a look, which she misses. I get going on the broken dog, mixing paste and trying to form new legs from chicken wire. The dog's tail is okay, his coat is made of brown and white tissue. I plow into the trash pile to find more of those colors.

The murmur of Joe's questions and Mama's fast, high-pitched answers sounds like the television is on a news station. Mama gets up to find some books. Joe turns to me where I am sitting cross-legged fashioning dog paws.

"This dog is going to have to have some black paws. I can't find more of the brown."

"He looks like Scooby Doo. Make some black spots. People won't think twice about his paws being black."

"Are you the Scooby Doo fan club president?"

"Actually, I'm more Davey and Goliath." He says this seriously, as if he is admitting a deep secret. "Here, let me." He takes the body and works the chicken wire opened so that he can make hooks for the legs to hang from. "How's this?"

"Pathetic, but with Mama's expert information, our brilliant writing and technical skills, and Scooby, don't you think Christabel will love our report?"

Mama returns with three books, two in Spanish. "Use this one," she says. "I'll be outside picking tomatoes for salsa. You like salsa, Joe? Are the books okay, Carmen?"

"Yes and yes," I answer for Joe so that she'll go outside and leave us alone for a minute. I need a kiss. I need to hold him.

I open the old children's book. We can get the facts quickly and simply and make the piñata report sound like it was a lot more work than it is.

"Joe, you want the Spanish ones?" I ask.

"What if Christabel challenges our sources?"

"We could tell her my mom translated. We can put Mama's interview in the bibliography as a separate source."

"Awesome."

The clock ticks loudly. I remember days in high school that if I wanted to go to see friends and I was working with Mama, the seconds ticked by so slowly. I would put on music to distract myself.

Now I am not hurrying the clock but holding on to time. I am home. Mama is somewhat happy. Joe is here. I'm not surrounded by screeching girls, and I don't have to worry about Salt sleeping in my bed. Joe will be sleeping in the living room. How to join him? That is the question.

Maybe I should talk it out with Mama, that I'm no longer a virgin, that Joe is my guy. Am I ready to talk about the adult me? Can't she see it? Doesn't she know what's it's like to want someone so badly you feel it burning. That song, "Fire and Ice." I've known both this quarter. I prefer fire.

Joe snaps his fingers under my nose. "Day dreaming?"

"Planning."

"That's frightening. Carmen is making a plan. Does it have to do with me?"

"Sort of."

He kisses me, and I curl into him. The couch is small. We hear Mama outside with her basket talking to the tomatoes, talking to the sunshine, telling the plants she will help them grow their fruit. She scolds a tomato worm, "Not on my tomatoes, *aruga.* Go somewhere else to change into the *mariposa.*"

"What did she find?" asks Joe.

"Tomato worms. They're big, fat, green caterpillars. Who would expect such a thing could become the mariposa, the butterfly?"

Joe tightens his arm around my shoulders. "Look at me, Carmen. I would believe that. Remember the scared skinny girl I met on the freeway?"

"Are you going to tell me I got fat?"

"No, I'm going to tell you that you are more beautiful with the freshman fear scrubbed away. I've watched you become a butterfly, what's the Spanish word, *marzipan*?"

"*Mariposa.*"

"You have wings now, Carmen, *mi mariposo.*"

"*MariposA.*"

"*A*?"

"For female."

"That you are," he says, kissing me again. Mama makes a a noisy entrance, banging the screen door and calling in to us.

"The *arugas* are terrible this year! Carmen, Joe, come see how many I dumped into the cage." She pads from the kitchen into the living room. Joe and I sit up straight.

"You cage caterpillars?"

"I don't want them in my tomatoes. But who would kill a butterfly?"

Joe smiles and takes my hand. "No one I know would kill a butterfly." He stops for a moment. "Well, maybe certain guys at school."

"Ernesto used to stomp them to watch their guts fly out. That's a bad thing Ernesto did when he was little. I'm glad you don't hurt them, Joe. "People," she sits down by us, "are fragile like mariposas. And they need a place to grow. For Carmen here, I thought she was growing up fine in our little town. But it was squeezing her, the way the cocoon squeezes the caterpillar, I guess. She wanted more and she wanted bigger and now, look at her!"

"Mama, you make me feel as if I'm on exhibit."

"No, *mi hija.* You are home."

"The university is like a gigantic exhibit, isn't it?" says Joe. "We're all expected to do this and do that with every step getting graded. We're supposed to grow up and find ourselves as if it's as easy as picking a project from a list."

"Right," I say, "That's exactly right. I'm glad you made this trip to San Ysidro with me to see my home."

"Me too." He hesitates. "My house tomorrow?"

"Fair is fair."

"You are a very brave mariposa, *mi querida.*" Joe kisses my forehead.

Mama dips her chin, glances towards me. A smile tickles the edge of her lips. "Oh, I knew it, Carmen! I'm not too old to know that look. You two, be careful with one another's hearts the way I am careful with the *arguas*. Be careful with your mothers' hearts too, *por favor.*"

Chapter 33

After dinner, Joe and I wash dishes. I scrub. He dries. Mama turns on Telemundo. The agitated, overly dramatic voices tell me she's watching her favorite soap.

Coastal fog rolls in, and the sun disappears. Goosebumps break out on my arms and shoulders.

"Do you need a sweater?"

"Check on the sideboard behind the table. Mama leaves *serapes* there."

"I said sweater not sweeter."

"And I said *serape* not syrup."

Joe leaves and returns with the striped blanket Mama has held on to since San Miguel. I want to tell Joe about San Miguel, the beautiful city I left, the hopes I have to return. He places the *serape* around me, resting his chin against my shoulder, turning his head to kiss my neck, my ears.

"Don't," I say without much force.

"You smell so good, Carmen. You and your *serape* and your kitchen and your house and your mom."

"That's quite a list. We're lucky the dry wind isn't blowing from Dairy Mart Road or the pig farms."

"We are lucky." His arms around me, we rock back and forth to music no one else hears. When the television clicks off, we push apart and busy ourselves with the clatter of putting dishes away.

"What about this iron skillet? This thing weighs a ton." Joe takes a few swings with it as if it's a bat.

"Leave it out on the stove. That's our #1 pan. Tortillas, chicken, you name it, we cook in that."

Mama peeks around the door. "I'm going to bed. Tomorrow starts early for me. Don't stay up too late, Carmen."

"Honestly, do you remember that I am in college? I know when to go to bed."

"Oh, yes, the college girl who knows so much about the world. Find clean linens and blankets for the couch. I put an extra towel in the bathroom."

This is my chance to say that everything would be much easier if I slept with Joe in my bed. But I hold back. It's hard to open up about my sex life, especially to my mother, especially in front of Joe.

"Say your prayers, *mi hija*. You too Joe," she says as an afterthought. She shuffles off to her bedroom. I hear her light a match for the candles on a family altar, to protect her mother, my aunts and uncles, my cousins, the mariposas, me.

"Will she care that I'm not Catholic?"

"Do I care?"

"I don't think so, but parents, you know."

"My mom is a Catholic with a heart that embraces everybody. She wouldn't care if you were Hare Krishna. Well, she might not like the bald and begging part of that."

"Ommm," says Joe. "I embrace the light of the soul."

"Now you sound like Franco. Just be you, Joe. Don't mock anybody's religion. People believe what they believe, and it doesn't hurt anyone else."

"Right. I'm glad you learned that. Was this great awakening before or after *Firstlings?*"

"Both. I don't want to talk about that again. You go shower, and I'll make up your bed."

Joe finds his overnight bag and disappears into the bathroom. He flips both switches, one for the light, one for the exhaust fan. It's so small and old-fashioned. I should have warned him. The next thing I hear after the toilet flushes is Joe singing in the shower. I swear he's singing "Girls Just Wanna Have Fun." I hope Mama can't hear him and get herself wound up about the lyrics.

He opens the bathroom door, whipping his towel to push the steam out towards me. He leaves the light and the fan on. I close my eyes, afraid to look. Did he bring pajamas?

Does he sleep in his briefs? He drops his backpack. He turns off the lamp.

"All yours, Caramel." He climbs onto the bed I've made on the pulled-out couch. He's wearing flannel boxer shorts. "You should have asked me to help you with this."

"Girls just wanna have fun," I sing to him off-key. I kiss him, making sure I am far enough away that he can't pull me into bed with him because I would not have the will power to get out. He smells so good, like some manly soap. "Nighty night, Joe Schmo." I run for the bathroom.

The privacy of our own bathroom fills me with relief. I am sick of waiting in line for showers and sinks and bathroom stalls. From the opened window, gardenias send their scent in. It is so lovely to run the hot water over my body, my shoulders, my arms, my legs, using the soap Joe left behind. The perfume in it is strong, like pine, and I am weak in the knees. I sit down in the tub, shaving long arcs up my legs, carefully under my arms.

I wash and rinse my hair with Mama's hair products. She buys gigantic bottles of shampoo and conditioner. The bottles are too large for my hands, and I drop one with a thump. A knock at the bathroom door.

"Are you okay, Caramel?"

"Yes, dropped the shampoo."

"Okay, good night." The door clicks shut.

I step out of the shower, wind a towel around my wet hair, and find that I haven't brought my pajamas in here. Fine. I wrap a wet towel around me. It is one of our old towels, frayed at the edges and stiff from being dried on the clothesline. It smells like my childhood, and I realize that's because it smells like home. Bleach, gardenias, and spice.

Rushing half-nude down the hall, I pull pajamas out of my overnight bag. They smell like the U, which is my grown-up smell, Obsession perfume, books, ink, musky clothes. I grab Mama's towel, damp as it is, and cover my pillow with it. I am sure I will find a way to embarrass myself with Joe during the night, sneaking into his couch bed or standing over him to watch him sleep for a few minutes. The house is quiet except

Joe is snoring. Light flickers from Mama's room, and I smell the wax of her candles. My head drops back on the pillow. Contentment sinks into my body and bones. I sleep. I dream of mariposa piñatas.

A rooster crows from across the street. I stumble to the bathroom. My hair sticks flat to the side of my head that rested against Mama's damp towel. I duck my head under the bathtub spout and re-wet it so it can be styled.

Mama is frying bacon and tortillas, filling the house with more delicious scents of childhood. I finish styling my hair, give it a squirt of hairspray, tuck my tee-shirt into my jeans, and decide how to greet Joe with Mama around the corner.

When I get to the living room, the couch is folded in and the linens are folded and stacked.

"Where's Joe, Mama?"

"Don't try to fool your mother."

"What are you talking about?"

"I saw how he never used the bed."

"He did. He's just polite. He made the bed."

"And I'm a *palemera*, a popcorn seller. You think you go to college to get smart and come home to a stupid mother? Mothers are not stupid about their daughters."

"Mama, we respect your house. Joe slept on the couch. I slept in my bed. Go look at the pillows if you want. Look at the sheets if you think that's what we did."

I turn away to set the table, slamming plates and silverware for the noise of it. Someone knocks on the front door. I open it ready to spill the latest from Mama onto Joe's shoulder. But it's Gayla, a poochy tummy, pregnant Gayla? I hug her, and we sit on the front steps.

"You didn't tell me, Gayla. Mama didn't tell me either."

"I know. Junior college isn't very exciting, so I quit. I work a lot for me and the, you know, the baby."

"Who's the father?"

"Todd. Remember my date for prom? That Navy guy, I met at the gas station? We broke up just before he shipped out in October."

"Did you tell him?" She shakes her head. "God, Gayla. I'm so sorry."

"It's okay. Your mom has been helping me." A scared look flutters across her face. She breathes deeply and straightens her shoulders.

"What about you?"

"What about me?"

She giggles. "That sexy guy!"

"You saw him?"

"He was jogging. He had one of those fancy Walkman things everybody wants. Is he rich?"

"Sort of, but he doesn't act like it matters. I hope he doesn't get lost."

Joe comes loping up the street, sweating in the cool morning air.

"Ladies! Hello!" He doesn't blink at Gaya's condition. "Introduce us, Carmen."

So I do, and he excuses himself for a shower.

Mama calls out, "Breakfast! You too, Gayla. You must eat for yourself and the little one."

I can't believe she's being so nice when she had been rude to me, her own daughter, five minutes ago.

Joe has taken the world's shortest shower. He appears in his OP corduroy shorts and a polo shirt with the Ralph Lauren insignia.

"I knew he was really rich," Gayla whispers to me.

"Come eat," says Mama. "Everybody is too skinny."

The storm has passed, Joe digs into his food. How does he know that eating everything he's served is the way to my mother's heart? I eat too because now I'm hungry, thinking of all the salty, flat food we eat in the dorms.

Gayla leaves first. She promises to write to tell me about the baby shower Mama is planning, hoping that I can come. I forgot to ask her if she knows if it's a boy or girl? I'll make something yellow, good for either one.

The sound of church bells alerts us that our time is really up. "Mama, we have to get going now. I'll see you soon. I'm sorry I can't stay for *El Dia*."

"Why not? That's terrible."

"I know. The quarter will be over, and I'll be home."

Mama tears up. "You'll come for Thanksgiving? That's sooner than end of term. *Mi hija*, I miss you so much."

"Um, Thanksgiving. I might need to stay at school, depending on projects and papers. I miss you more," I lie. "By the end of Winter break you'll be glad to take me back. I wish you had told me about Gayla."

"It's better to see for yourself. Will you call me after exams to come to get you?"

Joe smiles. "I'll drive her home on Winter Break too. My family comes down here for some holidays, not quite this far south, but Coronado. We have a vacation place there."

Mama frowns. I can see a thought bubble, "vacation place?"

We carry our Scooby Doo to the car, sitting him in the back like a real dog looking out the window. Mama waves from the door. Joe toots the horn and yells, "Adios, Senora Gracia!"

The tires squeal as Joe pulls out too fast. "Damn clutch," he says. "Your mom's going to think I'm a wild man."

"She'll add it to the list. I bet she's already on the phone with my Aunt Ines. I do miss home though." I'm quiet as we reach the corner of Tequila. "Do you miss home, Joe?"

"Nah. I'm too busy to be homesick. You'll see next year. Everything will be different by then."

Chapter 34

Joe rubs his eyes. He pulls over before we get to Oceanside. "Carmen, could you drive? I'm worn out. I kept waking up and hoping you'd come in to see me."

"Sorry. I had planned to. My bed felt so good, and I fell asleep so fast. Of course I'll drive."

We exchange places. Joe reclines the passenger's seat. I slip the *serape* off my shoulders and tuck it in around him. "Mmmm," he says. I need to help him expand his vocabulary of sounds he makes when he's happy.

"I'll wake you up in San Clemente if we're still going to visit your folks."

"Yeah, okay. You decide."

He's zonks, breathing deeply. A smile teases the corners of his mouth the way a dog shivers in his dreams. I jerk the steering wheel hard left when somebody honks at me for lane drifting. Joe doesn't wake. I wish I could attach the car to a track and snuggle up next to Joe.

Traffic eases. Soon, the exits for San Clemente are coming up. We need gas so I stop, and when I cut the engine, Joe sits up straight, arms out front like the walking dead.

"What happened?"

"Gas station? Pit stop? San Clemente?"

"Ah, super. I'm starving. You?"

I shake my head. "No more food." I dash for the bathrooms. Joe starts the pump and makes his way inside to the cashier and the snack shop. When I'm back, I climb into the warm seat, pull the *serape* up.

Joe returns with a hot dog that smells like onions. "Next stop, my house," he says. "If you still want to?"

I don't want to, but I can't let it show. He just spent twenty-four hours with my mom. Fair is fair. "Do I look okay?"

"Carmen, remember? My mom is this beach babe. She probably doesn't know Capezio shoes from Hush Puppies."

"Sounds like I'll love her. What about the whole Mexican deal?"

"What Mexican?" He chomps half the hot dog in one bite, chews, swallows.

"The only one, I believe, that you know intimately enough to introduce to your mother?"

"Caramel, my mother is the original peace-out person on Earth. She only gets radical about big surf and feminism."

"For or against feminisim?"

"Duh."

"So why doesn't she work? Like a career?"

"Why would she if she can surf all day?"

"Religious issues?"

"Earth Mother Gaiea." He stuffs the second half of the hot dog down his gullet.

"Catholics?"

"Follow their own path as instructed by Buddha."

I end the inquisition. Sounds like this should be easy and fun and a good thing for us to meet one another's parents.

Joe takes Pacific Coast Highway. The Miata slides around the bends of a neighborhood in Laguna. The houses here are not concrete blocks with dirt yards. Each one is distinct, not a housing tract in sight.

"Wow!"

"Wow, my driving, or wow, my good looks?"

"Wow, the houses."

"Big deal." He burps. "Sorry. Anyway, some people spend money on houses, some people spend money on cars."

"And some people spend money on both?"

"True." He pulls into the driveway of an ultra-modern house with windows across the top. The house is painted blue, everything is outlined in chrome, and two surfboards lean against the garage door. One is pink floral, the other is jet black.

"Ready?"

I hand him a breath mint. "One kiss for luck."

He exhales into his hand after chewing the mint, kisses me, and sings the rest of the lyric, "'and we're on our way.' I didn't know you liked White Bread music."

"See? That's exactly what not to say around your parents or my mom."

"I-I-I will refrain, will refrain" to the tune of "Stayin' Alive.'" He opens my door and pulls me close. "Re-lax, Caramel."

"Tryin'."

Joe opens the front door to the entry way. The stairs sweep into the living room. Sunlight floods in from floor-to-ceiling windows in the back. A blender growls against something chunky. We enter the kitchen, which is like a spread from a magazine brought into real life. Wide counters, an island, ceramic tiles, huge appliances. Shiny pots hang like a mobile over the stove. And standing with her back to us, chugging from the blender container, a pixie of a woman who must be Joe's mom. Joe sneaks up behind her and yells in her ear, "I'm home!"

She spits some of the green glop into the sink. "Joe, will you ever learn?"

"That's why you sent me to WPC!" he says, "And today I've brought to meet you my friend from the U, Carmen. Carmen, my mom. Mom, Carmen."

"You have no manners, Joe. You couldn't warn us you'd be coming by with a friend?"

"Since when have I done that?"

"Since I started shopping to feed two instead of two plus a hulk." She smiles at me. "Hello." We shake hands again. Her hands are sticky; my palm is sweaty. "Are you named after the opera, you know, Dido and Aeneas with the little gypsy girl?"

"Uh, I think I'm named for the the Ballet Folklorico's version of the opera, *Carmen*."

"Oops! I was an oceanography major. I wish they had had a surfing major! Joe's father and I aren't big theater buffs. Movies, but not symphonies or any of those things my neighbors love. Are you staying?" she asks.

"No, ma'am," I say.

"Oh, please don't call me ma'am. If somebody heard that on the beach, I'd never live it down."

"Yes, Mrs. Sneed, sure."

"How about calling me Tate?"

"Tate?"

"It's her surf name, as in little potato. A tator tot, thus, Tate."

I almost roll my eyes at the overload of cute, but okay. "Hello, Tate."

"Much better. Now, Joe, are you two hungry? I have some seagrass-spinach-pineapple smoothie left." She gets out two fruit juice glasses. I am ready to lose my breakfast, but Joe assures her we've eaten.

"You can never get too many natural vitamins."

"We're set on the vitamin front. Where's Dad anyway? I saw his board?"

"Good question. He's probably over at Shubie's trading surf stories. I'll call Martha." She picks up a receiver on the wall phone in the kitchen. Joe takes my hand and leads me down a ramp and out to the deck overlooking the Pacific. The breeze is strong.

"Where's your *serape*?"

"Car. I didn't think I'd need it." The truth is that I didn't want to appear more Mexican than I am, coming in with the whole serape deal.

"Let's sit in the sun on the far side. Dad built a good wind break over there." We sit down under a striped blue-and-white beach umbrella at a table tiled like the kitchen.

I tilt my chin towards the sun. My mind spins the images of Joe's house in a collage with images of my house; Joe's mom, Tate, with images of Mama; surfboards and a glossy kitchen versus a dirt yard with tomato plants and a tomato-worminator and a kitchen too small for three people with one big pan for cooking anything we need.

Just as I've decided this is a very bad idea, not just visiting but the idea that Joe and I could be a serious couple, his father calls out from the front door, "Hey, Squirt!"

Joe laughs and moves to the door. In a wheelchair, his father slowly maneuvers himself to the deck level and as close as he can get to me. "Hi, please forgive my bad manners. I'm not able to stand."

"Oh." I take his hand, look around for answers. "I'm Carmen."

"So Tate told me. I'm Joe Senior. Most people call me Joe." My Joe comes around to the side by his father.

"When we're both home, he's Joe, and I'm Squirt. And that is something you should not tell my frat brothers."

Tate eases out the door with a tray. Four glasses, a pitcher of what looks like lemonade, and a ceramic tray with veggies lined up. "Alcohol-free lemonade and no adding vodka, my dear Squirt. Hummus with your veggies?" She points to a red dip and a yellow dip.

"Hummus?" I ask, which I realize is stupid because I should act as if I know something instead of letting them see I'm an idiot.

"Oh, sorry. I thought you were Arabic. Squirt here has introduced us to about every known religion and racial type since he was in high school." Tate narrows her eyes at him.

"I'm more used to salsa. We make our own at home, *pico de gallo*!" I can see this is a little too much enthusiasm. I fiddle with the cross around my neck. "Mama is Mexican. I'm Mexican."

"And your father?"

"American, but not in the picture." I feel my heart drop. This is not going well. I would never call Tate the Earth Mother type unless that simply means goddess. Her eye makeup is flawless, she probably weighs ninety pounds, and her arms are tanned. Her muscles are amazing.

"Well, that's the way it is today, isn't it Joe? Half the couples on our block have divorced and remarried."

I don't interrupt to tell her I have never met my father.

"So, tell us about yourself, your family. Do you have a lot of brothers and sisters? What does your mother do?" Tate leans forward on her elbows. Her husband gestures to her, and she turns his chair so that the sun isn't in his eyes.

"Well, there's not so much to tell. I'm an only child. I have tons of cousins though in LA, San Diego, and San Miguel de Allende. Do you know that city in Mexico? It's famous for art. My mom's an artisan."

My Joe, Squirt, adds, "We're doing a report together on piñatas. We've been down visiting Mrs. Gracia, the world-famous piñata-maker. I interviewed her while Carmen finished up our piñata. It's for our Hispanic Studies class."

"Did you bring us some?"

"Some what?"

"Piñatas."

"We have the one, for our report."

"I could eat a hundred of them," says Tate.

"Piñatas?" I ask, confused.

"Those little fried dough sandwiches, right?"

Joe's face turns red. "No, Mom, piñatas, like the game where you hit a decorated container with a stick. I don't know what you're talking about."

"*Empanadas*?" I offer.

Tate hits herself in the forehead. "I'm such a ditz. Yeah, *empanadas*. So anyway, you have a project for what?"

"Hispanic Studies," Joe and I say at the same time.

A look zips between Tate and Mr. Joe. Tate rubs her hand across her lips. She provides a drinking straw for Mr. Joe. The lemonade drips out the side of his mouth. "I see," she says without inflection. "Hispanic Studies, Squirt?"

"Cross-cultural studies. Required at WPC. I love it. I've met a lot of great people like Caramel here and my T.A. Christabel, and this weird philosophy dude, Franco."

"Now there's a useless major," says Mr. Joe. I am afraid he's going to slap me with something derogatory about ethnic studies. "Philosophy. He'll be selling encyclopedias all his life."

"Nah, he's brilliant, pre-med plus philosophy, right Caramel?"

"He is."

"Is this how you got involved in the little fracas Friday night?"

My Joe, Squirt, turns white. "Fracas?" Fake innocence.

"Your coach called to mention you'd be doing some community service. Your frat president called too. Everybody's worried about team eligibility."

"For Christ's sake, Dad, it was nothing. I swear. Nobody was booked. There were no charges. I saw some people taking advantage of other people, and just like you taught me, I stepped in on the side of reason." My Joe is sweating. He lifts his polo shirt to wipe his face and hair. I admire his beautiful body. Who knows, this could be the last I see of it.

"We're proud of you, son," says Mr. Joe. "Exactly what I would have done, back in the day before this." He raps his knuckle against the wheelchair. "Did he tell you this part, Carmen?"

I shake my head.

"Don't surf a south swell in a winter storm."

Tate is still thinking about *Firstlings*. She gives us a tight smile. "I agree you should help others, no matter who they may be. I do, however," she pauses, "draw the line at getting carted off in a paddy wagon like a common criminal."

"I guess they told you the whole story?" My Joe's voice sounds constricted.

"A sorority sister gave me a call." She smiles again, the sunny Californian housewife. "Tell me, Carmen, which sorority did you pledge?"

I wish I were faster with the repartee. "*La Raza*," I answer truthfully.

Tate frowns. "Oh, it must be new. Lots of changes are coming to Greek life, I hear."

Joe pulls his shirt up again and wipes more sweat. "Thanks for the lemonade. Carmen and I need to push on, lots of studies and a report to finish. Wait, before we go, do you have Halloween candy to spare? We need some for the piñata."

Tate goes into the kitchen, stands on a stool, and takes half-a dozen candy bags out of the cupboard. "I bought your favorites, Joe, so don't you eat all the Reese's."

"Who me? Never!" It must be a family joke because they all laugh. Tate shakes my hand, "Glad to have met you,

Carne." She hugs her son. "We love you, Squirt." As we get into the car she calls out, "Next time, bring the piñata-maker too, or at least a piñata for us!"

Joe pulls out with the tires shrieking. "Sorry they gave you the third degree beyond acceptable limits. I think you passed."

I lean the passenger chair back, cover myself with my *serape*, and ask, "Why would I not? Poor girl, rich boy; Mexican girl, White Bread boy; what more could a parent ask for? A mom who thinks my name is Meat."

"Exactly." Joe pats my cold hand and holds it until he has to downshift again.

Chapter 35

Pre-Final Blues have descended. Franco wants new goals and more meetings, but no one attends except me and Christabel and Anaissa. He rants about fear of *the Man* and our payback service hours after the demonstration.

Joe gave me the notes from his interview with Mama. I'm preparing note cards that we can split in half between us as speakers. I have Scooby Doo perched on my desk where he draws a lot of attention from Salt, Shirley, and Norine, especially since he's filled with candy. I left two bags of mini-Snickers out just for them. Now they want to have a piñata party for Cinco de Mayo. I tell them fine, I can deal with May requests.

What I can't deal with right now are more requests for anything from me, well, except if Joe would like to see me more often, a thought beyond beautiful. But it seems like every class has upped the requirements we started out with. I work. I go to the library. I go to class. I type. I wait for Joe to call. I sleep.

Shirley is worn out from all the activities after *Firstlings,* including Greek Week athletics. She sleeps twelve hours every day. I have to sneak around the room and type in the lounge so that I don't disturb her. From the amount of dope she smokes, I know she's hurting. She hasn't said a word about *La Raza* and *Firstlings*. Either she didn't connect me to it or she's too high to remember.

We did talk about Salt sleeping in my bed. She promised it won't happen again. Her main thing is that she had a lot of pain and wanted him to stay and hold her hand, sing a song, strum the guitar. She's sorry he fell asleep. Shirley says she doesn't think he smells funky.

So now we're back to class, pushing towards finals. I call Joe to see if he wants to practice the report one time.

"No, can't," he says. "Practice, classes, the frat. Busy."

"We don't want to mess this up, Joe."

"As in the report?"

"Yeah, and as in us, you and me."

"You worry too much, Caramel."

"I know. That's the way I am."

"What good does it do to worry? It's like throwing mud all over your pretty face."

"Huh?"

"Something like that. I mean don't ruin today by thinking of bad stuff that could happen tomorrow."

"I still want to practice the report one time. Ten minutes, Joe, maybe fifteen?"

"When are we scheduled in class?"

"Tomorrow."

Silence. I hear him shuffling around in his backpack. Paper crinkles. He picks the phone back up. "Maybe. I can meet you before anthro, or we could cut. At Berkebile?"

I think about seeing Franco when I don't want to see Franco. "Not too early. I work. Al's?"

"Opens at 11. Berkebile stairs?"

"Too noisy. Library."

"I'd never find you."

"Guido can maybe help me get off early. I'll wait in the main reading room. You wait there if you're there first. We can go down in the stacks to practice."

"That's what I'm talking about! Practice what again?"

"You are so bad. The report that will keep me from failing this class. We are not practicing kissing, fondling, or any other nifty tricks to enhance my knowledge of *el sexo*!"

"Okay. Library. Try to get there half an hour before class."

"I will."

"Bring the stuff. Bring Scooby."

"Crap, Joe. I have to walk to campus with our report typed out, our note cards written out and color coded, *and* carry Scooby?"

"You are a woman of many talents, Caramel. There's my ride. Catch you tomorrow."

"I'll be the one with the big brown paper dog."

"Whew, right. Like I'd forget Scooby's sweet face." The phone disconnects.

And even though I'm annoyed, I'm smiling.

Joe meets me at the library as scheduled. We make a few changes to our report. I practice some of the Spanish words with him. We're ready.

In our Bramble classroom, Scooby sits between us like our pup, like our baby. I am putting way too much emotion into this piñata.

Christabel arrives. She asks if we want a projector (we should have thought of that), a record player or tape deck (we should have thought of that), or any other devices to enhance the class's participation.

"No," I say. "We're going to teach them the history of the piñata and then play the piñata game and sing the piñata song." Christabel unlocks the door and goes in to clear her desk.

Joe wrinkles his forehead. "There's no note card for the piñata song."

"I'll write it on the board."

"We have to swing Scooby from something."

I dig into my backpack and produce a skein of heavy-duty yarn. "This should work. You string it up now, and I'll get the song on the chalk board."

"Write big."

All of a sudden, I'm nervous. I break into a cold sweat. This all seemed so easy with Mama there to tell us the stories and now it's just me with Joe. But he heard all of Mama's answers. He should be okay. He's standing on a desk, looping the yarn into Scooby's head ring. He tosses the skein across the light fixture three times so that Scooby should hold. Joe pulls, and Scooby bobs. In the corner, there's a window opener for the high bank of side windows.

"That okay to bash with? I brought a ruler, but it's so short."

Christabel purses her lips, and she grimaces. "The window opener looks dangerous. Somebody could break the lights or hit another student. What else could you use?"

"An umbrella? A yardstick? A broom?"

"In my office."

"Could you please get us the broom?"

The bell rings. We have ten minutes until show time. Joe and I move the desks into a semi-circle so that there's room for Scooby and the piñata game and still the class won't have a problem reading the board when we sing. I have to sing. The cold sweat is back. Before I heave, Christabel returns to hand me the broom. She stands by the door, welcoming our victims. Joe is experimenting with the raising and lowering of Scooby. He wraps the yarn at an angle and ties it to Christabel's desk leg.

Our classmates are mocking our Scooby in a friendly way. Before she claps her hands for quiet, Christabel whispers to me that Franco was at her office to leave a note, so she invited him for our presentation. That's what I need today, more pressure. I am sure Christabel is well aware that she's made this harder. She's smiling at me like a spider with a fly.

Joe puts one finger over his lips. The room falls silent.

Christabel sweeps her right arm out, "Take it away!"

First, I hand our typewritten report to Christabel. She flips through it, making sure we have a bibliography. No bibliography, no credit. She smiles and says, "Proceed."

Joe starts with the history card. He tells the class, speaking in a normal tone of voice like he's used to being in the spotlight. He explains that the piñata is a religious relic. It carries a history over 400 years old. Then he asks, "What country did the piñata come from?"

Hands go up.

"Spain."

"Mexico."

"Argentina."

"Brazil."

After each wrong answer, Joe makes a buzzer sound. We should have brought a buzzer.

"One more guess?"

"Italy, but then to Spain and Mexico," says Maria.

"A treat for the brainy lady," says Joe, throwing her a Hershey's kiss. This is totally unrehearsed and wildly accepted.

"Now listen carefully to the next part."

I step in to talk about how to make a piñata, the change from open-mouthed clay pots to papier-mache, the way this revolutionized the shapes and figures of the piñata into the colorful cartoon characters seen today.

"My question to you is about the fiesta of the piñata. Are you ready? When are piñatas used today?"

"Birthdays!"

"Weddings!"

"Christmas!"

"*Cinco de Mayo*!"

Students are frantically waving their hands to answer as if a single Hershey's kiss is going to make their day.

"You're all correct. The piñata custom is part of almost any celebration in a Hispanic household. Pass out the treats, Joe." He empties the bag of Hershey's onto the desk, we grab as many as we can carry and walk around distributing the goodies.

"Now here's the fun part." I point to the words of the song on the board and sing-talk them. "C'mon, everybody sing with me."

The class joins in. We sing, and it's as if the desks move closer together, as if we are holding hands, singing this silly song as one.

"Time to play the piñata game," Joe says. "Who will be our first volunteer?"

No hands.

"Wouldn't it do your heart good to bash something and break it?" Joe tugs Sister Rosalie to the middle of the circle. I tie a handkerchief around her eyes. Joe spins her three times, hands her the broom. I grab the skein of yarn and run past, lowering Scooby to give him a big push. Then it's up and down and around and around. The class is hysterical, singing off-tune, ducking for no reason, as Sister Rosalie flails away.

She gives her turn up to Christabel. This is the best part. I love it that Christabel is willing to be seen acting silly. She gives Scooby a big whack and his treats fall to the floor. Our classmates scramble to recover the goodies inside, hard candy, See's suckers, Reese's, Snickers, and more Hershey's kisses.

Christabel pulls the blindfold up, which makes her look like a pirate. "Back to your seats. We have time to sing the song one more time."

Before that can happen the door opens. Franco stands silhouetted by sunlight.

"Teaching the dignity of Mexican culture?" He makes a disparaging noise, "Chuh. Right."

I turn to him. "Franco, life has laughter. Who laughs more than Mexicans?"

"Laugh all you want. See how far that takes you."

What a storm cloud on our fun. I erase the chalkboard and pick up the remnants of Scooby.

Joe waves at Franco's retreating back, turns his hat backwards, and raps:

Adios, Franco, amigo.
I'm not goin' where you go.
I'm not showin' no disrespect,
I'm just saying, let me interject,
Lessons don't gotta be so perfect,
Me and Carmen, it's our project,
So disappear, you're incorrect,
It's not about intellect,
Circumspect, dialect, retrospect.
It's your big frown that we REJECT.

Christabel claps, our classmates cheer, and Sister Rosalie covers her mouth as she laughs. Joe kisses me in front of everybody. I hug him.

"Nice finish."

"I'm getting there, huh?"

"You're there." I kiss him again.

Chapter 36

We should celebrate our successful piñata presentation with pizza out, but Joe says he has the Christmas frat formal to coordinate. He's in charge of the venue.

"My house president says it has to be somewhere new. But all the new places are totally thumbs down on the Frat party scene. Old guys tell us *Animal House* totally killed our image."

"The truth hurts." I punch him. "Who's your date? Do I know her?"

"You really want to know?"

"Yeah, then I can stalk her and break her ankle."

"Carmen, you know by now you can trust me."

"So it's okay if I go out with Franco?"

Joe stops walking. He turns my shoulders towards him and nudges my chin up with his hand. The walkway is crowded with students, and they flow around us like we're a rock in a river. "No, it's not okay if you go out with Franco. I know him. I know his history with the ladies."

"And I know yours." I poke him in the chest.

"That was pre-you." And I think about the night when it was Franco and then Joe, and that time with Joe was absolutely it. Franco was also a "pre-you," and Joe doesn't know. He stands firmer. "No Franco. I don't want you to obsess about this. I'm in a frat. I do activities with my frat, have fun with my brothers. The girls are just girls. Not one of them is you."

"But you can't take me to their events?"

"Not yet. Maybe next year."

"What?"

"When I'm an upperclassman, I'll have more say in what I do or don't do. Who knows, maybe I'll quit, join *La Raza*."

"Maybe I'll pledge Shirley's sorority next fall."

Joe thinks a long moment. "Carmen, the sororities work a different game."

"Meaning?"

"They pay attention to stuff like where your father works, what's your family background, are you a Daughter of the American Revolution. Heredity counts big-time."

"So I fail on all counts. But Tri Chi took Maria."

"Maria's father owns an oil company. You could try the new chapters, the special sororities."

"Like Special Olympics?"

"I didn't say that! I don't want anyone breaking your heart."

"That's sweet. Just like Mama said."

"True." He kisses me. We walk to the Student Union where he turns towards the Al's. "We could get pizza here."

"Al's does not count as *out* out. I mean somewhere not here, not campus."

"We'll have pizza every night at Thanksgiving, our condo weekend."

"I like Indian curry and Mexican food too."

"Now, you're getting expensive."

"Me? As if! I'll cook for you. Tamales! How long until we go?"

"Three weeks." He gives me a hug. "Call me. I like talking about Thanksgiving together." He smiles his Joe smile. The skin around his eyes crinkles.

"Bye." I walk away about two steps. "Joe?"

He turns back towards me.

"Your date for the formal? Could you take Shirley?"

"First rule of University dating: Do not date roommates."

"Even if I asked you to?"

"I'll think about it."

"'Cause for *Firstlings*, she had a date problem. Her sisters finally found somebody who was okay with," I stop, "her leg and everything."

"My date that night ended up with a date problem too. Since I was in lock up with you all."

"The sacrifices you make for me, Joe."

"Worth it. Now go, 'cause I'm late." He disappears into the Stu U.

Back at the dorm, Shirley is trying on a new dress. It's a black sheath, wide at the shoulders, tight, and short in the hips, so short that her prosthetic leg is exposed. She yanks at the hem.

"What do you think, Carmen?"

"Longer would be better."

"But all the sisters are going short and sexy with the hemlines."

"What about diagonal? Maybe long on the one side?"

"That's so obvious."

"It is."

"But you think this thing is gross?" She sits, pulls off the leg, and throws it against the door.

"You know I'm okay with your leg. I'm not a boy. I'm your roommate. I'm not Salt, who has known you from the start. Your party is sort of a blind date, right?" She nods. "So you want to have him reject you without even getting to know you? You have to cover the leg, Shirley."

"Nobody's that stupid."

"Shirley, are you telling me not one person has turned away from you since you arrived? Not one of your sorority sisters says mean stuff about your leg? Do you know how many people have changed their seats in my classes so they won't have to sit by the Mexican?"

"You're making a big deal out of nothing, Carmen."

"So don't ask for my opinion. Shirl, you are totally neurotic. Sometimes you make me crazy." I slam out of the room with my psych book, take the elevator down, and set up a study corner in the very back of the dorm library. I look up *displacement* in the back of the psych book. Bingo! Shirley is displacing her anger about her leg. She normally acts as if it's not a part of the equation, but when I talk to her in real world terms about her leg, she gets mad at me. I try to think of things in my life that would compare since nobody has cut off one of my legs. Big deal if I'm brown as caramel. Mama has been accepting of Joe so far. Joe has been accepting of crazy me. He doesn't get mad at me unless I get clingy. How can I not get clingy? He doesn't want me to date Franco. Did I date Franco as displacement? I settle in to read the assigned chapters, using my highlighter for notes, marking my lectures with the page numbers that correspond in the text. The library door opens. I hunker lower in my cubicle. A shrill voice starts a conversation with someone who's either listening or can't get a word in. The shrill voice is Norine's.

"Oh, my God. Did you see that dress on Shirley. Eew! That plastic leg! And the end where the doctor cut it off, now it's sort of calloused, and she's gained weight and there's this ridge of blubber that hangs over the peg leg." She snorts. "Seriously, I about peed my pants. Who's going to tell her that dress will not do? I was like,'Wow, Shirley, that dress is awesome,' and the whole time I'm about to puke looking at THE LEG. Wouldn't she have a clue by now that nobody wants to see her grody leg? Cover the damn thing. Wear a pants suit, wear a longer dress. Do not sit anywhere that some unsuspecting person might actually touch that, eeeewww, that cold, hard rubber thing. Speaking of hard and rubbers." She trails off.

A low murmur replies. I can't hear a word. I lean as quietly to the right as I can to see if I can glimpse the other person. All I can see are black boots. Salt.

Norine sits on the couch. "C'mere, my Salty one. Let me have a little cow-lick of your delicious neck."

I hear the springs of the crummy couch. I hear moans and groans and "Oh honey" and "Oh baby" and shoes/boots coming off and hitting the floor, and zip, there goes Norine's dress, and zip, there go Salt's pants. I can stand up, walk out, and pretend I don't even see them. Or I can toss their clothes at them, catch them as Sydney Sheldon would say *in flagrante delicto,* and let them deal with whether I heard Shirley's best friends talking about her behind her back. Yes, that's it. At least if I have something to say, I say it to her face.

"Nice ass," I say to Salt. His back is peppered with pimples. "Maybe people in glass houses shouldn't throw stones."

They both turn their heads towards me. Salt pulls his pants up and drags his hand along the floor, trying to find Norine's dress.

"If you're going to talk about my roommate and your friend, maybe you should be nicer about it. It's not like Shirley asked for cancer. You two make me sick."

I walk out, go up to the room, and tell Shirley I'm sorry about critiquing her dress.

"At least you're honest with me, Carmen," she says, hugging me. We sit down on her bed with a copy of *Seventeen.* We scan the ads for dresses we like. "See how this one goes diagonally, is that what you meant?"

"Yeah. We could add a piece in on the bias. That would be so cute. And we don't have to worry about matching the fabric. See how they're using bright colors? Call your grandmother and ask her if she has time to help you with this."

"They're on a cruise."

"I could do it. Who has a sewing machine? Probably nobody."

"Sister Rosalie!" Shirley pumps her fist, which gives me a rush, not a sorority rush that leaves people out but a heart rush that pulls people in. I'm glad I got back to being gentle with Shirley's heart.

Chapter 37

Shirley's massaging her stump with a new pungent liniment, something with eucalyptus oil. She's doing that a lot recently. I pull her quilt around her shoulders. I wish I could help her more. I can take my psych book to the laundry room, study there, try to catch up after a three-day cold, plus be a good roommate. I hope she doesn't catch my cold.

"Shirl, any laundry?"

"No. You could throw my leg in though."

"You're kidding."

"Yes, Carmen, I'm kidding. Go away. Let me sleep."

When the first load is in the dryer, I shake out a white shirt of Shirley's. It should be ironed, and I like to iron, so I set up the ironing board. Anyone can see that I'm in my displacement mood, substituting one task for another. I am sick of psych. There's probably a good word for that, like psychophobia. Shirley's white shirt is easy to iron, except around the buttons. The smell of the spray-on starch and the hot iron remind me of home and Mama. I think about the trip Joe and I are taking over Thanksgiving. Mama will spend the holiday in the kitchen with her sisters arguing about the men and the kids and the recipes. The men watch football, drink beer, and talk about the women in the commercials, yipping like coyotes when one is sexy.

I'll miss it, but being with Joe in a room with a view and walks on the beach and talks in the sunset, well, who wouldn't take option B? I told Mama it was a once-in-a-lifetime trip to be invited skiing with Norine. I should feel guilty about lying, but I don't, not even after lying about *El Dia*, which is a pretty bad thing to lie about.

I open the dryer to see if there's anything else to iron. This load is all jeans. From one pair, a washed-out piece of paper and some dollar bills have fallen out of the pocket. I hold up the jeans. They're Shirley's. I put her money back into her pocket and sneak a glance at the paper. It's an appointment form of some kind.

The heading is bold type: Dr. Wellman. That's a better name than Dr. Pain, I guess. Dr. Wellman, oncologist. A cancer doctor. Shirley must have check-ups scheduled. I try to make out the rest of the writing, but it's blurred. *SCAN* I can read. What would they need to scan after cutting her leg off? Hey, Dr. Wellman, go scan someone else's body parts and leave Shirley alone. She's fine, except she sleeps a lot, like now when I return.

I put the laundry basket on my bed with her jeans on top. On her desk, I put the washed-out appointment reminder with a note from me, "What's up with this?"

Even if I'm not going to study, I decide to chill in the library. I'll find my place in the stacks and learn some more about Diego Rivera. I stop by the Stu U to pick up next quarter's schedule. Once I'm settled in my favorite place with the Rivera book, I wonder what classes I should take next. I pat my pockets, find change for the pay phone and call the Frat house. No one answers. The dime rattles down the return shoot.

It's dusty in the stacks, which makes my nose run. My cough barks out and echoes. I take Diego with me to the upstairs reading room, hoping I'll find someone to talk to. I take notes about Diego Rivera for no reason, for no test, just because I want to know. Wouldn't that be the best way to learn? You tell your advisor what you're interested in and then you read books and talk to people who know that stuff and you don't waste your time on all kinds of things you don't care about. I laugh at RINK and wonder if I should take ice skating. I can't remember if those PE classes are required or not.

My head begins to pound like migraine time, but it's not even close to when that should happen in terms of pre-menstrual hormones. I take an aspirin with a cup of water from the corner faucet. Over the drinking fountain, the bulletin board carries the usual sales announcements, roommate requests, drive partner queries, club meeting posters, silly graffiti A blue paper with a Women's Free Clinic logo invites young women in to talk about birth control. I think of Gayla's pregnancy and realize that for a smart girl I am extremely stupid about my own body. I'm going to spend four days with Joe, so probably a lot of sex in one weekend, 'cause he's so hot and I love his body even if he won't say he loves me yet, which I know he does, but I hope he'll say it soon so I can say it back and kiss him and make love like all day and all night and that brings me back to the clinic. They're around the corner from Student Health. I decide to save my academic life, my body, and my mental health by getting birth control pills.

I walk out and inhale the cool fall air. I crunch leaves on the downward path between the library and Berkebile. I stop for a coffee. The coffee is perfect for my aching throat. I should gargle with it. My tonsils luxuriate in the hot liquid, which I understand sounds ridiculous, but Mama always had me drink hot lemonade when I was sick and the hot coffee feels like that. When it hits my stomach though, the coffee makes my gut rumble. I keep what's left in case it goes down better when it's cooler.

My focus on the marvels of coffee continues as I stroll to the Medical Center. The upper offices hold the clinics for specialty diseases and conditions. There are several floors for cancer patients. I remember Shirley's note. Maybe she'll want me to go with her? Probably not. She handles stuff like her leg like I handle the grease drain at work. Got something yucky? Deal with it.

So I walk into the Women's Free Clinic office. It's a Sunday, it's early, and it's just me. The receptionist asks me to fill out a long survey about my health, my sex life (does one night with two guys count as a sex life?), my vital statistics and my family history. I have few answers under father, which is uncomfortable, but this lady with her helmet-hair has probably seen it all. She's about seventy.

The last page of the five-page history asks, "Why are you here?" There are some choices like amenorrhea (what?), hemorrhoids (dear God), and bleeding. How about I am here because I don't want to get pregnant like my friend at home, but I do want to have sex and why shouldn't I?

I write in "need birth control pills." Duh.

A nurse in her white cap and white belted uniform and white granny shoes opens the clinic's door and calls, "Carmen?" She scans the entire waiting room as if somebody might be hiding behind a chair.

"I'm right here," I say, getting up with my backpack and the Rivera book.

"Come in, dear," she says like I'm a toddler that she has to treat gently. "Step up on the scale, please."

I don't even look at the final damage as she flicks those weight things around. It does no good, "121" she announces to the world. She writes it in her chart. I was 112 when I left for college. No more pizza, no more cheese, no more cookies. Before I get too far with my resolutions, she leads me into a cubicle with a curtain.

"Undress completely. Put on this gown with the opening to the front. Cover yourself with the extra sheet. Doctor will be in soon."

What have I gotten myself into? Knowing I've gained nine pounds, I don't feel like showing my blobby body to a doctor. But of course I manage to get undressed and seated on the exam table with another paper sheet covering my lap. My heart starts pounding, and I am about to just get dressed and boogie out of here, when the door opens. A young doctor walks in. He has golden, curly hair, tanned skin, and I think I'm going to die if this guy does the pelvic.

"Ms. Principia, hello. I'm Dr. Fritz," he says, shaking my shaking hand. "Don't be nervous." He pushes the intercom button, "Assistance, please." The nurse comes in to hold my hand. "This will be over in a few minutes. Place your feet in these stirrups."

"Sure." My face turns hot.

He sits on a little wheely stool, adjusts a lamp so that it will shine on my internal cavities, shall we say. "Lay back," he instructs, and I think great, I get a doctor who can't conjugate lie/lay. "Relax now."

I hold my breath.

"You can't hold your breath and relax, Ms. Principia. You're okay." He wheels up to where he can speak to me face-to-face. He holds up something that looks like a knife. "This is a speculum to gather cervical cells. Once that's finished, I will palpate your uterus to measure it. Everything will be done quickly, no pain, and, assuming no abnormalities, you'll be on your way with a prescription in your hand."

"Thank you, Doctor." I try to relax. I count the foods I will no longer consume while he conducts the exam. And it's bull that it won't hurt because it does hurt, that cold metal thing pinching me. I breathe deeply and try not to flinch.

He turns to put the cells on a laboratory slide. From below my feet, he says, "A quick measurement, which won't be so uncomfortable."

I start to rise on my elbows. "Hold on," he says. He backs up his little stool. He adjusts my feet to stretch out higher and wider. The doctor puts himself at a better angle to study whatever it is he needs to see down there.

"Ms. Principia, when was your last period?"

"Last month? Maybe seven weeks. I'm not very regular."

"We'll be conducting some blood work and have you leave a urine sample. I don't think birth control pills are a good idea for you."

"Why not? That's why I'm here."

"Too late."

"I told you, I'm not regular, I'm often late."

"Too late for pills. You, Ms. Principia, present the bluish color on your cervix that indicates you are pregnant."

"No, I'm not."

He raises his eyebrows and shrugs his shoulders. "I'm the expert here. You came to me for help. You're not a virgin. What birth control were you using before coming to us?"

I'm silent. I'm stunned. I'm ashamed. I am pregnant.

"So, as I said, we'll do some labs and schedule pre-natal care. We can also provide the literature on abortion. Get dressed. The nurse will escort you to my office where we can talk." He leaves with the nurse.

Talk? I don't want to talk. How can I explain that I don't even know if it's Franco or it's Joe? I put on my clothes and consider a mad dash home to Mama.

The nurse knocks on the door. "Ready? I'll take you to the lab and then you can step into Dr. Fritz's office, Carmen." It's a good thing she's leading me because I can't see anything but my feet as I walk, my head is hangs down so low.

Chapter 38

My ears feel stuffed with cotton. I've made it through the lab. Now the doctor is talking. I hear nothing. I feel dizzy and disoriented. What to do? Where to go?

Dr. Fritz asks, "Any questions?" He hands me a folder stuffed with brochures.

I blink my eyes. "No." I can't verbalize the thousands of questions bombarding my brain.

"Think about your options. Think about your future. Come back to see us soon if you choose to terminate and in a month if you choose to proceed with the pregnancy." He stands and opens his door, ushers me out to the lobby. "Ms. Principia, everything will be all right no matter what you decide. Talk to your boyfriend. Talk to your family."

"Thank you, yeah, I'll talk it over with my mom."

"Don't forget the father. The father has rights. Bring him next time."

"I will." I make it to the bus stop bench before I break down crying. There's a bus heading my way, and when it stops, I get on, pay too much because I don't have exact change. I wonder where the bus is going. I could ask the driver, but I don't. At the next stop three old ladies slowly get in, show their passes, sit down. They cluck and coo like pigeons. I move back a few seats to get out of their noise. I bury my nose in the Diego Rivera book.

Two hours ago, I thought I could go to Mexico. I'd see the works of Diego Rivera. I'd get a Ph.D. in art. I'd join the Hispanic Studies Department at a big university. I'd buy a family home in San Miguel where we would vacation in the brilliant sunshine.

Now, I don't know what to do. I'm stuck, like Gayla. I'll be back in my bedroom. I'll be making piñatas. Dirt yards and tomato worms and baby diapers are my future. Dr. Fritz says I have choices. Dr. Fritz says bring the father, not even considering that a girl like me might not know who's the daddy.

The bus swings around in a bus zone and comes to a stop. "End of the line," the bus driver says, eyeing me in the mirror. The old ladies have gotten off without my noticing. I go out through the middle doors, to avoid interaction with the bus driver. It's cold here, like on Joe's patio, and foggy. Across the street, runners disappear down stairs, but other runners come up the stairs, a conveyer belt of runners. I cross the street and lean against the railing. We've reached the end of the line because we've reached the beach. All this time at WPC, and I haven't gone to the beach. I pull my sweatshirt on. My hair blows back, and I throw it into a scrunchy to keep it off my face.

I join the line of runners going down towards the shore.

"Move it," says a mom with a baby in a front sling-pack. She's tanned and toned. The baby is quiet.

"Go ahead." I move aside like a robot, CP30.

The lady jogs forward. I finish the stairs and see the bike path, the roller skaters in bathing suits. Why are they not freezing? I am so cold I can't stand it. If I jog the stairs a few times, maybe I'll warm up. If I'm not very pregnant, maybe the running will bring my period, and I won't have to think about being pregnant, my ruined life, sitting around with Gayla in San Ysidro until I'm old and gray.

I cram the shiny folder full of brochures, numbers to call, and papers into my backpack noticing the headings: To Terminate; Your First Trimester; Seeing Your Doctor; Nutrition.

Whatever. I run up the stairs. I run down the stairs. I take off my sweatshirt and throw it on my backpack. I do five more sets of stairs until I can hardly breathe. I sit down on my sweatshirt.

The fog has lifted. The sun dries my sweat. I put my backpack under my head. I hear the waves, the sea gulls, the roller skates.

Sleep overcomes me so that when I wake up, the fitness parade is over. I should get back to campus, make some phone calls. I pull the doctor's handbook out and glance through the stuff he wants me to know. Is there a paper here for morons? Or one for hot shot academics who think they're so smart and end up like any other pregnant girl just out of high school? Is there one about finding out paternity? Actually, there is one like that. I read it over.

I could wait to tell people. I'll buy some bigger clothes at Goodwill. Mama doesn't have to know yet. Joe and Franco don't have to know yet. Maybe I'll go to Coronado with Joe over Thanksgiving, act like everything's fine, see where that takes me? We can still have fun there. There's plenty of time for explaining everything to everybody, and maybe I'll be lucky, and this baby could go away and this is just a scare.

Which is a mean thought, a selfish thought, and I get up, take the stairs, walk into the church across the street. A homeless guy has his shopping basket in the aisle next to where he's praying on his knees. I nudge it, the wheels squeak, and he turns towards me. Seeing that I am not stealing from him, he smiles. He reminds me of Jesus except for the gray hair and the missing front teeth and the dirt encrusted into his neck. His smell isn't very godly either. I hurry to the sacristy. I sit on the bench and knock on the little window, which slides open.

"Welcome, Child of the Church," says the disembodied tenor of a man. The curtain silhouettes his profile.

"Thank you, Father. I have not confessed for a month. I have been rude to my mother. I have been jealous of my roommate."

"Impatience is a habit to conquer."

"Yes, father."

"Is there more you wish to confess?"

There is so much more, but if I say it, the baby will be real, not just some lump of cells Dr. Fritz told me are there, growing with every minute that passes.

"I must confess to you that I have had sexual thoughts about someone not my spouse, and I have had sexual relations with someone not my spouse." I hesitate.

"Yes?"

"I'm pregnant."

"I see. How old are you?"

I want to tell him fourteen so that I can pretend I didn't know much and someone took advantage of me. But I can't lie to the priest. "I'm eighteen. I don't know what to do."

"Remember that God loves you. God loves the child you carry. Do everything in your power to love your child. Do everything in your power to keep the Father in your life. Carnal sins require much penitence. Will you pray with me?"

"Yes, Father."

We say the Lord's Prayer together. He adds a benediction to me for my courage and to the baby for its strength. He gives me my penance and tells me to go with God.

"Please come back to us for support and fellowship," he whispers. "Find the bulletin board in the foyer. We host a support group for unwed mothers."

I walk out feeling lighter, more hopeful, hand the homeless guy a dollar. "Keep the Father in my life." I know he meant God, but I think of the baby. I grew up without a father. Shouldn't my baby have a father, a real one? Joe or Franco? Does either one want to be a father? Not yet, neither one. Right now, it's me and God and this little peanut who will grow to be my baby. God will see me through unless I choose to terminate, which I won't. I've already given the baby a nickname, Peanut.

I wait for the bus back to campus. When I get on, I smile at the driver and over-pay my fare and sit in a window seat, watching the mobs of people living their city lives, people in cars zooming, people shopping, people talking. Not one knows what I know about me, that I am going to face Truth, place my life in the hands of God, Jesus, the Holy Spirit, the Virgin Mary. I wonder if my mom will buy the story of a second Virgin birth? The idea is ridiculous. I laugh out loud. The driver checks the mirror at the next stoplight to be sure I'm not some wacko on drugs. I wave at him and pull the Diego Rivera out of my backpack. *Mother and Child* makes the child so big, he burdens the mother although her face is serene. *Motherhood* is a peaceful, loving picture. The baby is new. The mother is young, calm, sleeping with her baby in her arms. This is the one I will turn to. This one makes me believe Our Father watches over mothers and children.

I turn the page. The next page shows a piñata-party with dancing children in orange. A little boy in blue has broken the piñata, and all the children rush in for the treats. I lean in closer to the book. Does that little boy look like Franco or like Joe? He certainly looks a lot like me.

Chapter 39

I wait a week to build my nerve and call Mama. The phone rings and rings and rings. I slam the stupid receiver down and curse that she doesn't have an answering machine like a normal person. That's stupid too because who wants a message that says, "Hi Mom, guess what? I'm pregnant, and I don't know who the father is. Aren't you thrilled?" She'd go into hysterics. She's going to anyway, but I should be there with her.

I kick my chair. I throw my pillows to the foot of the bed. I weed through my closet for the loosest clothes I own, stuff I can hide myself under until after finals. My pants are too tight from flab and baby. It's so hopeless. I want to call Gayla and ask her about this stuff, but she'd tell.

Shaking the pamphlets out of the folder, I start reading one about the support group. Support as in money or support as in emotions? I pick up the next one, "Deciding to Terminate." The paper makes it sound easy. I could miss one day of class. I could go back to being Carmen, instead of Carmen plus one.

The phone rings. Let it ring. I don't feel like talking to anybody, well, except maybe Joe, but that scares me too. I pick up.

"What?" I say rudely.

"Carmen? Is that you? It's Salt."

"Who else would it be if it's not Shirley? You're such a dork."

"Is Shirley there?"

"Nope."

"Good."

"What?"

"I need to talk to you about Shirley."

"Maybe you need to talk to me about Norine."

"No, Shirley. Look, could you just come downstairs?"

"I had the flu. I've got to catch up in every class."

"Ten minutes?"

"Fine." I put the receiver down, hide my pregnancy info folder in my backpack, and take all of it with me down stairs. Salt is sitting in the lobby. Franco is there. God, Franco, how would he like it if I walked up and told him that he's about to become a father? Wouldn't I love to see his face? Actually, no, because he'd blame me.

"Yo, Salt. Hey Franco," I say.

Salt stands up and gives Franco a friendly flip off. "Later." Franco's eyes are sleepy, his black eyelashes flutter against his brown cheeks. He lifts a lazy hand, wiggles his fingers.

Salt and I walk to the empty dorm library. He scouts around the cubicles, returns to the couch. "Sorry about the other night, Carmen."

"You should be. Shirley needs her friends even when she acts so blasé."

"Um, yeah. A lot more now."

"What gives?"

"She had that scan. It's bad. There's new cancer."

"No. She's fine."

"She's not. She's going to finish this semester and go back into chemo."

"Is it her other leg?"

"It's her liver. Do you think they'll take out part of it? Maybe it's like a lung. Lots of people lose a lung, and they're okay for a long time, like John Wayne."

"Where do you get this stuff?"

"Film classes. Anyway, Shirley wasn't going to tell you, but I said it's stupid to keep secrets, especially from your roommate. Secrets never solved a problem. Well, maybe during World War II, you know, loose lips sink ships."

"What are you talking about?"

"Shirley and cancer. It's back. We're her rocks, somebody she can lean on."

"You, me, and who else?"

"Not Norine. She makes everything into a pervy joke. I couldn't have said *rock* to her."

"Do the Woosters know?"

"She's said she's waiting until they get back from their cruise."

"Life is so totally unfair. She was on her way with the sorority and all. Is she telling the sorority?"

"I suppose. But if she does that, she might as well put the news in a headline in the school paper. Those girls never shut up."

"They could help her if money's a problem, like doing a fundraiser."

"Money's not the problem. Her body's the problem. I don't think they'll hold a give-a-liver-lobe event."

"Got it. Okay. Thanks for being straight with me, Salt." I hesitate, thinking about the baby. I want to scream and go to kick-boxing and not have to have this baby or if I am going to, I need to talk to somebody besides that priest about it. All this flashes through my mind, and all I do is give Salt a hug. "Yeah, thanks for letting me know," I tell him, like I need another problem hanging around my neck.

Salt gets up and stops at the door. "Keep the faith, Carmen. Things may turn out all right."

"I wish." I open the Rivera book. That picture, *Motherhood.* I stare and stare at it. I crease the page along the interior margin, folding it back and forth, back and forth. I rummage through my back pack and find a ruler. With tender care, I place the ruler across the fold and tear the picture out of the book. I slip it into my pregnancy folder. I touch the mother's face and the baby. That picture will be there for me, and when I get depressed or worried or stupid mad, I'll use its silent solace to calm myself. And once again, I know I've made my decision about the peanut no matter what Franco or Joe might say. I'll use the Rivera picture to start the discussion with Joe, then Joe and I will tell Franco. I hope they don't fight. How does the doctor figure out who's the father? Something about blood chemistry?

In the folder, there's a booklet about using amniocentesis, the reasons and the risks of using it, which is for women way older than I am, thirty-five and up. I can't imagine sticking a needle through my skin, through the uterus, and into the fetus. We aren't looking for a genetic disease, so I don't need amnio. The fathers can damn well wait. The pamphlet says most tests for paternity are done after the baby is born. After? Franco won't even know my name by then.

I stash all my info away and slink through the lobby. Franco has his feet up on the couch. He's sleeping like a hunting dog after a long day. I could change that attitude with one sentence, "Hey, Franco! You're going to be a father!" Or not. Why ruin a perfectly good friendship? Things will be changing soon enough.

There's no reason not to wait and tell Mama after Christmas. Why ruin a perfectly good Christmas?

Back on the fifth floor, in the hallway something goes WHUMP, followed by a screech. I run towards the noise. It's our room.

Shirley stands in the middle of piles of clothes, books, tapes, and paper. Her head is tilted back. She is screaming. A trunk lies between the bed and the closet. She's rubbing her toe. I envelope her in my arms. "Shirley, Shirl, what honey?"

"I think I broke my toe. That trunk fell on it."

"Do you want ice?"

"No, I hope it's broken, and the doctors chop it off."

"What?"

"I'm packing. I'm going home."

"You can't do that."

"Watch me." She stops screaming and shaking, sits on her bed, sorting through her stuff, making piles of shirts, skirts, pants, towels, notebooks, books.

"Salt said you went for more tests, not that you were quitting school. Was he wrong?"

"Salt is stupid."

"Goofy, not stupid. So what's with all this?"

"I went to the registrar this morning. I took incompletes in all my classes. The cancer is in my liver. Carmen, I can't take more chemo."

"Yes, you can. You can do anything. Look at you! Did you think for one minute last year when you applied to WPC that you'd get here, have a ton of friends, a weird roommate, and join a sorority? Did you consider that you are among the bravest people at this whole school, an example of courage?"

"Help me pack this stuff, okay? I hear you, Carmen. I got in as a legacy, my mom went here, my grandmother too. The sorority is everything I thought it would be. Mostly, chemo and college do not mix. This next round, I'll need blood transfusions and maybe a bone marrow transplant."

"Well, maybe that's why you're a Tri Chi? Maybe fate or karma or God or Buddha could see the road ahead and wanted to be sure you had sisters to run blood drives and marrow matching. What do you think of that?"

"Bullshit, and you know it. Now, help me pack."

"I'll give blood this afternoon. *La Raza* will stand behind you. I'll call Franco and Anaissa. I'll call Joe, get his frat too." I rub her back in circles as Mama does for me when I'm having a bad day.

A bad day. Shirley doesn't even know about the reality of my recent days. Considering her condition could be fatal, my problem's not close This baby is not in my plan. Shirley's new condition wasn't in hers. I've never heard her say one word that wasn't positive about her full recovery, minus one leg. I have to be strong for Shirley and for me and for the peanut and for the father if I only knew which one was the father so I'd better try to accept either candidate.

"Have you talked to your grandma?"

"Sent a telegram to the ship. They'll fly home from the next port. Even if the chemo doesn't kill me this time, it will kill my grandma. She gets so afraid when I look like death, all pale and skinny and puking and hairless."

"Shirley, let's pray, okay, just you and me?"

She crosses her eyes. "You know I'm not religious."

"Me either, but we need all the help we can get." I find my book of novenas. "Whoa, the patron saint of cancer patients is St. Peregrine." I kneel by her bed.

She bows her head, shifts her eyes towards me. "What's a peregrine?"

"A bird."

"Perfect. I'll give cancer the bird."

"Be serious. Don't mess with God. Let's read this together." I place the book across our laps. We say the Novena, slowly, like kids learning to read aloud. "We need to say this for nine days."

After the prayer, Shirley blows her nose and crutches her way to the bathroom. I flip to the index in the novenas to find the saint of pregnancy. Gerard. Yay, that's real inspiring. I kiss the cross around my neck and say a silent prayer to St. Gerard, "I want to believe you know what is best for me. Please watch over me, St. Gerard."

I'll buy matching necklaces with a falcon on them for Shirley and me. I'll search for a medallion of St. Gerard. Most people won't know Gerard from St. Christopher, except my mom and Gayla and all my aunts, Sisters Rosalie and Octavia. I stop. No St. Gerard for me; I'll find a medallion to wear for Peanut and say it's for Gayla's baby, which is more like equivocation than a lie, unlike the other stuff I've been saying.

Chapter 40

Double-crosser, Shirley lied. I come back from classes on Thursday to find her side of the room empty. She's gone home. A note on my desk has her home address and her home phone and a bunch of X's and O's and smileys. And a directive, "I left you a cute suitcase. Please finish the novenas for me." I call the number, but the answering machine goes off, and I can't think what to say so I hang up.

I open my desk drawer to write her something inspirational to keep her spirits up. On top of my pens, there's a personal check written out to me. A sticky note on the back says, "Thank you for being such a good roommate for Shirley." Mrs. Wooster's signature is on it. I check the amount. It's clear she noticed that I'm not rich even though five hundred dollars is ridiculous amount for me being me. I staple the check into my pregnancy folder.

The Residence Advisor slips a pink sheet under my door. I guess she doesn't want to talk about cancer. It says I don't have to pay for a single room, and they'll give me a new roommate next quarter. Right. I'll have a new roommate after spring quarter, the peanut. I open the door to ask the RA if we could hold a car wash or a blood drive, but she has disappeared around the corner to the other wing, and I'm way too tired to chase her. I crash on my bed.

Norine walks right in. "Bummer. Shirley was fun."

"Shirley IS fun. She's not dead. She'll be okay."

"Exactly. So who are you moving in here?"

That's a leading question. I don't want her to think she can move in. A lot of bad stuff has happened this week. The last thing I need is Norine for a roommate with revolving boys every night.

"No one is moving in. Shirley could change her mind. I hope she'll come back for finals."

"And in the meantime, which hunk are you having up here?"

"Are you crazy?"

"A little. About boys. I wish Jennifer hadn't broken up with her boyfriend. It was rad when she was shacking with him and the room was mine. What I wouldn't give to go back to no roommate at all, except it's great having more of her clothes to wear. We could work out a deal like that one movie. Salt took me to a retrospective festival. Don't you think old films in black and white are romantic?"

"Would you shut up? Do you have a brain? This is serious."

"I bet you bring Franco the delicious up here this weekend."

"No, I won't. And I won't be humping him in the dorm library either."

"Yeah, Salt, you know, he's like, 'Wanna screw?' and I'm like, 'Sure.'"

"Ew. I am not into casual sex." At least not anymore, which I don't say. "Norine, are you on the pill?"

"Since I was fourteen. Are you?"

"No, IUD. It's supposedly safer." I don't think I have to confess this as a lie since I sort of do have an internal uterine device, a human one.

"Are you going home Thanksgiving?"

I pause before I answer, trying to avoid a trap. "Yeah, home."

"Can I come with you?"

She looks all sad and forlorn like a little lost girl.

"Uh, no, sorry. The whole family is coming. Thirty of us cousins try to sleep in the living room."

"One more wouldn't matter then."

"Are you majoring in debate?"

"Are you majoring in poli sci and then law school? You're going to have to work on your shifty eyes. When you lie, you don't look at me."

"Done arguing. You cannot come home with me on Thanksgiving."

She yanks the blanket off my bed and curls up into a fetal ball. "I hate going home. I told you about the ski trip, right? My parents love skiing. I hate skiing, all cold and your nose running. The people they're going with have this way gross son." She peeks out of the blanket. Her mascara drips down her face like a she's in the band, KISS.

"Worse than Salt?"

"Salt has a heart. He's downstairs talking to the desk people about doing a blood drive for Shirley."

"Awesome. We should help." I tug her hand. She lands on the floor.

"For a Latino, you're such an Ice Queen."

"For a middle-class white chick, you're such a wannabe."

"Taco head."

"Hair spray brain."

"Brown noser."

"Slacker."

"Um, um, wait, I'll think of one."

"Too bad, so sad. I win."

"Are you sure I can't come to Thanksgiving with you?"

"One hundred percent sure. There's no way, Norine. Go ask Salt."

"Yeah, okay." She uses my cotton and my astringent to clean up her face. She smiles into the mirror and fluffs up her hair. She leaves. I call Joe. He's still not at the frat, probably diving practice, so I start packing for our trip to Coronado. I try on all my jeans to see which ones still fit. It's getting hard to breathe in these things. Bathing suit, still okay, since it fits below my belly button. My stomach pooches out more than that day a hundred years ago at the pool with Franco. How soon will Joe notice? I throw in a little sundress that I can wear as a cover up, add a beach towel, and shorts. The rest of the stuff has to wait until the morning we leave. I add the pregnancy folder at the last minute because he might want to know some of this stuff. He's out there diving, and he doesn't even know his world is about to implode.

I count off on my fingers the four days of Thanksgiving weekend. I will tell him on the Friday. Wednesday we'll be tired and Thursday should be romantic. I'll tell him Friday morning and then we'll have all day to discuss our choices. We can walk around Coronado. The town is full of old people so we won't have a baby in our face every time we turn around.

On my calendar, I go back to the Friday night that ruined my life, sex with Franco, then Joe. I've run out of names to call myself. So I'm six weeks now, thirty-two to go. The baby is due in July. We could get married this spring. I picture a wedding on the deck of Joe's parents' house. Mama wouldn't like that. Pregnant or not, she's going to want us married in the Church.

All of this feels like a bad dream, with scenes of kissing, scenes of running, scenes of being scared. I wish I could be my own dream director and could cut certain scenes, like the scene where I tell Mama and the one where I tell Joe, and the one where I find out if the baby's father is Joe or Franco. I haven't dreamed a scene with an actual baby yet or of me as mother in a Rivera painting.

I pull the folder out of my suitcase and find the paper for termination. I pick up the phone, dial the number. A man's voice says, "Hello, peace be with you. How may I help you today?" I drop the phone to cut the connection.

If I did that, I wouldn't have to tell anyone, but God knows. God already knows I am thinking about termination, sort of, even if I'm not really. Abortion is way up there on the sin meter, even thinking about it. Going through with it, God's not going to forgive me that one with a few Hail Marys. I am a doomed sinner. I'm not just screwed but double-screwed for not regarding my body as a sacred vessel, so should I go for the triple screw and terminate? I call the number back, and this time I stay on the line.

The same man answers.

"I just called a minute ago."

"I hoped you'd call back. How may I help you?"

"You set up terminations?"

"After counseling."

"How much counseling?"

"As much as it takes for you to make a choice."

"Will I be okay after?"

"That depends on a lot of things and that's why we do counseling."

"You mean I might not be able to have a family someday?"

"The aftermath of an abortion will affect you in body and soul."

"Oh."

"Should I schedule you in for tomorrow, Miss?"

"No, I'll call you back." I ease the phone down again. If I go to see them, I want Joe to go with me. Even if it's Franco's baby, I want Joe to go with me. Franco, he'd be like "Well, aren't you the archetypal idiot?"

I am an idiot. I am a pregnant idiot. I hope the Peanut turns out smarter than me. I go down the hall to talk to the Sisters. Their door board says, "Blessings to all. Home for the holiday!" Even nuns have better things to do than pray with the likes of me

Chapter 41

Wednesday before Thanksgiving. I haven't gone out with Joe. We've been phoning and seeing one another in class. He's compassionate when he hears about Shirley. The frat will help Salt with the blood drives. But he's always on the run, and I am always tired. At 6 in the morning, Joe calls. "Pick you up at what time?"

"You're the driver. Traffic sucks on holidays."

"You packed?"

"Yeah, you?"

"Locked and loaded."

"What?"

"I'll be there in three minutes."

My dorm floor echoes with emptiness. I drop a pile of books just for noise. Everybody took off on Monday if they could. Joe had practice, so I've been stuck too. Too much time with my books, my folder, and my peanut. To tell the truth though, I've been sleeping fourteen hours plus naps. Only one cafeteria is open this week, and Mitchell was hoping most of us would beg off our shifts so that he didn't have to choose who works and who doesn't. When I get dinner, I wave to Anaissa, but I bring my tray to my room, sit and eat alone. I'm not in the mood to act silly with Norine or listen to her mindless schemes. She's become best buddies with her roommate all of a sudden anyway. I avoid Franco in the lobby by coming in through the other door. I'm going to have a nervous breakdown before I find out the paternity of this baby.

Joe is parked out front. I think about the day I met him, how I judged him as a smart ass and a spoiled brat. When did I fall in love with him? Am I in love with him? Joe opens the trunk and I put my little suitcase in. He opens my passenger door. My *serape* waits on the seat.

"One kiss and we'll go," he says, putting his hands in my hair, caressing my cheeks. "I've missed you, Caramel."

My heart is pounding seeing him again until my brain reminds me of the peanut. "Me too. I've been alone a lot."

"What do you want to do first in Coronado?"

"Sleep."

"Really?"

"Really."

"What's the second thing you want to do in Coronado?"

"Walk on the beach. Depends on the weather."

Joe smiles. "Maybe it will rain the whole time 'cause what I want to do is hold you while you sleep and listen to music and watch football and every now and then call for room service to bring us something to eat and then go back to bed and get to know every inch of you."

"That's romantic," I say, knowing that we'll have one day of this and then I will change everything and all we'll do is sit around wondering about the peanut.

"Our condo has a fireplace."

"Delicious."

I fall asleep, warm under the serape. I dream of Joe and I dream of me, but in the dream, the due date is past and I think I look like an elephant, the way their sides bulge out, like the baby is lying sideways.

"Carmen," Joes touches my shoulder. "You were crying in your sleep."

"Was I talking?"

"No."

I am relieved that I wasn't talking about babies or lies.

"Go back to sleep because we'll be at the big, scary bridge in ten minutes."

"Now I'm not sleepy. Once we get on it, I'll freak."

"I'm driving. Put your trust in me. Let's see if you can get over this phobia. I want you to take in the whole view. It's fabulous at the peak of the bridge."

"What'll you give me if I pass your test?"

"The same thing I'm going to give you if you don't."

We laugh, and a shot of desire runs through me. I haven't felt anything but numb since meeting Dr. Fritz. Telling Joe might not be so hard after all.

"Here we go." He takes the off ramp. The bridge climbs upward. I focus on the sail boats bouncing in the deep blue of the harbor. Wind blows the water into white caps.

"Top, now we descend," says Joe. "See the Hotel Del Coronado?"

From here the Victorian turrets shimmer in the gray morning clouds like a palace in a fairy tale. "Is that where your condo is?"

"No, we're right here." We drive along the water front. Joe makes a turn into an underground garage. He grabs the luggage. In the elevator, he pushes the button for the top floor. The elevator is all glass. I slump against him, hiding my eyes. The swoop upward has made me dizzy.

"Easy, Carmen. Almost there, Baby.

That word, *baby*. He says it all the time. How are we going to have any fun if all I can think of is the bad news I have to deliver about the baby I am going to deliver. My churning stomach scares me. Barfing in the elevator would not be okay. We stop with a ding. We step into a hallway encased in glass windows.

"Wow, Joe, this is totally beyond my expectations."

"Not exactly the dorm is it?" He beams and opens the front door.

We walk into a suite of rooms bigger than my whole house. The windows run floor to ceiling, there's a piano, a window seat overlooking the bay, a velvet sectional couch, and stairs up to the bedrooms.

I follow Joe upstairs. The master bedroom has a huge bed, the biggest bed I've ever seen. The bed is turned down like it's just waiting for me. Joe sets my suitcase on a luggage rack and throws his overnight bag into a corner.

"Check out the master bath." He leads me into a tile-covered room with a claw-footed bath tub. The faucets shine. Along one wall, the shower has no curtain. It has an open surround made of pebbles. Joe pulls me in. "See," he points to all the nozzles, "we can shower together."

"Could I shower now, just me?"

"Sure, I'll call room service. What would be your wish, my lady?"

"Tea and crumpets?" I tease.

"How about a margarita and quesadillas?"

Oops, I hadn't thought about alcohol. If I say no, Joe will ask what's the problem. It's too soon to talk about what's the problem. "Sure." A sip or two will cover me without hurting the peanut.

The bathroom is filled with the biggest, softest white towels I've ever seen. I think about the towel I gave Joe to use at my house, scratchy as a gym towel, and a niggle of shame creeps up from my stomach. On the back of the door hang two absolutely fluffy white plush robes hang. I shower. The soap says it was milled in France. I sniff it, lemon and basil? Heavenly. I step into the shower and zone out in the warm water, adjusting the nozzles to caress aching my back. I wash my hair with shampoo of the same lemony basil scent. I could seriously stay in here all day, but Joe opens the door.

"Food's here."

"I'll be right out. You go ahead. I know you're always starving."

I fold myself into one of the cuddly robes and wrap a towel around my wet hair. When I see myself in the mirror, I change my mind and blow dry my hair even if it's a curly frizz, it's still better than the towel.

Joe's sitting in front of a colossal television. The room service food is on the side table. He balances a plate on his lap, the remote in his hand, a pitcher of margaritas on the coffee table.

I sneak up behind him and put my hands over his eyes. "Guess who!" I remember when he did that to me and I didn't know him well and I was kind of mad.

Joe starts naming every girl's name he can think of to tease me. When he says, "I give up, who is it?" I come around to the other side of the coffee table out of reach and open the robe.

"You sexy thing! Get over here this minute."

"I guess that wasn't fair."

"Right you are because you're going to need some food and drink before we get busy." He lifts his eyebrows up and down, and he's way too cute to resist. He puts his plate down and opens his arms to me. I fly into his embrace. We forget about everything except the next touch, the next kiss, the absolute joy of the two of us.

We wake up as the sun is setting. "Sunset. Want to sit on the balcony?" Joe asks.

"I'm not moving anywhere. Sightsee tomorrow."

"Cool. I have plenty of sight seeing to do right here."

I wake up to stripes of morning sunshine. We never closed the drapes. We did manage to get ourselves upstairs and into the bed with its sheets as soft as kisses.

I get up and wander around the condo. Joe has left a note that he is out for a run and that I should order room service. Could I be any happier, which is when I remember that tomorrow is the day I've promised myself to tell Joe about the baby. We're about to enjoy our last perfect day.

By the time room service arrives, I'm not even hungry anymore. I force myself to eat some oatmeal with brown sugar and to drink cranapple juice. I peel an orange. I go upstairs to get dressed for the day, it's windy, so I put on sweats. I make a sudden decision. I will tell him today. I arrange the pregnancy folder on the coffee table, turn on the television to the Macy's parade, and curl up on the couch, waiting for Joe to come in, waiting to ruin his life.

Chapter 42

A key rattles in the door lock. I'm so nervous that I knock my water glass on the floor. Time's up, and I'm going to face the issues with Joe. I run to the bathroom to double check my hair and dash on a little make-up, not too much 'cause he likes the natural look.

The refrigerator door opens, bottles clink, and I think how nice it is that Joe will bring me a drink too. That's a natural segue into opening our baby talk.

I slide down the banister, which is totally childish, but I want to make Joe laugh. I slip around the curve, the momentum is too much, and I land with a smack on my butt. "Sorry, Peanut," I whisper. I'm rubbing my aching ass when there's a voice from the kitchen, a female voice.

"Hello?"

What? Maybe it's the maid. I edge from the living room through the swinging doors to the kitchen. No Joe, well, there is a Joe but not my Joe. It's Joe, senior. And Tate. I'm dead.

I could run back upstairs. I don't.

"Hi, Mrs. Sneed. It's nice to see you." I'm such a liar.

"Hi, Carne, right? Joe said you all were going skiing." She glances at her husband. "Isn't that what he said?"

"You know Squirt. Changes his mind in two flicks of a lamb's tail." He wheels over to the counter and puts the daily paper there.

What? Joe better get here fast because I'm going to lose it. I pick up the paper and stroll it over to the coffee table to cover up the evidence folder.

"Anybody hungry?" asks Mrs. Sneed.

"Joe will be after his run."

"He's always hungry, day or night. What's in the 'fridge?" Tate leans in, opening drawers, switches to the freezer, same result.

"Um, we didn't shop yet."

"Today's Thanksgiving. Joe, honey, is that market on Orange open on holidays?"

"Don't know. Call room service. You're on vacation." He wheels into the living room and picks up the paper, clicks on the remote, and goes off into man-land, football.

"Carne, what sounds good?"

"Joe likes pizza."

Tate puts her finger down her throat. "The worst! I guess I'll have some work to do in the nutritional studies with you two. How about green salads and turkey sandwiches?"

"What time is it?"

"Eight."

"I already ate. What else would Joe want? Do they have yogurt?"

"Super idea! I'll have them send up yogurt and figs. We have a blender around here somewhere." She shouts out to her Joe, "Fig smoothie okay, dear?"

"Make sure they bring honey."

"Honey for my honey!"

She's positively witty this morning. A fig smoothie sounds about as appealing as garlic toast for breakfast. I cannot barf in front of them.

Which reminds me of the folder that I have to get out of there like now. I sit on the couch closest to Joe Sr.'s chair. I dig through the paper towards the bottom of the stack to retrieve the folder and extra sections from the tons of Black Friday ads. I slide my hand around. The folder got scooped up with whatever it is Joe Sr. is reading. I can't take it right off his lap. I walk to the window to see if I can spot Joe coming back from his run. What did he do, run to San Ysidro to pop in on my mom?

Mr. Sneed calls out to his wife, "Tate! Could you or Carmen supervise my transfer from this chair into the recliner, do you think?"

"Carmen! Not Carne! Hey, honey, sorry I've been calling you the wrong name." She puts her arm around my shoulders. "Want to stand by?"

"I'm pretty strong," I say.

She looks me up and down. "Yes, you are. Me too. I like a girl with muscles and grit, not some weeping willow with a hankie in her hand." She reaches for the papers on her husband's lap.

"Here, I'll take those. Joe will want to do his sports analysis." I toss the multi-inch Tribune to the chair.

"Save the crossword for me," says Tate. "Unless you want it, Carmen?"

"Oh, no, not at all." I rummage through the papers, still feeling for the folder and examining the inserts. "Which section for the crossword?"

"I'll find it. Let's see if Joe can get himself settled."

He rolls the wheelchair over next to the recliner. He's sweating from the effort of pushing the chair through the thick-piled carpet. "How would you like new flooring for Christmas?"

"That's what you said way back on the 4th of July weekend that I'd get new carpet by my birthday. But that was last summer. Look how expert you are now." She wipes his brow with his handkerchief, and Mr. Joe completes the maneuver.

"Whew. Better! Should have taken the shoes off," he says. "They weigh about ten pounds. Did you know an elephant's heart weighs 200 pounds? Man, oh Manochevitz, the world is full of wonders."

The doorbell rings, and I pray it's Joe. It's room service with the figs, orange juice, milk, granola, honey. Tate yells, "In the kitchen," signs the bill, and turns back to us. "Where's that crossword?"

"I'm still looking for it," I barter for some time. "Do you need help with the figs?" which is the last thing my stomach wants.

"That's considerate, Carmen," she says, taking the papers away from me. "The drive down this morning just about wore me out. Holler when you have the figs ready. I'll feel better once I get something to eat. Why do we have to leave for trips at the crack of dawn, Joe?"

He doesn't answer. He's nodded off in the chair. Tate opens the coat closet, finds a blanket, and covers him. "Sleep well, my sweet," she says, kissing his forehead. She takes the pile of newspapers and sits in the recliner next to him. I walk into the kitchen and pound my head with my fists. She cannot be the one to find the folder, especially since I haven't even talked to Joe about Peanut yet. I go back out with the interlopers, which isn't nice since it is their house. "Could you show me one fig peeling? I don't want to mess up."

"Lord save me from young women who don't cook," she grumbles. But she does get up. She leaves the mound of papers in the chair. She grabs a fig and a small knife. "See you start right here." She slices through the fig and chops the slice into pieces. "No one peels figs. The skin is edible and extremely nutritious."

"I'm so embarrassed. I'll come right back and do them all. I just need the restroom." Tate watches me slink off into the living room. I take the bottom half of the papers with me upstairs and leave them on the bed, making sure the folder is there. It is. I wash my hands and face in the bathroom. I have newsprint spotting my arms like chicken pox.

Chicken. Not a word I need to think right now.

By the time I'm back downstairs, the blender is blending. So much for my helpfulness in the kitchen. The door opens, and my Joe walks in, dripping with sweat.

"Squirt. Do not come into this room so disgusting and sweaty," Tate hollers as she throws towels at him. She slams the door in his face. "He knows the rules about hygiene. He's such a slob."

"But a sweet one," I say, trying to offer peace. I slide toward the hallway.

"Tell him we have breakfast waiting."

"Yes, ma'am." That and about a hundred other things, like now what do we do with our romantic weekend? Well, it wasn't going to be romantic anyway once I broke the news about Peanut.

Joe's wiped down, like an auto after a car wash. "Think she'll let me in now?" he asks, kissing me.

"Why didn't you tell me they'd be here?"

"Why didn't they tell me they'd be here? Our family lives very spur-of-the-moment."

Is this my lead in?

"Did they ask you about the skiing trip?"

"They did. I didn't even know what to say."

"Should have said no snow."

"Like I know that. Joe, we can't stay here."

"Why not? They're cool with my girls."

"Your girls, plural?"

"I mean any of them one by one."

"That would be how many?"

"Carmen, stop. You are the one, right now. I love you. We'll have a great weekend with or without them. They have a million friends here in Coronado. We probably won't see them much. My dad still loves to surf. He belly rides. He spends hours out there. And when he gets tired, he watches my mom surfing, showing up all the gremlins half her age." He hugs me. "Want to learn to surf?"

"There's something I want to show you as soon as we go in and have breakfast. Then we can talk about surfing or whatever. Are you ready?"

"Ready Eddie."

"You are such a goof."

"You are such a goody two-shoes."

And I think, nah, not two shoes. Four shoes.

He opens the door for me. As I cross the threshold, I know this is probably our last really happy moment.

Chapter 43

Joe sings in the shower. He's probably rocking his air guitar too. I peek in. A fist jabs into the steam, "Da da da daren't dent, daren't dent. . . GHOSTERBUSTERS! Who ya gonna call? GHOSTBUSTERS."

Live it up, Joe Sneed. You're going to need a Ghostbuster power pack. The water shushes off. He comes flying into the bedroom and dives into the middle of the bed. "Who ya gonna call, Caramel?"

"Someone who can carry a tune," I answer. I throw his clothes at him. "Let's walk on the beach."

"Let's roll in the hay."

"Joe, your parents."

"My parents have the other master all the way across the condo. It's not going to be any fun if you go all virginal on me due to the presence of parental units."

"I'm getting to that."

"What?"

I sit on the edge of the bed. Joe tumbles me backwards into his arms. He strokes my hair, kisses the top of my head, kisses my closed eyelids. I twist away. "Wait, Joe."

His eyes have taken on his sexy look I love so much. "Joe, there's something I have to tell you."

"So tell."

"I'm pregnant."

He sits up. He's very still. "You're pregnant? How?"

"Um, sexual intercourse? There's more."

"Please don't say twins."

"I won't," and I stop to swallow a burst of tears and shame, "I can't be sure who's the father."

"Carmen? What? Who else? What about birth control pills?"

"I went to get them, for this weekend, you know, and the doctor at the clinic said I couldn't have them because I don't need them because I'm already pregnant."

He buries his face in his hands. "A baby? But maybe not mine? Were you hooking up with somebody before college? Carmen, who were you with besides me?"

"Franco." My voice squeaks.

"That bastard. He's such a player."

"It was just one time. Same as you, until we came here, just one time. But the doctor gave me this packet so we can look at our options."

"I don't want to talk about options. I want to talk about how soon I can kill Franco."

"Don't be like that. It's going to be months and months before we know. It's safer to wait until after the baby is born."

"I have to know."

"Or what? You won't love me anymore?"

He paces around the room. He throws his body on the floor and cranks out push ups. He does sit-ups and burpees. Finally, he stops. He sits beside me and picks through the papers I've laid out in a line. He crumples one and then another. "I know it's your body, Caramel, but it could be my baby too. Can we throw away this termination paper? Please don't terminate our baby, the baby."

"I haven't decided what to do. I want to talk to my mom."

"You're Catholic, right? So no abortion."

"Catholics do a lot of things the Church doesn't agree with."

Joe lets the papers fall to the floor. He drums his fists into the down pillows. He picks a pillow up and hits me over the head with it. I grab another and swat at him. We run around the room in a full-fledged pillow fight until one of the pillows bursts open. Down flies everywhere, sticking to our skin and hair, to the acoustic ceiling, to the carpeting.

"Do I get a vote?"

"If you do, so does Franco. Maybe all three of us should meet."

"No way."

"When's the baby due?"

"July."

"C'mere." He crooks his finger and indicates the place he wants me to sit. "Carmen, nobody used their brain here. I assumed you were using birth control, you assumed what? That it was a safe time of the month? There's no doubt that you're pregnant?"

"No doubt, except which man provided the daddy's sperm."

He reads the papers one by one. He reads about support groups and the trimesters. He reads everything twice. He rolls to the floor and sits back on his feet. He tears a strip of paper off the termination hand-out, twists it into a loop. "Carmen Principia, Caramel, Pinata-Head, will you marry me?"

I'm in shock. "You don't have to marry me, Joe."

"I want to marry you. We'll handle this. The parents, they'll just have to deal with it. When the baby comes, they won't be mad. A little Carmen. A little Joe. If it's a Joe, we are not naming the kid Joe. So, Carmen, I'm asking you again, will you marry me?" He slips the twisted paper over my left ring finger. "Let's go tell the 'rents. And call your mom. We'll have a family dinner."

"Wait. I haven't said yes. And our house is full of family, so Mama can't come today. Plus, you're still assuming your parents will be speaking to us. What's your mom going to say to her sorority friends?"

"Okay. In order. Will you marry me, yes or no?"

"Yes. I love you."

"I love you too. And I will love the baby no matter what, do you hear me? *No matter what,* so maybe we can keep Franco out of the picture. Second, when's your mom going to be free?"

"Tomorrow by noon."

"All right. Let's plan a little fiesta for tomorrow night. My parents will be at the beach all day, you can make sure your mom will come, and you and I can put dinner on the table with a little help from our friends in room service."

"Really? You think?"

"If they're together when we tell them, it won't turn into a shouting match between me and my mom. She'll put all the blame on me, so don't worry your sweet self about my mom. Don't stress out our baby."

"I call it Peanut."

"Don't stress out Peanut." He leans over and speaks to my belly. "Hey you in there, Peanut. Be cool. We're cool. No stress, got it?" He rubs my belly for good measure. "You don't look pregnant."

"I'm just a few weeks in. Count it out, Joe. The baby is due in July."

He closes his eyes and gestures like he's carrying a one. "July. A summer baby. I'm going to be a father in July?" He shakes his head, disbelieving.

"Either you or Franco."

"I requested we leave Franco out of this."

"I can't agree to that. I grew up without a father. Peanut has to know the full history."

"That'll be hard to explain to a kid."

The laugh erupts from somewhere inside me. "Our talk with the Peanut is a lot of years off, Joe. Let's concentrate on now. So what happened to the last of my questions?"

"Remind me."

"What's your mother going to tell her sorority sisters about her son marrying the girl from San Ysidro whose main attributes are that she can make a piñata, that she can cook tamales, and that she got into WPC with you?"

"My mother is going to tell them she'll be a grandmother in July, and she can't wait to teach Peanut to surf."

"As if."

"Carmen, sometimes you simply have to trust people. My mom's a lot of things, but spiteful isn't one of them. Do you want to tell them today?"

"No, I like your idea better, about the dinner. Could you tell them that we're cooking tomorrow, and we're going shopping? I'll change into something beachy."

He hugs me. "Beachy is good. I don't want you trying to show off and learn to surf this trip. My mom will beg you, it's sort of a test, so we should stay away from the beach with them. Or you could belly board with my dad. You're not afraid of the water are you?"

"Only the water that's cushioning our peanut. That's the only water that worries me at all. But no belly boarding. I can feel Peanut like a hard little apple when I lie on my stomach."

"Wow, you can? Show me."

"Not now, you get too carried away."

"I know. Okay, see you in five minutes. I have to make some chitchat out there, and I don't want to start any true confessions, because Carmen, this is really scary but it's sort of cool too. Take care of Peanut while I'm away."

"Okay. Joe?" He turns back to me. "Don't spill the beans or the peanuts or any other substance." I take off the paper circle. "It's probably best if I don't put this back on until tomorrow. Go now. Let me make myself into someone who doesn't look like she's been through the washing cycle."

"You can do that?"

"Watch it, Mister. You're talking to the mother of your (I show him my crossed fingers) child. Half my good looks go into this project. Let's hope Peanut doesn't get your nose."

"Hey! Nose observations are out of bounds."

"This entire event is out of bounds."

"Guess we'll have to write some new rules, Caramel."

"Yep. Make a new plan, Stan."

He leaves the room, singing "We are the Champions." We are?

Chapter 44

After too much food and drink, the parents are relaxed. We have served our meal of lobster tacos, cheating with prepared side dishes and two cooked lobsters from room service. I made the tacos from fresh tortillas Mama brought. Even though she did not want to come, Mama praised our efforts as *sabroso* after chastising us, "This food, too much money." In her black shirtwaist dress with the white Peter Pan collar and cuffs, her hose and heels, she appears to have dressed for a funeral while the rest of us are beach casual

The three parents have about thirty seconds before the world changes. Joe whispers to me, "Be strong." I squeeze his hand. Three pairs of eyes laser in on us. My Joe is standing with his wine glass raised. I am by his side with my tumbler of water. I hope my water isn't already a giveaway.

Clink, clink, clink, he raps his spoon against his glass. "Carmen and I want to thank you for being the best parents in the world." The Sneeds cheer themselves. Mama gives me a skeptical eye brow raise. "We have some big news, well actually, important news because the news isn't exactly big."

Tate, slightly tipsy, giggles. "Did anyone follow that train of thought?" She swoops the air across her head with a flat hand. "Whoosh, went right by me." Joe senior catches her flying hand and holds it.

"Go on, Squirt. The suspense is killing us." He reaches across the table to hold Mama's hand too. She starts to pull away, but doesn't. She takes hold of Tate's hand. With her tan, Tate's skin is the same shade of brown as Mama's.

"Friendships make a circle," says Mama.

"Yes, right, exactly, Mrs.Gracia, a circle of memories. Carmen and I would like to announce to you. . . ."

Tate interrupts. "Wait, Squirt. I want my camera." She withdraws from the circle and rummages around in her beach bag. "Somebody take a picture of us at the table holding hands." The three parents join their hands again, smile on cue, and click goes the camera.

"Now, Squirt, let your father take a picture of you and Carmen." She leans across the table and informs Mama, "He's going to tell us she's pinned, you know, like a pre-pre-pre engagement." This remark is supposed to be *sotto voce.* We all hear her.

"Not quite, Mom. Take a few 'pre's' out."

Joe senior is no longer smiling."Don't tell me," he begins.

"Carmen and I have gotten you together to tell you three things about ourselves. The first is that this is more than a friendship. We love one another." He kisses me. "The second is that we're going to get married." I hold up my hand with the paper engagement ring on it. The parents react with wrinkled brows. "And the biggest news is that. . . ," Joe stops. He gazes at me. His hands are sweaty. He takes a drink of his wine. "The biggest news." He stops again.

"I'm pregnant," I say.

Gasps all around. Tate gulps her wine and pours herself another glass. Mama's mouth is opened like she's struggling for breath.

I go on. "The baby is due in July. It's not a planned pregnancy. We aren't afraid. We're excited. For now, we're calling the baby our Peanut." I sit down, feeling light-headed. Mama scoots her chair away from mine so that she can look me in the eyes. Her jaw is set firmly in a frown.

Mr. Joe recovers first. "I'm going to be a grandpa next summer? And my Tate here and Lucia are going to be grandmothers? "

"Don't you call me Grandma," says Tate. "Are you two sure? Who's your doctor? What were you thinking? You're babies yourselves." She stops to sigh and dab at her eyes. "Won't Carne get to do the candle-lighting in her sorority? I loved that, it's so romantic. You don't want to miss that do you? Which sorority was it again?"

"*La Raza*. They're not big on ceremony," I assure her.

Joe comes around the table to sit by my mother. "Mrs. Gracia, I promise you that Carmen will finish her education, and I will do my best to be a good husband and a good father."

"What about your education, Joe? You have two more years of undergrad and three years of law school." Joe's father has pulled a calculator out of his pocket.

"I'll transfer here to San Diego. Law school has to wait. I can go at night. We don't have all the answers yet."

"Mrs. Sneed, Tate, we've grown up a lot in a few weeks. I'm coming home to live with Mama. We'll manage. We're not the first college kids to have a baby."

"Lucia, it's your daughter. You're probably not as shocked as we are since you people are used to having families young. What do you think?" Tate pours herself another glass of wine.

Mama straightens her shoulders. "My people? Are you saying Mexicans are baby factories?"

"Well, now, typically, aren't they?"

I sit in Mama's lap before she can throw a punch. I nuzzle into her shoulder.

Tate is still talking. "Look, it's as easy to fall in love with a rich girl as a poor one, you know. That's the whole point of going Greek."

My Joe's cheeks flame red as they do when he's angry. "Mom, please tell me you're drunk. Apologize to Mrs. Gracia and Carmen."

"What are you talking about? Apologize? How about you and your girlfriend of the month tell us you're sorry. How about you tell us you're in the twentieth century, that you aren't really going to go through with this baby you obviously aren't ready for?"

"Out of the question," I say. "We are having this baby."

Mama moves me back over to my chair. She holds my hand. "What am I supposed to say? That I'm shocked?

Disappointed? Happy because I like Joe? Sad because his parents think my daughter and I are low class? I need time to think. Carmen was going to be the smart one, the college graduate, the first one in our family. Now she is like everyone else. Carmen, you're not even smarter than Gayla?" Mama fingers the medallion around her neck. She unclasps it and puts it on me. "The blessing of John De La Salle upon you. I have worn this since I left you at your college. Aunt Ines gave it to me. This Saint will see you through your degree. Even with a baby, you can get your degree. Don't give up your dreams for a baby. Let the baby be part of your dreams." She looks at the Sneeds. "That's what I did with Carmen. I made her part of my dreams, to come to America where she could get the best education, to be more than a piñata-maker."

Tate scrapes her chair back from the table. "Statistics show too many of you choose that path. This is all a bit much for me. What am I going to tell my sorority sisters, Joe?" Her husband chucks her chin.

"You'll tell them and everyone else that we've been blessed. We'll have a smart and beautiful daughter-in-law to go with our impetuous son. We'll have a grandbaby! Carmen, are you feeling okay?"

"I get very tired."

"Carmen," Mama says, "You come with me tonight."

"But."

"We need private time. Joe, come over Saturday."

"I'd like to be with you. We should talk."

"No, Saturday. For one night, give us time, me and my smart daughter." She stares at me so silently that I feel like I've ruined her life.

"Mama, I'll be home full time as soon as I take my finals this quarter. I'll ask for a leave of absence. If I don't go back to WPC, the credits will still transfer. I'll get a job."

"You know nothing about money. You know nothing about babies. You, Carmen, are a selfish little girl. How can such a girl raise a baby? Enough. We are leaving. Get your things."

"The baby is our little Peanut," says Joe. "Be happy for us. We'll make things work. Carmen and I, we're a great team. We got an A on our piñata report."

"A baby is not a piñata, Joe," says Mama. "It was brave to tell us. It was brave not to choose abortion." She looks Tate in the eye. "For now," she holds her hands palms up, "I must have time with my daughter."

Joe and I exchange glances. I leave the table, pretending to go upstairs to pack, but I sit on the lowest stair to listen.

"Everybody, calm down." says Mr. Sneed. "We can have a celebration after the baby comes. All I ask is that you get married soon. I want Joe's name on the birth certificate, not an X or a blank space for unnamed."

Does he know my history? That I have only a name for my father, no knowledge. This is the first time I have considered that I am repeating my mother's life choices, except I believe I have chosen a better man, as long as the father is Joe.

"I vote for a wedding the weekend before Christmas. What do you think, Mrs. Gracia? We'll keep the gathering small. And then in July when Peanut is born, we'll party hardy."

Tate points her finger at her son. "Your partying days are over when that baby is born. And Carmen up there, she's not going be your pretty, perky little bride for long. How are we going to tell our friends about this beaner baby? What about all the wedding plans I've dreamed of? Why didn't you think before causing this big mess?"

"Mom," Joe interrupts, but my mother cuts him off.

"A baby is not a mess. A baby is a person." Mama scoffs. "The baby is already a soul" She dabs at her eyes with her napkin. "Worrying about a wedding? A wedding does not matter. The vows matter. Carmen will focus on getting ready to be a mother. This is not a time to look through magazines for white dresses and wedding cake. She will have penances to the Church."

I want to tell Mama to butt out. Joe Sr. has taken this so well. Mrs. Sneed is typically selfish. My mom, not so selfish, but disappointed and angry and worried. How will we ever become a family? Tate will probably hammer Joe with talk of my becoming one more fat *mamasita*. I know he'll be the best father in the world. I watch him kneel by his father's wheelchair, rest his head against his father's chest. They reach to include his mom, but she storms out the door.

Mama calls up to me as if I have been packing all this time, "Carmen, hurry."

I run into the bedroom, throw a few things in a bag, and scribble a note for Joe to bring the rest. All the fears I've lived with since Dr. Fritz gave me the news, every moment comes back, added to Mama's broken heart and Tate's disdain that Mama and I, our entire family, we are not good enough for her side of the family.

The voice calling me now is Joe's. "Caramel, come down here." I go to him with my suitcase. We face my mama and his father. "We know we're way young. We know this was not your plan for us. But we're brave. We'll learn to become parents, maybe different from you, but parents to our one little baby. Not everything in life worth knowing is learned in a classroom, you know?"

He winks at me. He seems to think everything will be all right. Tate runs along the waterfront, slapping her thighs with each stride, shaking her head, talking to herself. I don't know how I can forgive her. She is a bigot. She doesn't even know us, and she sees us as dirt.

I admire Mr. Joe, who has tears in his eyes. To create a family, we're going to have to construct a labor of love. I believe love is stronger than hate. I believe I am stronger than Tate. I'd rap out a rhyme like Franco if I didn't want to forget him completely.

Chapter 45

Mama gasps as the elevator shoots downward as if the floor has fallen out from under us. The sparkling harbor and spinnakered sailboats blur into one mosaic.

The parking attendant greets us, and to my surprise Mama produces a claim check Usually, she'd drive ten blocks to find free parking. She fumbles in her purse for tip money. "How much, Carmen?"

"Don't know. Five bucks?"

She swears in Spanish and hands me the money. "You and your rich friends."

We're going to argue later anyway, so I don't respond. The parking guy pulls our truck up in front of us, opens both doors, and I hand him the money. "Thank you very much," he says, kind of surprised. "This truck is a classic. If you ever want to sell it, you can find me right here. It's radical."

As Mama pulls out onto the main street, the Chevy pops a burst of black smoke. Any other day, we would laugh. We inch through Coronado, full of traffic and tourists for the holiday weekend. Pedestrians amble every which way near the Hotel del Coronado, and Mama stomps on the brakes as a family jaywalks. More swearing in Spanish.

That's it for highlights of the drive home. The silence in the car settles around us like a lead blanket.

"Put your suitcase in your room, Carmen, and come sit outside with me."

"Yes, Mama." I worry about Gayla's super-spy eyes. "How about inside so Gayla doesn't come over yet?"

"Outside."

I can tell this isn't going to go well. She seats herself on the double swing out back. Washing my face, I use a cold wash cloth on my puffy eyes, check the medicine cabinet for aspirin, and take two. Next time at the doctor's office, I need to ask about the migraine meds and the peanut. Having delayed as long as I can, I join Mama on the swing.

"So," says Mama.

"So here we are."

"That university was your decision, Carmen. I trusted you. I trusted them. A good religious school like that, how does this happen anyway?"

"This meaning the baby, or this meaning sex?"

"Don't talk like that to your mother."

"I meant no disrespect. I meant only honesty. How can we work through this if I'm not supposed to mention sex to you?"

"It's such a sin. You aren't married."

"Were you?"

"That's the point. Wait here, Carmen." She hurries into the house. Gayla waves to me, and I meet her half-way as she crosses the street. Her pregnancy must be going well because she is huge in front, and it looks as if she will tip forward from gravity alone. Mama is opening and shutting drawers and doors

"I'm home for a couple days. I'll come see you. Mama has some things to tell me."

Gayla's eyes open wider. "She's going to tell you about her boyfriend?"

"What boyfriend?"

Gayla whistles a little tune. "The one who comes on Fridays and Saturdays. She probably wants you to meet him."

"Really?" I cannot picture my mother with a man.

"It's not like she's too old, Carmen."

"Just too old-fashioned."

"That's what you think."

"I'll come over as soon as I can, give you the latest."

"Righteous." She waddles back into her house.

Our door slams. Mama rocks on the swing with a big photo album in her lap.

"Sit by me," says Mama. "You know this book has photos of your childhood. I've added one you haven't seen before. It's your father."

"Why did you wait until now to tell me more about my father?"

"It seems like it is time."

She flips through the book, pointing at pictures of herself from childhood, bright eyes and black hair, and a little pudgy. "My mama was a good cook. I ate too much *menudo* and *mole pablano*." She turns the page.

"This is the only picture I have of your father." She shows me a portrait, like one taken at school or the mall. "He was twenty then."

"Handsome," I say, admiring his slicked back hair, his aristocratic, elegant facial features, the aquiline nose and almond-shaped brown eyes like Franco's. His lips are delicate, almost feminine, but maybe that's the pose that makes him look like that.

"He was handsome. He is probably still handsome. What he had in looks he lacked in character, I am sorry to say. He took me out for seven wonderful weeks when he was in San Miguel with friends. I was seventeen, younger than you, Carmen, and he took advantage of my youth with his syrupy words and stormy ways. He would pitch a fit of jealousy whenever I talked to other men. I thought that was a good thing that he was possessive of me. I thought that meant he would want to keep me as his wife forever."

"I know someone like that, but it isn't Joe, Mama."

"Wait. We will get to Joe. Your father, Jacobo Principia, even his name is some kind of joke. The man had no principles, and from what I have heard of him in his career, he hasn't learned much."

"And you, Mama? You have no blame?"

"No, for two months, I was a foolish girl in love with a rich and handsome man. He gave me too much to drink. He took advantage of me and then he left town. I couldn't think how to find him, to tell him about you, and I waited a long time to decide whether to bother telling him about you."

"Were you ashamed of me?"

"Ashamed of no father for you. Never ashamed of you, until maybe today, Carmen, you making the same mistake as I did except I don't know if you were made drunk to lose your morals."

She turns the page, filled with pictures of a youthful Lucia holding a fat baby with full cheeks. As we move through the album, the pictures show the baby growing into a toddler and then the child I remember as me. The pictures are black and white, but I feel the colors of San Miguel and the warm sun.

"This is my favorite picture, Mama." We are holding hands, walking home from the market. My hair is pulled into twin pony tails. Mama is fat. Our love connects us right there for anyone to see. What have I done to her love for me?

"Carmen, this father of yours was a scoundrel. He makes so much money in Colorado. But he would never send a single peso to help you. The only honest and good thing he did was notarize his signature on your birth certificate to help you if you came to America. He is a writer, he owns land and a second home in New York. Under all his handsomeness beats a heart that values himself too much."

"I know someone like that," I tell her again. "But it isn't Joe. Joe is the kind of man who will make a good father. He makes me laugh even when I am sad. He takes time to learn our culture." I debate telling her about *Firstlings*. "He joined one of the Mexican clubs and one of the Mexican classes at WPC. He's not a snob."

"His mother is."

I'm silent. I cannot rebut this. Tate is not someone I would choose to be in my family. "Mr. Joe is kind like my Joe. And Joe's mother is devoted to Mr. Joe, isn't that a good thing?"

"A wife's duty, Carmen."

"So you would have been devoted to Jacobo if he had married you, even if he was harsh and cruel?"

"He was that. I would not have married him if he came back or if I thought he would hurt you. When he left, it was adios, except for the letters I sent him when I found that raising a baby costs money. I asked the art dealers in San Miguel if he had made purchases, and I got his address. He only answered one letter about your birth certificate. A man will pay for his sins. Jacobo thought he was above all that, above the Church, like a god."

"Tate seems to think that too."

"She thinks she is smart, but she is stupid about people, about the world. If you marry Joe, you will have a second child, his mother. The mother will be more trouble than a baby."

"July is a long way off, Mama. I'll have some time to charm her. Joe too because you know Joe is not afraid of his mother. He is doing things a man would do for someone he loves, someone he loves and respects"

I dig my toes into the warm dirt under the swing. The bougainvillea is bursting with bright pink and gold. Honey bees flit around the lemon tree. My home in San Ysidro is warm. My people are warm, and Joe knows this. He comes from the cold, damp coast and his frivolous, artificial mother.

"So, then, Carmen, what now for you?"

"Forms and exams. I will come home. I will learn from you and from Gayla. And I will work at a job somewhere so that we don't ask for money from Joe's family. Tate will like me better if she doesn't think I am using Joe for money. She may even like the Peanut."

"Everyone loves a baby, Carmen."

"You think she will love a caramel-colored baby, a half-Mexican baby?"

"Yes, because your baby will be beautiful." For the first time since I stood up to tell the parents about being pregnant, Mama smiles. "Your baby will be very beautiful, and maybe she will be smarter than her mother or her *abuelas*."

"Can you imagine calling Tate *abulea*?"

We start laughing. "She will want a fancier name," says Mama. Mama puts her nose in the air and raises her hankie in two fingers.

"*Nana, Bubbala, Booma, MiMa, Grandmere*?"

"Whatever she chooses will be fine with me, says Mama. "Because I know in my heart that I will be the main *abuela*. I will be by your side every moment as I have always been, *mi hija*." Mama puts her arms around me.

"You're not mad at me anymore?"

"Only about the college."

"I will finish college, you wait and see. I won't quit."

"I remember when I didn't want you to go to the college so far away. But then I was so proud of you, and I bragged to everyone you were at Western Pacific Concordia, learning to be someone great, someone famous. That was the wrong thing to tell them. Jacobo is great and famous, but what good is that if he is not willing to be a father to his child? So you went to the University, and what did you learn there?"

"I learned the world is a big place with all kinds of people. I learned that we are all brothers and sisters, *uno mundo.* When I go back, I will know better what to study. I want to help the world, to help all people to understand Hispanic pride." Pride reminds me of Franco. He sounds so much like Jacobo. "I am glad to be marrying a good man like Joe."

"The Peanut will be brought up Catholic?"

"Yes. The Church has been a source of strength in all this."

"And who else?"

"Joe, and now you, Mama. Our *familia* will be too. Mr. Sneed."

"We have to wait for Tate?"

"We are patient, especially you, Mama."

"Come," she says.

Mama and I walk to the corner of the yard where we have a statue of the Virgin Mary. We say a prayer, asking for patience and kindness to help us accept and love Mrs. Sneed so that she may also love Peanut Sneed.

"Mama?"

"Yes?"

"Gayla told me you have another secret, about a man?"

"Gayla has a mouth that holds too much and flaps like a pelican's. The man is an artist. He works with me on my piñatas. He is helping me to increase my technique."

"Technique? As in piñata?"

Mama smiles a secret smile. "Yes, my art. And maybe my kissing." Her cheeks are rosy. "Life is full of surprises, yes, Carmen? Love is the biggest surprise, *el diablo de amore*!"

I sit on the couch to watch soccer. Mama hums a song as she prepares our dinner.

Chapter 46

Gayla calls out, "Carmen?" I picture her wedging herself through our broken screen door. It doesn't open all the way. I hold my breath to help her fit.

"Right here," I mumble, not even opening my eyes until the couch dips at the end by my feet. "I must have fallen asleep here last night." Gayla lifts my feet into her lap and massages my toes.

"Your mom told my mom." She smiles like we have conspired to be pregnant at the same time. "It will be okay, Carmen. It will be good. You'll see. And your baby has a foxy father!"

"Gayla, stop. I have to drop out of college. I love WPC. The baby will be fine. I will be fine. I'm mostly worried about the grandparents."

"Pffft to them. You don't need them."

"Joe loves his parents. I don't want to cause a war."

"Babies have a way of making things better."

"You could be right." I sit up, pulling my feet back. "We'll see. My baby's due in July. Yours?"

"March."

"They'll be practically cousins unless I move."

"Why would you?"

"Joe. His parents. His school."

"He can go to State."

We're quiet. Mama is outside tending her garden. She has her radio on and is singing along, loudly and off key, "Like a Virgin." Gayla and I can't help laughing. The irony is probably lost on Mama.

"Come over, later, Carmen. Borrow some clothes. It's amazing how great it is to have clothes that don't squeeze your belly." Gayla kisses my cheek. I watch her out in the yard talking to Mama. The radio's too loud. I can't hear them.

By the time I'm out of the shower, dressed, picked a few things from Gayla's preg wardrobe, Joe's car is at the curb. I run to kiss him. He holds me tightly, his scrubby beard chafing my cheeks. He smells so good, soapy and fresh. His old high school tee-shirt is soft from hundreds of washings.

"De-li-cious, Joe, I want this shirt."

He pulls it over his head and gives it to me.

"I didn't mean this minute!"

"Be careful what you wish for around me, Caramel. Your wish is my command."

"Too bad wishes can't go backwards."

"Wait. Think about it. Where would people be if they could take back anything they wanted to undo?"

"How about one thing?"

"Not even one."

Mama calls to us, "Come in! We have much to discuss. There's little time to get yourselves back to school."

"Ready Freddie?" I ask him.

"As ever. Wait one sec." He dashes to the car where he puts on another tee. I pull his tee-shirt on over my tank top. It covers me better, and I don't have to think about the Peanut showing. All my skinny tank tops will stay home.

Mama sits at the table. She has put out a pitcher of watermelon agua fresca and a plate of fruit. "I will help you eat right, Carmen. Not so many *churros* for a while."

"I like *churros*," Joe says sadly.

"Then I will give you some to eat by yourself. *Churros* are not best for Carmen. Too much indigestion, gas, and farting."

"Mama! Stop!"

"You're going to be married. You're going to be a mother. As you wanted, we don't talk like you are a little girl any more. You listen to Madonna?"

"Sure," we both say.

"That's good. She teaches lessons in her songs. She speaks frankly. I like that." Mama picks up Joe's hand. "I like you, Joe. I think you are a good man. I want you to know this one thing. You are not required to marry Carmen."

"What?" That's basically not her business.

"Mrs. Gracia, my parents said the same, that no one has to get married any more. Carmen and I, we decided this for ourselves. We're better together. And we want the Peanut to have two parents."

"Especially me, Mama. I don't want my baby not to know the father until it's too late to care." I look at the album in the middle of the table. "Joe, Mama and I talked about my father last night. Here's his picture." I turn to the page.

"Good-looking dude, big deal. I believe being a father is more than getting a girl pregnant. My father is a really good father." He closes the album. "You, Mrs. Gracia, all by yourself you raised Carmen. I will be proud to be your son-in-law."

"And your parents, Joe? They will be proud to have my Carmen in their family?"

"My mom said cruel things. She gets drunk. She gets mean. When the Peanut is born, she won't resist any more. She'll make it up to you."

Mama takes the dishes to the sink. She stops behind Joe to hug him. "*Sabroso*, you smell good!" she says.

"Hey, that's my line!"

"It's Irish Spring soap."

"Maybe I'll give some to your new piñata advisor, Mama."

Joe glances at me with a raised eyebrow. Mama drops a glass in the sink. It's a good thing it's plastic. Her hair is bunched in a clip on top of her head. We watch a flush flash up her neck.

"I'll buy that soap. When you come home, that's something to remind you of Joe." She hesitates. "Ignacio might move in by then."

"What?" we ask as a couple.

"Your Mama is not too old to love a man."

How do I find an answer to that? Of course, she's not too old. I don't even know this guy. I wish I could stay home starting now, watch over this new phase of life Mama has entered without one word to me.

Joe breaks out into song, "Ch-ch-ch-changes!" He pulls Mama from by the sink and waltzes her around the table. He knows all the words. He doesn't look a thing like David Bowie, doesn't sound like him either, but it is a darling scene that I would like on videotape.

"Joe, where did you learn such a fine waltz?" Mama flaps her apron to cool her face.

"My dad before his accident. He thinks a gentleman should know ballroom dancing, the old charm school style. My mom misses dancing with him."

"We will have many men at your wedding to dance with Tate, and not just the Mexican hat dance," says Mama.

"I'll make sure she knows that too. Could I ask for one more thing, Mrs. Gracia?"

"Anything."

"A piñata for our wedding?"

"Of course. Ignacio will have some special ideas."

"I was thinking it should represent us, Carmen and me."

This could be interesting. "How about another Scooby?"

"You know I like Goliath better."

"What represents best for you two together?" asks Mama.

Joe wraps his arms around me and rests his head on my head. He turns me to face him. His face is a concentration of seriousness. "Carmen? You know, right?" His hands float down to encircle my abdomen. He rocks me back and forth, foot to foot, sideways.

"A peanut piñata?"

"A peanut piñata!"

Joe swivels in front of me, talking to my belly. "Hey, Peanut. We're going to make you the centerpiece at our wedding!" He looks up at me. "Take a guess, Carmen. Pink or blue?"

"I refuse to choose. I vote for yellow."

"Yellow peanut? Gag."

"You two are too silly to be parents," says Mama. "You have seven months to grow up."

"I hope we're always a little bit silly," I say because I do.

"Ignacio and I will make you a fine multi-colored peanut piñata. Joe, you will waltz at your wedding with all of Carmen's aunts and me, and your mother, we hope will do a Mexican hat dance. Won't it be a grand fiesta?"

"Well, we'd better do it soon, or the bride won't be in the mood to celebrate her own wedding," I grouse, thinking of Gayla's ponderous body.

"The day after Christmas?"

"A blessed day."

"Joe Sneed, I was so sad and angry with my Carmen's choices. Now I am as happy as a butterfly, the mariposa." We cling to one another in a three-way hug, and I imagine what it will be like when there's a little baby cuddled in with us. A family circle grows. There's always room for more love.

Chapter 47

Dead week. How appropriately named. We have no classes, no papers, no events. We are to study for finals. Without Shirley, my room in Ortega echoes. I try playing my tapes to fill in the empty space, but I'm not in the mood for any of the songs Shirley and I danced to, laughed to, dissed with one another.

Salt drops by. His hang-dog features have morphed into those of an orphaned pup. He does and he doesn't want to talk about Shirley.

He sits like a zombie for hours, playing a hand-held video game or sleeping on her bed. She took her linens with her so I don't worry about his sleeping there.

"Carmen, want to visit Shirley," he asks, awakening from a snooze.

"Like where?"

"Her house is close. We could take the bus. Unless she's having chemo. Then I sit with her. It's eighth floor of the med center, same building as student health."

"Call her grandmother and find out when would be okay."

"Tonight. I'll call tonight. Plan for a morning?"

"Sure." I aerate the room the minute he leaves.

When I hear Norine come shrieking down the hall, I make sure my lights are off. I cannot deal with her. Once I hear her door close, I sneak off to the library, coming back late to fall asleep the minute I'm in bed.

Joe asked if I wanted him to come along as I met with each of the offices to request a leave of absence. I said no. It's not that I didn't want him with me, of course I do. It's the lie

I'm telling about why I'm taking time off. Peanut is not part of my conversation with anyone here.

Getting out of the U is much easier than getting in. My advisor, Jesus, signed my withdrawal form, saying, "I hope your mother's health improves soon." Yeah, I said my mom is sick, and I'm needed at home. After Jesus, it's Marlene at work-study and the people at financial aid and the residence advisor at the dorm. Check, check, check, my list is completed, and as soon as I finish my last final, I'm on a leave-of-absence until further notice. They guarantee I can come back in any semester. There aren't any mommy and me dorms here.

Santa Ana winds have stripped the trees of their fall leaves. The winds blow down the dorm corridors, moaning in the empty tunnels. The library keeps the windows open because Santa Ana winds are hot winds. People's papers fly everywhere when the gusts are too strong. That's how I lost my *Mother and Child* picture. I had it in front of me while I studied. The picture blew away out the window. I hope the finder loves it too.

Al's is closed until next semester. The U tries to ensure that we are not tempted away from our books. Coffee is still available at Berkebile. I wander down the main walkway. It's noon, and what used to be the student body's favorite meeting spot is as empty as my energy reservoir. No one is spouting off in the free speech area. The offices in Berkebile are closed except the student paper.

Coffee in hand, I peek into the *La Raza* office. Franco sleeps at the desk, head down on his crossed arms. If he had been awake, I might have gone in. Or not. I don't really want to deal with anything Franco, and I don't want to tell him I'm leaving school. I'll mail him a letter. He can hear it through the grapevine.

In the two weeks since Thanksgiving, I've gained only a pound. Gayla's jeans are so comfortable. I walk on out of Berkebile and decide to drop in on Dr. Fritz, let him know the Peanut is going to be well taken care of as opposed to gotten out of the way.

The walk to the Free Women's Health Center energizes me. I should be walking more every day. I owe it to Peanut to be the healthiest mom I can be.

I fill in a form for returning patients. Two girls sit in the chairs in the back corner, talking quietly. I can guess which one is pregnant by her slumping shoulders. Her friend asks her the questions on the survey and writes the answers down.

The nurse calls for Cheryl. She goes in. Her friend twists her long hair around her finger and waits.

The nurse calls for me. "How are you, Carmen?" she asks.

"Okay, I guess."

"No exam today?"

"Like class or here?"

"Class."

"No, nothing until next Monday. Is Dr. Fritz going to have to do the whole procedure, the stirrups and all?"

"Not today. Follow me. You can talk to doctor in his office. This is a consultation, not a check-up."

"Cool." The chairs in Dr. Fritz's office are better than the plastic ones in the waiting room. They aren't new, but they're wide and comfortable. He knocks. It's his own office, he knows I'm dressed, so why is knocking? Maybe he thinks I'm studying my belly button or feeling my breasts. He enters quickly and takes a seat, my chart in his hand. He says, "A moment, please," reviewing whatever it is he wrote last time. He looks up. "Hello, Carmen."

"Hi."

"I hoped you would bring your boyfriend this time."

"Spur-of-the-moment, coming over here."

"Oh? Did you come to a decision?"

"Yes. The father and I have talked. We told our parents too."

"Good, good."

"We've decided to keep the baby."

Dr. Fritz smiles a wide, boyish grin."Congratulations. Do you want to schedule your monthly visits? Do you have questions?"

"I have a million questions. I'm taking a leave of absence though. I'll be seeing my doctor at home."

"Good choice. When you get settled, send me your doctor's information and I'll send him a copy of your chart. There's not a lot in there, but it gives him a starting point. He'll be glad to see that you came in early for pre-natal care."

"He doesn't have to know I might have considered abortion?"

"It's not in your file unless that is the choice you and the father make. You're young and healthy, and there's no reason to worry about your pregnancy, Carmen. Since you have the support of your parents and your boyfriend, you're better off than most of the women we see."

"That's good. I feel fine. Just tired. My mom and my boyfriend took the news pretty well, better than I did actually."

"Outstanding." Dr. Fritz gets up and comes to me. He shakes my hand. "I hope you'll stay in touch. The baby's due when?"

"July."

"I work here year-round, so send me a picture. And tell me what you name your baby. Oh, also, about the tiredness. Take a nap when you're tired. You don't have to make excuses. And here's the brand of vitamins I recommend." He hands me a jar full of capsules that look big enough for horses.

"Thank you, Dr. Fritz. It must be hard working here with confused women every day."

"We serve a community that needs us. WPC doesn't like our location so close to campus, but it's the best place for us."

"If you'd been far away, I might not have come."

"That's true of lots of women. Good luck to you and your baby," he says before entering the next exam room. "Remember to send your home doctor's information." He gives my shoulder a reassuring squeeze.

He makes it sound like I can do this. Through the power of positive thinking, I seem to have a number of people on Team Peanut.

Chapter 48

Salt carries a bouquet of sunflowers. I carry three swirly-colored balloons.The admissions desk lady says Shirley is on the eighth floor. Her door is propped open, and we walk in. She's leaned over in her bed, puking into a mustard-yellow vomit catcher. People who make hospital equipment should think more about colors.

Salt goes right in. He holds her hair back until she's through retching. He pours a glass of water. She shakes her head, points at the fruit juice box.

"Shirl," he says, "look who came to see you."

"In a minute." She barfs again. Salt is quick with the vomit catcher. He wets a washcloth at the sink and wipes her face.

"Better?"

"Way better. Who's here?"

"Carmen." I step in with the balloons. "Is it okay to hug you?"

We hug.

"So how are you, Carmen?"

"Good. Exams next Monday, Wednesday, Friday. It's dead week." I am immediately sorry to have said *dead.*

"Every week is dead week in here," says Shirley. "Do you think I smell?"

"Uh, no. No way."

"I feel smelly, like the chemo chemicals sweat our through my skin."

Salt asks a nurse about the vomit dish. She tells him to dump it into the toilet if he wouldn't mind. He disappears into the bathroom.

"How can I help you, Shirl?"

"There is no help. I finish this chemo, go home, die."

"Stop talking like that."

"Truth."

"I'll visit every day."

"Not every day. Call first. Between my grandparents, the sorority, and Salt, I am way over the limit for visitors." She sighs. "I wish I could be back in the dorm with you, Carmen. You're the best roommate."

"You'll be back for spring."

"No, I won't."

"Next fall?"

"No."

"Oh." I want to tell her not to feel bad, tell her how I messed up with Peanut, that I won't be back either. "Think positive."

"It's okay. Look at all the stuff people have brought me." She points to flowers, a bulletin board full of pictures from Sorority events, my balloons hanging out with other people's. The ones I brought are the only ones still inflated, swaying in the air conditioning. The others lie limply on the floor.

Salt opens the bathroom door. He sets the mustard-colored plastic thing next to Shirley's water and juice box.

"Thanks, Salt."

"No problem."

"You guys?"

Salt and I answer together, "Shirl?"

"I'm really, really tired. Do you mind cutting this visit short?"

"You need your sleep." I fluff up her pillows as she adjusts the bed to a flat position. "Do you want another blanket?"

"They're in the closet."

Salt retrieves a blanket. "Shoulders or full length?"

"My bed robe works for my shoulders. Let me have the blanket here." She indicates the side of the bed facing the window. "Kind of roll it, like a sleeping bag, so I can rest my arm on it." She turns on her side, IV'd arm up over the blanket roll.

"Is there anything I can bring next time?"

She's almost asleep. Her front teeth hold her bottom lip as if she's going to say the letter *F*.

"Shirl?" I ask quietly.

No answer. She's conked.

"Salt? Do we stay while she sleeps?"

"I don't. My mom died of lung cancer. She liked to have quiet time without people talking and asking questions she didn't have answers for."

"I'm sorry, Salt. I didn't know that."

"Yeah." He pats Shirley's hand. She doesn't move. I place my cheek next to hers. Her skin is clammy, moist and cool.

I whisper in her ear. She blinks, falls asleep again. "C'mon, Salt." We walk out into the bright white corridor. The nurses are working on charts behind their counter. I wish I could ask them about Shirley.

"Should we talk to them?"

"They aren't allowed to tell us anything."

"I get that." We take the elevators down. We don't talk to one another. "Want to walk through the art gallery, Salt?"

"Nah, finals."

"I don't even know your major. I don't know Shirley's major. Where have I been all semester?"

"Living your own life. That's how it is here. Stupid WPC is so God damn big."

"Star #1 just fell from the sky."

He laughs. It wasn't that funny, but I laugh too.

Salt takes the path towards campus. "See you whenever, Carmen."

"You know where to find me."

"Yep."

I stand and watch him until he goes around the corner near Berkebile. I have a flash of inspiration. The elevator zooms me back upstairs. The nurse on duty tilts her head as if to ask me a question.

"I'll be right out, two minutes," I say, entering Shirley's room. I edge towards her bed. She is sleeping soundly. Her wispy hair is all gone now. She is thin like a starving Ethiopian.

Her wrist is so small, her hospital i.d. is in danger of sliding right off. My heart hurts. Shirley has a million things left to do in her life. What about her career? Her wedding? Her babies?

Kneeling by her bed, I say a prayer to St. Jude. I sing Mama's favorite lullabye. Peanut floats inside me in his safe little private place where he's growing, cell by cell, and my tears fall because I'm pretty sure Shirley will never see my baby or have her own. Shirley's not the girl who left our dorm room, shouting and fighting mad. She's fragile as a newborn. She needs her sleep.

When I reenroll in school, I'll take philosophy. I do not understand the meaning of life and death, why her and not me, why Peanut, not a tumor. I sort of understand Franco's philosophy minor if he's going to be a doctor.

I sit back on my heels. "Shirl," I whisper, "Joe and I are getting married. I'm going to have a baby. If it's a girl, her middle name is going to be something that reminds me of you. If it's a girl, I want her to be crazy and funny and a fighter and someone confident, who can deal with life without a bunch of lies. You're amazing, Shirley. I want her to be brave like you." I kiss her again. She doesn't blink back, and I hope my words have fought their way through the chemicals and the cancer.

Chapter 49
April, 1985

Every day is the same. When Gayla comes over, we watch quiz shows and old movies. We talk about babies. She had hers early, a six-pound boy, which caused a lot of worry. She chose the name Cirilo Juan, which I think sounds too feminine, but it's not my baby. She asks Mama for her advice. Does the baby need a sweater to walk around the block in his limo stroller-baby buggy? She asks me stuff I have no idea about. Do I think he smiled? When can he eat solid food? On and on and on.

I am tired of talking about babies. Peanut is growing. He's more like a gourd now, a gourd with pointy ends that kick and pinch me. That's the good part. Looking like a pumpkin is not so good. Joe visits every other weekend. He loves feeling the baby kick. We lie on the couch, Joe's head in my lap. He sings crazy songs to the baby. When Joe is here, I'm fine. I can't wait for Spring Quarter to end. I can't wait for July.

Mama introduced me to Ignacio. What a shock! He's not tall and handsome like my father. He's only as tall as Mama, rugged looking, with gray hair, flat Indian cheekbones, and a really loud laugh. When they work on piñatas together, they talk and laugh. They take a nap like a siesta every day. Ignacio says it's because he has so recently arrived in America and is getting used to American time, rush, rush, rush. I imagine it's because they like to cuddle and more. I try to go to Gayla's during their siestas, which get a little noisy, and not with snoring.

We had a little emergency change to the wedding plans. I was spotting, and my doctor said I need as much bed rest as possible. Mama enforced this for weeks. We never even sent invitations. The actual wedding to Joe was nothing big deal to talk about. The ceremony in City Hall lasted like two minutes. Joe's father was his best man. His mother didn't come. We kept my side of the family down to Mama, Aunt Ines, and Ignacio. If Joe saw our entire clan together, he'd probably run for the Canadian border. Someday, we'll get married in the Church.

Today, it's April 2nd. The weather is stormy, and I'm stuck inside. Gayla taught me to crochet, so I'm working on a baby blanket in yellow and green. I'm now an expert making granny squares.

Salt calls, which is weird. He's speaking in a soft mumble.

"Carmen?"

"Yeah."

"You know Shirley?"

"What about Shirl?"

"She died."

"No, no, no way, Salt."

"She died, this morning. Her grandma called me. Could you come up here? Norine told me you were home taking care of your mom. But, it would be nice if you could come to speak at Shirley's funeral."

Now I'm stuck. I am quite obviously pregnant. If I go, everyone will know.

"It would mean a lot to the grandparents, Carmen."

"What day?"

"Thursday."

"Where?"

"Um, Shirley wanted to be cremated, so it's that Methodist church in Hollywood. We liked to go there sometimes. Shirl loved the organ music."

"I should come."

"That's why I called."

"The weather is really bad.'

"Her grandmother said you could stay over with them if you want to."

"I'll stay with my aunt. That's so nice though."

"They're nice people. They're having a hard time. This last week, Shirl was in hospice. She didn't want visitors, not even me." He stops. I hear him crying.

"Are you okay?"

"Sort of."

"Tell the Woosters I'll be there. What time?"

"Ten. You should come up Wednesday night. Traffic and all that."

"Thanks for calling, Salt. See you Thursday. Um, I guess I should tell you the truth. About leaving school? I'm pregnant."

"Whoa. Didn't expect that. Are you okay? Oh, Franco is one of the speakers too. Do you care?"

"It's not about me or Franco. I'd do anything for Shirl. It's okay." We say bye.

I ask Mama if I can drive to LA. She says no. She says she will go with me. She doesn't want me driving so far alone.

"I'd be fine, Mama."

"And I'd be nervous."

"I'm supposed to talk. What should I say?"

"Whatever is in your heart, *mi hija.* I wish I had known your friend."

"Me too, Mama. She was special. I really want to do this alone, okay?"

"You are carrying my grandchild. No. End of argument."

Mama starts making phone calls, Ignacio, Ines, on and on. I knock on Gayla's door. She comes to the door with her blouse open, the baby latched onto her breast, making slurping, sucking sounds like a piglet. I think maybe I won't nurse my baby.

"Do you have a black dress?" I ask.

"Oh, oh. Wait, okay?" She slips her finger under her nipple to get it out of the baby's mouth. It comes out with an audible pop, and she lays him into a crib in the living room. "I don't want to talk about death while I hold Cirilo." She pats his back. "Let's check my closet."

The baby is sucking his fist. His shaggy black hair is totally cute. Gayla has him dressed in a striped onesie that has seen better days. She swears by the prices at the GoodWill. We go through her dresses, most of which I have already rejected as not a necessary part of my pregnancy wardrobe based on being butt ugly.

She pulls out one that is navy blue. "I don't have black, Carmen. Black is not good for pregnant mothers. Who died?"

"My college roommate."

She makes the sign of the cross. "That's terrible, like losing a sister, huh?"

"It is. I know. It's so sad. I promised I'd speak at her funeral." I picture the church and all those people. Somehow I'll have to let the stares and whispers slide off me like I'm Teflon girl.

We leave as soon as we can. We stay with Aunt Rosa. Thursday morning, Mama drops me off in front of a gray stone church in Hollywood at nine. She says she would like to come in with me, but I tell her she would make me more nervous, and I might puke again. Cars plus pregnancy don't work very well for me, just ask the freeway between home and Hollywood. She will meet me at the reception. I'm wearing the navy blue dress and very low heels that don't quite fit. The shoes rub my pinkie toes. My feet are swollen and ugly.

The Woosters greet me in the cool, shadowed sanctuary. A few older people are already in the pews. If they notice I'm pregnant, they're keeping it to themselves. No surprised fluttering around me and none of the usual stupid questions.

"Carmen, dear, here's the program. If you'll sit in the front pew, you can get to the pulpit easily."

"I'm so sorry," I say to each of them.

Their eyes sparkle with tears. They look much older and frailer. I check the program: welcome, slide show to celebrate Shirley's life, comments from friends. I sit up front on the left aisle, leaving room for others. An organist begins to play solemn hymns. I'm thinking Shirley liked this? I almost miss the fact that Salt is to speak because he's listed by his real name, *Morton.* Franco is next, and I'm after him. The program has an amazing picture of Shirley on the front, a yearbook portrait. The words to a Keats' sonnet are included in the program, "When I Have Fears." That does seem like a Shirley choice; it's all about dying young.

Salt sits down beside me, reaching into his suit pocket to be sure he has his speech. Norine wanders up the aisle. We move over to make room for her. She is dressed in a black sheath, which is shockingly neither low cut nor too tight.

"You'll be fine," I say to Salt.

"Hope so." He sniffles and pulls out a handkerchief. He hasn't really looked at me yet.

I take his hand. I look down at my non-existent lap, hold the program on the edge of my knees.

A lot of people are arriving now. Someone comes from the right aisle to sit next to me, placing a box of Kleenex between us. "Hello, Carmen," says Franco. "Glad to see you here." He glances askance at my belly. "Anything new in your life?"

"Later," I tell him. "This time is all about Shirley."

"Absolutely," he says. "Where's Joe?"

"He didn't really know Shirl. I told him I'm better here with just me. Don't start, okay, Franco?"

"Far be it from me to argue with you." His smile is a bit snide. "Is your mom still sick?"

"Later."

More people have come in. Sister Rosalie sits by Franco. The sorority sisters enter in a group, all in their lime green, and I swear it is every member. Some of them cry into their boyfriends' shoulders. Shirley's grandparents sit at the other end of the front pew. Her grandfather goes up to consult with the preacher. The clock ticks away. At ten, the organist does something that makes the organ swell out loud and proud. A choir joins in. The vibrations of the music come right through the floor, through the pews, and into me. I begin to cry. Franco hands me Kleenex.

The pastor opens with a prayer. Mr. Wooster talks and shows slides. He talks about raising Shirley the baby, the toddler, the gangly kid, the teen with two legs, the teen with one leg, sorority pictures. The music during the slide show is Michael Jackson's greatest hits.

Salt goes up to talk about how much Shirley loved her grandparents, how much Shirley loved college, how much Shirley loved music. He kind of rambles around, but his speech is sincere and beautiful.

Franco goes up to read a poem. Why he chose Dylan Thomas's "Do Not Go Gentle" is beyond me. That poem is about an old man. That poem emphasizes too much of what was not accomplished. Well, okay, I give him points for the idea of fighting against death. He starts to end with a short rap: "Shirley wasn't ever my girl,/She was too smart, a true, pure pearl." He stops. "Sorry," he says, "I thought I could, but I can't finish this." He pulls a handkerchief from his suit pocket and wipes his eyes.

My turn. Franco waits to take my arm as I negotiate up the low stairs. I walk to the podium, trying not to do the pregnant waddle, trying not to limp. I tell the crowd about Shirley being my roommate, some of our big moments, some of the little ones. I tell them about meeting her, how her sorority gave her the answer to a prayer (all the lime-green Tri Chi's dab their eyes, nodding, yes, yes), visiting her in the hospital, knowing I would have to say goodbye. I tell them I told her a secret that's not such a secret anymore. There's a murmur of laughter. I recite a verse of Auden's "With Rue My Heart Is Laden," from memory. I love the simplicity of the verse. The poem is about golden friends, light-footed boys, girls like roses.

When I stop, everyone is crying. Shirley's urn is a simple bronzed vase with a lid, surrounded by flowers. The flowers are sunflowers and baby's breath. No roses, no gladiolas, no funeral wreaths. I take five of the sunflowers and hand them out with a hug to the Woosters, to Salt, to Franco. One flower is for me.

This is how we say goodbye to Shirley. When we leave in the limo, Salt asks if the driver could power the roof window open. The storm is moving on, and in the ragged clouds I swear I see a laughing girl like a rose.

Chapter 50

Brenda Wooster cries softly, staring out the window. Rolf strokes her hair, saying, "It's okay. It's better. No more suffering. No more anger. Peace, pure and restful peace. Our Shirley is happy again." He kisses her hair and kisses the St. Peregrine medallion around his neck.

I unclasp mine and give it to Mrs. Wooster.

She whispers, "Thank you, Carmen. Thank you all. Eternal love, eternal life."

Salt and Franco and I sit uncomfortably close together in the seat that faces them. Franco throws his arm across the seat. If he drops the hand down to my shoulder, I'll punch him. I inch closer to Salt, trying to arrange this dress discretely so that it doesn't pooch out over my belly.

The limo turns left on Franklin. Traffic crawls through Hollywood. The silence in the limo is draped with words unspoken. We don't want to be rude to the Woosters, so we sit like statues, which is hard for me when Peanut decides it's time to take a womb-tour. The tumbling around is okay until the Peanut finds the spot that pushes against my bladder.

We turn onto Doheny, making our way up into the hills. Beverly Hills? I wonder. The limo stops in front of a huge white mansion with a circular driveway. Valets are on hand to help people park. I see one of them parking Mama's truck. Mama is standing on the Woosters' porch, waiting for me, obviously unsure about walking into this party of rich people. I wish I had asked her if she wanted to bring Ignacio.

The driver stops and opens our doors. The Woosters walk up their front stairs to greet Mama and a few other early arrivals. Franco gets out and offers his hand to help hoist me out of the car. Salt follows. On a normal day, Salt would say something about my ass. Today is not a normal day.

I'm desperate for a bathroom, so I scuttle over to Mama, whisper to her. She asks the butler in the foyer. He directs us down a long hall, a hall with pictures on the wall, a gallery of their family life. I see an old picture that looks like

Shirley. It must be her mom. We never told each other those stories. We always thought there would be time enough someday.

Mama asks, "Was it okay, Carmen?"

"Yes, beautiful. The two guys in the limo with me spoke too. And there was a slide show of Shirley. Wait here for me, 'kay?" I rush into the bathroom, relieve myself, strip off the panty hose, and put the damn things into my purse. Please, God and St. Gerard, do not make me wear pantyhose again when I am pregnant. I have indentions in my middle from that tight elastic. I wish I had thought to bring other shoes. My little toes are bleeding. I wrap them with toilet paper and stuff my feet back into the shoes. Torture.

When Mama takes her turn in the bathroom, I follow the crowd into the backyard. The Woosters' backyard is landscaped as an Asian garden. There are bridges and little brooks. There's a wishing well. Every table is centered with a small, trickling fountain and sunflowers.

A buffet is set up. Before my friends line up where most of the crowd has gathered, they tell me to take it easy. They'll serve me. I can relax. I kick off my shoes and rub my toes against the soft grass. It feels like velvet, not scratchy like our patchy wild Bermuda grass at home. Salt, Norine, and Franco return, each carrying two plates. They set the extras next to me. Salt asks, "Beer?" and Franco answers for me, "Punch, no alcohol."

A harpist plays softly. I don't know any of the music, it's something classical, so anti-Shirley. But so was the organ, so what do I know? I read about grief in my psych book, something about funerals are for the living not the dead. The Woosters can have any music they want after all they've been through. Norine, Salt, and Franco are back with a bottle of wine, a six-pack of beer, and three lemonades. They arrange the lemonades in front of me, popping open their beer.

We eat like hungry children.

"Hunger is a natural reaction to grief," announces Franco.

"Hunger is a natural reaction to hunger," Salt agrees.

"I'm always hungry, but for weird stuff," I say.

"You've gained a lot of weight," states Norine.

Before I answer her or flip her off, some older people sit opposite us, probably friends of the Woosters. I wish Mama would hurry up and find me, but I see her asking questions of the servers, pointing and asking. There are exotic foods here. I'm the one who thought the caviar on toast was berries. Franco got a good laugh out of that. The Chinese dumplings and fruit kabobs with dipping sauces are way better.

The harpist stops playing. Mr. Wooster steps up on a platform. He says simply, "Brenda and I welcome you. Thank you for coming. We hope you celebrate Shirley's life with your memories and sign our books in the main room. Shirley told us how much she loved all of you, that each of you made her life better. We thank you for your friendship. We lost her parents too young in a plane crash on their first vacation without the baby. From that loss, Brenda and I became parents to this wonderful child, Shirley, who lit up old our lives. Without her friends, she would have lost her battle with cancer long ago." He wipes his eyes. "Thank you."

The people across from us get up to talk to him. Salt and Norine meander away in the direction of the bar. Mama waves at me and takes a seat with Sister Rosalie near the buffet. She holds a champagne glass, draining it too fast, and chatting Sister Rosalie's ear off. I'll be driving home with a silent, sleeping Mama, bless you, Sister Rosalie.

I guess it's time to talk to Franco about Peanut. Now, I wish Joe were here. "So, yeah, Franco, my mom isn't sick. I'm not either, just pregnant."

"Obviously."

"I'm going to have the baby."

"Why?"

"How can you go to WPC and even think someone would have an abortion?"

"How can you go to WPC and get pregnant, smart girl like you?"

"And you're not the least bit curious about the baby's father?"

"I assume it's Joe Sneed."

"Have you forgotten our little escapade so quickly?"

"No, not forgotten, just not applicable."

"That's self-righteous talk, Franco. You know we didn't use any birth control."

"So you're saying this baby could be mine? Is there anyone else on your list I should know about?"

"It's either you and Joe."

"It looks like you've made your decision," he says, holding my left hand with the wedding ring on it. "You married him? What if the baby is mine?"

"Joe would adopt the baby as his own."

"Wow, what a guy. Now me, if some girl says I got her pregnant, I wouldn't marry her. I'd take her to court to prove it."

"What?"

"Listen, Carmen. For one, I asked you if we should stop and you said no. For two, it's your body and you should respect your body enough to protect yourself. For three, I'm not getting married until I'm thirty."

"That's like seven years. The baby will be in school already. How could you say that? Children need fathers."

"I agree, but it wouldn't work for me. I'll be in med school and internship and all the stuff that goes with getting an M.D. I could be on the East Coast next August. Johns Hopkins is my first choice school."

"Your degree matters more than a child's life?"

"I'm planning for the future in every move I make."

I laugh sarcastically. "Right, like when you put the moves on the new freshman?"

Franco stares around him, at all the fancy people. "Carmen, you were never in any danger with me. I told you up front how I felt about marriage."

"Then you shouldn't have seduced me."

"Is that what I did? I seem to remember some hot and heavy moments with you wanting more, not less."

"But men have responsibilities too."

"Sure. I'm Machiavellian about power. A woman is my business once she marries me. She can choose her own adventures until then. So if you're not married to me, I have no concern for the results of sex with me."

"Good speech for a debate, Franco. Joe loves me. I love him. We're married. We are going to be just fine with our lives while you're still out there chasing rainbows."

"Wrong allusion."

"Wrong man, in every way." I wave at Mama. "I think I'll be going now. Have a nice life, Franco."

"Carmen, let me tell you a secret."

"Now he gets up close and personal." I start to walk away. He jumps up to place himself in front of me and takes my hands. "Let me go!" I hiss the words through my teeth.

"Hear me out. I am not your baby's father." I start to protest, but he says, "Hush. Listen. I caught mumps right after high school when I was volunteering with Rosalie in Guatemala. She was in my senior class, not a word back then about becoming a nun. Anyway, the point is that down there I caught severe mumps called *mumps orchitis*, meaning the testicles were affected. And while it's rare, it can happen. I've been tested ever since. I'm still not producing sperm. None of my sperm were making babies in October last fall. Do you understand now?"

"There's no way the baby is yours?"

"Not this year."

"Absolutely, positively not?"

"Do you want copies of my test results? I can mail them. I'm still shooting blanks. No sweat, not right now anyway."

I am so happy that I hug him. "I can't wait to tell Joe."

"That's good you told him about me, you and me, I mean. Marriages are founded on trust." He pats my rounded tummy

"Yes. He didn't care. No one else, not Salt or my mom or Joe's parents know. Shirley knew, but Shirl took this secret to her, um, urn."

"Does that mean we can be friends again?"

"I'll think about it," I say sternly, but I'm grinning. "You're Catholic, right? Maybe you'll be a god parent."

"As long as a god parent doesn't change diapers. I'll read to the kid from my radical books. I'll put him in a Che Guevara tee-shirt. I'll buy him Mao's *Little Red Book*. Will you call me when he's born?"

"It could be a she. And if so, I'm naming her for Shirley."

"That's the worst name, and you know it."

"But the nicest person." I tip my head to the sky to see if I can find my angel cloud with the laughing girl. "I'll call you."

"When?"

"July."

"Do your best to have your baby on the 4th of July!"

"You think?"

"I'll pray. I love you, Carmen. You're a shining spirit. You'll be a great mom. Don't give up on your education. Get your degree. I would like to visit the piñata-maker when I come to see the piñata-maker's daughter. And the kid."

I finger my remaining medallions and find the one with John de LaSalle. I unclasp it and give it to Franco. "May you be a fine doctor someday, Franco. You'll be an inspiration for this baby and many others."

He kisses my cheek, we say goodbye. Salt is leaning on Norine, but staggers over, where I hug him.

Sister Rosalie greets me with a kiss for each cheek. "I'm sorry for your loss, Carmen. Shirley was a lovely girl."

"Yes, thank you. The Church brings me comfort."

"Bless you and your baby. When are you due?"

"July. Joe Sneed is the father." I smile and show her my wedding ring.

"More blessings! Did Franco tell you about his mumps?"

I blush fiercely red. "He did."

"God is good. He works in mysterious ways. Franco's mumps turned into a miracle for me. That story is part of how I chose to become a nun. After Franco was on his feet again, I spent too much time knowing the beautiful devil before we returned from Guatemala. Yes, Carmen, the Biblical *knowing* with all that implies." She blushes a shade redder than I am. "Those chances that I took could have turned out differently. I was a very ignorant and trusting girl. God watched over me. I pledged my life to the Church once I realized I had been blessed in this way as you have been blessed in yours."

Our lives hold such secrets. I drive Mama, who is tipsy and sleepy, home to San Ysidro, and count the hours until Joe calls me. For once, I'll have something interesting to talk about.

Epilogue

August, 1985

Our baby is here, born on the 14th of July. He's not a peanut. He's a nine-pound firecracker. The months of waiting and swollen tired feet don't feel real. For the labor and delivery, Joe was there, holding my hand. I was not brave at all even though we had taken the Lamaze classes. I screamed and thrashed until they gave me the spinal.

From those hours, I remember my first look at this baby, with his thick black hair, big black eyes that are a little almond-shaped, teensy fingers, perfect toes.

I remember the smile on Joe's face when the nurse handed him our baby. Joe, Senior, said that the baby looks like Joe. Mama says he looks like our family, like Miguel. I think he looks like a baby.

We had been writing down names and getting suggestions from everyone who knows us. The baby books and the family tree and the advice of others made no difference. Joe and I decided he would be called Daryll David. The whole name together sounds like music, Daryll David Sneed. We are proud that we have chosen an unusual name. Everything about our baby is unusual from how he was conceived to how he's been received. Seriously, I should have named him Jesus. I am relieved not to have to name a girl Shirley, though I would have honored that promise, something like Shirl Lee Sneed.

Shirley died, and I gave birth. Life is not fair.

Gayla brings Cirilo over. We rock our babies and nurse them and watch the grass grow. Joe planted a lawn in our dusty backyard so Daryll can have a swing set. The butterflies have flown away, like my ignorance and youth. Growing up is not about leaving home. It is about learning to make a peaceful life, full of gratitude for every person, every experience, every minute. Joe has moved into the main house. Ignacio converted the garage into a workroom with a bedroom. Mama is living there because she says that too many cooks spoil the broth. The saying doesn't fit with babies. I know better than to correct her. She is much smarter than I am about life.

I nuzzle Daryll's fat chins, inhale the scent of him, baby soap and cinnamon, milk and his daddy's shirt.

Joe has sculpted Daryll's hair into a Mohawk with hair gel and dressed him in a San Diego Chargers onesie. "He'll play quarterback," said Joe on his way out the door to his job. Next month he starts classes at San Diego State and will have one more challenge to juggle.

Mr. Sneed comes over twice a week. He toes a ball from his wheelchair to the baby on the blanket. He puts the baby in his lap in the wheelchair and rolls around the block, stopping for the neighbors to admire Daryll. He wants us to spend a week at his house so that he can walk the baby in his own neighborhood and introduce him to his other grandmother. I worry about Tate, but I know she will fall in love with Daryll. Who wouldn't? Tate doesn't pretend to be a big expert on babies. She wrote a note to me to do what I think is right because I am the mother. She says mothers know best. I don't know if she's being mean, but this remark made Mama smile and turn away. Did I mention that July 14th is also Tate's birthday? How could she resist a present such as Daryll?

Life can be full and good even if you are only the neighborhood Piñata-Maker. Or the Piñata -Maker's daughter. No one thinks to call me that anyway. I am Carmen, Carmen Sneed. It makes me laugh to say my name, Mrs. Sneed. I am Daryll's mom and Joe's wife.

I want Franco to visit. He's helping Sister Rosalie at the orphanage in Tijuana. He will come for the baptism in August before he begins med school at UCSD. He asks if I know that the baby's birthday is Bastille Day, the opening of the French Revolution. Franco says to watch out because his god son is going to be someone strong enough to break down walls and fight for people's rights. Franco needs to see this little baby before pronouncing such big plans. One thing Daryll won't be is a cynic who agrees with Machiavelli.

One year ago, all I wanted was a degree. If life adds to my accomplishments, like my college degree I still want to earn, that will be good. I will be proud. Mama reminds me that I have accomplished much just by being me, Carmen. I've taught Joe and his father that Mexicans are more like them than unlike them, *uno mundo*, one world. We are all the same under our skin. We don't need to set ourselves apart in sororities and fraternities and secret rituals. "*Todos somos hermanos y hermanas.*" We are all brothers and sisters. Daryll will know this all his life because I say it to him every night with our good night prayer.

There's something even better though. I have learned to respect life and choices and people of all kinds, from silly Norine to stay-at-home Gayla to peasant Ignacio and my miraculous, brave Mama. When the baby cries too much, Mama sings to him. She calms him like no one else can. His blankets have paste stains on them.

He is a lucky baby to have every one of us, a multicultural family. We each add something to his world. Who knew such a miracle would come to me, the Piñata-Maker's daughter?

A note to my readers:

Some Rivers End on the Day of the Dead was written and published in 2010. I had planned a trilogy, but I began working on other novels. When I came back to writing *The Pinata-Maker's Daughter,* I found that the story had changed immensely in my mind over the three previous years. While the Sneed family as introduced in *Some Rivers End on the Day of the Dead* is this same family, I have changed Carmen's maiden name from Garcia to Gracia and on her father's side, to Principia.

Similarly, as I worked through Carmen's conflicts in the novel, I found that I was no longer writing a young middle grade or YA novel. This prequel is definitely for late YA and adults although I am aware that other YA authors do include some frankly sexual scenes in their novels.

I hope you enjoy *The Pinata-Maker's Daughter.* The final book, *So You, Solimar,* has a new springboard to life!

About the Author

Eileen Clemens Granfors has written four novels, two anthologies of flash fiction, and two anthologies of poetry since retiring from teaching at Saugus High School in Santa Clarita, California. Growing up in Imperial Beach, California, she came to love the ocean and all water sports. Her grandmother and her teachers helped her fall in love with reading and writing. She and her husband hope to relocate soon to their dream house on Table Rock Lake in the Missouri Ozarks.

http://www.eileengranfors.blogspot.com, *Word Joy*
This web site carries up-to-date information on Ms. Granfors' books, giveaways, book club ideas, and recommendations on the best of new books to read.

About the Artist

Donna Dickson is a Canadian artist living full time in San Miguel de Allende, Mexico. She also teaches painting classes in *Plein air* or Studio and specializes in both water media and oils.

The cover art for ***The Pinata-Maker's Daughter*** is titled "Mother's Day."

Donna's other interests include meeting people, gardening, bird-watching, and learning about nutrition.

http://www.donnadickson.blogspot.com

Acknowledgements

My thanks to all who have helped me by editing, reading, researching, and offering emotional support. To Donna Dickson, thank you for the beautiful cover art that graces this book. To Kathleen Penrice and Immy Kwon for their reading and suggestions; to Eve Caram for her UCLA writing classes; to Marianne Wallace, Rachelle Staab, Yvette Johnson, Judi Turner, Caroline McCoy, and Elena Felix, writing *compadres*; to Denise Contreras Harder, Brenda Dubiniak Powers, Elaine Sick Vockrodt, Karen Ritchie Schimek, the late Victoria Takashima Popov, Cheryl Shealy Byrd, Barbara Gifford Mead, Joanne Gartner, Janie Ayers Bennett, and Barbara Maier, friends who grew up with me. To Dorothy Braus Palialogas, Kathy Dunlap, Elena de Lira Lima, roommates, who suffered my growing pains. To Marianne Murphy, the late Rochelle Paul Zidenberg, the late Howard Zidenberg, Kevin West, Bill Garwin, Roy and Judy Glickman, and Roger Cox, college friends. To Ron Portnoy, for our good years. To Alisha Portnoy Woodroof and Aaron Portnoy, who never expected their Moth to become a writer. To my 248 blog members, I appreciate your support. Special thanks to my husband Patrick for motivational speeches and wine opening as needed, and to Nilla and Kali, who listened to me reading every draft.

Printed in Great Britain
by Amazon